LAW OF THE JUNGLE

D0931938

LAW OF THE JUNGLE

DAVE SMEDS

ILLUSTRATIONS BY
MAX DOUGLAS

BYRON PREISS MULTIMEDIA COMPANY, INC.
NEW YORK

BERKLEY BOULEVARD BOOKS, NEW YORK

X-MEN: LAW OF THE JUNGLE

A Berkley Boulevard Book
A Byron Preiss Multimedia Company, Inc. Book

Special thanks to Ginjer Buchanan, Steve Roman, Michelle LaMarca, Howard Zimmerman, Emily Epstein, Ursula Ward, Mike Thomas, and Steve Behling.

PRINTING HISTORY
Berkley Boulevard paperback edition / March 1998

The Putnam Berkley World Wide Web site address is
http://www.berkley.com

Make sure to check out *PB Plug*, the science
fiction/fantasy newsletter, at
http://www.pbplug.com

Check out the Byron Preiss Multimedia Co., Inc. site on the
World Wide Web:
http://www.byronpreiss.com

ISBN: 0-425-16486-1

BERKLEY BOULEVARD
Berkley Boulevard Books are published by The Berkley Publishing Group, a member of Penguin Putnam Inc.,
200 Madison Avenue, New York, New York 10016.
BERKLEY BOULEVARD and its logo
are trademarks belonging to Berkley Publishing Corporation.

PRINTED IN THE UNITED STATES OF AMERICA

10   9   8   7   6   5   4   3   2

**For Werner Roth,
X-Men artist of the 1960s.**

He may not have been the best artist,
but something about him
appealed to me when I was eleven,
and turned *X-Men* into my
favorite comic book.

X·MEN®

LAW OF THE JUNGLE

CHAPTER 1

The Tyrannosaurus rex crashed into the clearing, jaws snapping. A young man—more of a boy, really, dressed in nothing more than a loincloth—scampered in front of her, with so little lead that the gust of the meat-eater's breath chilled the sweat on his supple young back. Now that they were in the open, the dinosaur could sprint, and would soon overtake her prey.

Just as the animal hit her full stride, a thick cord rose from the grass behind the fleeing teenager and was pulled taut. The tyrannosaur's ankle struck it, and down the beast went, flailing her ridiculously undersized arms. The huge body slammed to the earth.

Dazed, the gray-green theropod barely shifted as half a dozen powerful grown men raced from their hiding places in the brush and wrapped additional ropes around her huge, ostrichlike feet and around her snout to keep her vicious teeth in check. The savages darted away before a claw could swing their way and eviscerate them. They tugged in the direction the youth had been running.

A stone's throw away, the clearing ended at a steep slope. The dinosaur blinked, roared, and began to thrash. One man was yanked off balance. Another eight men joined the first six and continued pulling. The boy lent his effort as well.

The eight-ton monster need only have remained still and the men would have been hard-pressed to drag her massive body any distance at all, but her wriggling helped scoot it over the bedewed grass toward the slope. She glared at her tormentors, far too eager to nip one or ten of them to notice the precipice.

Under thick, tropical fronds at the edge of the clearing, a final pair of men waited, one a coppery-skinned, long-nosed figure like those fighting the dinosaur, the other a tanned blond in a set of cut-off Levi's and sandals.

The native hefted his spear. "A jab through the eye and we are rid of her, Lord Ka-Zar," he said, his words rendered in a gutteral language full of sharp breaks.

"Have you no confidence in your men, Tongah?" Ka-Zar asked in the same tongue.

"Of course I do. Did you not see how magnificently they brought down the longtail?"

"Exactly," said the blond. "So no spears. Not unless they lose their grip on those ropes." Ka-Zar could hardly blame Tongah or his people for struggling against his strange requests. Spare the life of a longtail? Counter-intuitive. But he had to insist. This part of the Savage Land was becoming overrun with large herbivores. Only predators as large as the T. rex could assure ecological balance. Besides, Ka-Zar merely wanted the animal out of the way so he and the Fall People could continue their mission. If they were actually hunting for food, it might be a different story. But the Fall People had no shortage of food this year.

The main party of men worked their way over to the slope's edge. At the last moment, the tyrannosaur dug for purchase in the loose soil, resulting in a primal tug-of-war across the gap. Tongah's warriors eyed the hard boulders at the bottom of the slope and tightened their grips, pulling until their muscles stood out in corded ripples. The creature roared one, two, three times. A last surge of effort from the humans sent her careening over the edge. Down tumbled the tyrannosaur and the trailing ends of the ropes.

The beast eventually came to rest awkwardly amid the boulders, flattening a mound of creek shrubs. She roared in pain. Ka-Zar worried she might have suffered a broken spine or major injury, but she rolled, twisted, and began pulling at the ropes entangling her legs. She soon broke free and stood up.

She didn't charge. The scrabbly ground made climbing back up impractical, and the rex had to have realized that. She rumbled off downstream, growling. The men jeered at her, tossed stones, laughed.

The monster would eventually find a spot where she could mount the banks, but to return to the clearing would take her an hour or more. By then, the tribesmen would be gone.

Ka-Zar and Tongah greeted the victors as they recrossed the chasm on the remaining log. The teenager who had baited the trap found himself the center of attention.

"You were not supposed to lead the beast so closely, Immono," chided the youth's father, shaking his head so emphatically the long stripe of hair along the center of his scalp flapped from side to side.

"The longtail was faster than I imagined," Immono said. His immature Adam's apple fluttered at his throat, and he turned so pale Ka-Zar stepped back in order to avoid the splatter should the lad abruptly lose his breakfast. Delayed fear. A natural, healthy response. What counted was that during the chase, he had remained calm and executed his role in a manner that brought success.

"You bring honor to your family, Immono," Ka-Zar said, squeezing the shoulders of both sire and offspring. "You will have plenty to talk about at the storytelling fires tonight. Tonight, and many nights to come."

"Thank you, Lord Ka-Zar," the young man said, and beamed.

"And," Ka-Zar said, rubbing his palms together, "now that we're finally rid of that nuisance, we can get back to following this trail."

The Lord of the Savage Land pointed to a cluster of footprints along the top of the bluff, not far from those created in the scuffle with the dinosaur. Some bore the outlines of human feet. One set was distorted in a vaguely wolflike pattern, complete with clawed toes. A final set looked like they had been made by a giant frog.

Ka-Zar bent down, touched the spoor, and frowned. Half a day old now, and no fresher thanks to that T. rex. Her arrival was probably coincidental, but either way, the trackers had been delayed while they dealt with her, and the small hope they had had of catching up with their quarry had grown ever more faint.

But what was there to do but make the attempt? "This way," he said, leading the men of the Fall People into the jungle.

The tracks took them up along one side of the little gorge where they had lured the dinosaur. The riot of footprints were plainly etched in the dirt. Small branches lay broken, the ends hanging by shreds of bark. The grass was still flat where it had been trampled. Even if Ka-Zar had been raised entirely in England as Lord Kevin Plunder and never escaped the protected, genteel lifestyle his cousins endured, he would have been able to follow a path such as this. His quarry had not tried to disguise where they had gone. They had chosen to flee as fast as possible, eliminating the delay inherent in avoiding soft ground or seeking out streams that would wash away spoor. This route made use of an animal trail, so that it had not even been necessary to hack away vines and fronds.

Tongah grunted and pointed to a shadow in a clump of grass. He picked up a broken leather necklace. "Ararisa," he said, caressing the pearly mussel shell that decorated the loop.

Ka-Zar nodded. Ararisa was one of the three members of the Fall People who had been kidnapped in the night raid. Her mate Kombo had been among those killed by the attackers.

At least the children had been spared. That was the only silver lining in the recent depredations. The raiders sought adults. And they wanted them alive if possible—Kombo apparently had been too quick for them, and had put up too much of a fight.

A mile up the slope, they came to a broad swath of volcanic rock. The trail vanished upon the dark, pitted surface, one of many scars from the catastrophic upheavals the Savage Land had survived in recent years. Tongah's warriors combed the perimeter of the area, but shook their heads. It was as if their quarry had vanished into the air.

Ka-Zar was sure they had.

Young Immono confirmed it. "Look!" he called. Ka-Zar ambled over to a crevice near the center of the flow field, and looked down where the boy pointed.

"Leatherwing droppings," he said. Pteranodon, or some other type of pterosaur, had left the pungent gift. "Like the last time."

Ka-Zar gazed skyward, toward the umbrella of clouds that perpetually hung over his realm. Out over the great central lake he spotted a flock of leaf-tailed rhamphorhynchus and several puffin-beaked dimorphodons. Over the foothills to his left he saw a pair of condors gliding the thermals. The creatures belonged there. They were merely going about their business of slurping up fish from the lake or carrion from the upland meadows. But Ka-Zar knew that earlier in the day he would have seen particularly large flying reptiles with saddles and riders, carrying away Ararisa and the two grown cousins who had shared the hut along with her late husband and their children.

Again. Ka-Zar clenched his teeth until the enamel threatened to crack. This search party had met with failure more profound than the previous one. Two days earlier, when a pair of Fall People brothers had been snatched from their raft while spear-fishing in the river near the village, sharp-eyed observers had seen the kidnappers and their winged mounts pause to rest on an islet out in the lake. The stygian blackness of Savage Land night had concealed where they went from there, but at least they had been seen. Should those raiders turn up in a village, some among the Fall People would recognize them.

Today, nothing. Only Ararisa's necklace to put on her empty grave. Though her abductors had taken care to carry her off alive, once their master had his way with her, she would be dead.

"Back to the village, my friends," Ka-Zar said. "Our vengeance will have to wait."

The mounting of the search, the snaring of the Tyrannosaurus rex, and the fruitless end of the chase had consumed most of the day. Twilight was nearing by the time the band of warriors slipped out of the jungle foliage into the fields of the Fall People.

Ka-Zar frowned at the rows of tiny corn stalks and the vegetable patches. He still wasn't certain how much he should have encouraged the Fall People to take up agriculture. They had not forgotten their hunter-gatherer ways yet, but the risk was there. Once they made the shift, their culture would never be the same.

Too many doubts. The day's mission had been a failure, so it was all too easy to question his lifework as well.

Preoccupied, so close to home, tired from an ordeal that had begun at first light, with the news of the raid, he failed to notice that the parrots and bowerbirds in the trees had gone silent.

Tongah was more alert. "Lord Ka-Zar! Beware!"

The tribesmen flung themselves flat. Abruptly a hail of axes and spears rained down from above. Ka-Zar whirled just in time to see talons descending. He leapt to the side.

Clever. Who would have expected a raid upon such a large group of warriors, coming so soon after the other attack? Wounded men screamed. Dust flew. Ka-Zar rolled to his feet and looked up.

A rider on a pteranodon had Immono and had already risen above the treeline. The youth kicked, swiping upward with his knife. The alert rider spurred his mount—

—and the flying reptile let go. Immono plummeted.

"No!" Ka-Zar screamed, sprinting forward.

He made it only four steps before a heavy weight landed on his back. His chin struck the path hard. Stars twinkled behind his eyelids.

"The Lord of the Savage Land himself." The exclamation grated like an obsidian knife dragged across granite, point down. The language was English. At one time, the voice had belonged to a friend. "I have been so looking forward to *touching* you."

Ka-Zar twisted, but could not free himself from the cold, scaly grip. He could see his attacker's face, however. It was elongated, green, with a bony protrusion extending its skull backward. The face of a pteranodon grotesquely combined with that of a man.

"Sauron," Ka-Zar grunted.

The monster answered with a smile. Checking to the side, it swept away Tongah, who had risen and drawn back his arm to fling his spear. Another warrior was sent tumbling on the other side, unable to react as fast as Sauron's long wings could whip outward. Other raiders had wheeled about on their pterosaur mounts and were keeping at bay anyone else who might try to interrupt their master at his amusement.

Tendrils of agony sprouted deep in Ka-Zar's body. From his spine, his heart, his joints. The strength poured from him. In seconds, even keeping his eyelids open was more than he could manage. Then, mercifully, everything went dark.

Shanna O'Hara sprinted through the gates of the village palisade. Some of the village warriors kept pace, but none were able to pull out ahead. Not after what she had seen in the sky.

She and her party leapt across an irrigation ditch and through a row of orchard crops into the corn and vegetable fields. It was as she had feared. Raiders on winged reptiles whirled and struck at the search party that had gone out with Ka-Zar. Limp bodies lay on the ground.

In the midst of them was the tall, blond form of her husband, pinned to the ground by a grotesque harpy, an enemy she had once thought dead.

She was within range now. She stopped, notched an arrow, and drew back her bowstring.

Sauron looked up, let go of Ka-Zar, and stared straight at her. Waves of nausea struck her. Something tugged at her mind, repeating a message so simple it was almost impossible to resist. *Sleep, sleep, sleep.*

LAW OF THE JUNGLE

She released the arrow. It sailed past Sauron's head. A clear miss, not even enough to make him flinch.

She and the warriors beside her stumbled forward, no longer completely dazed by his hypnotism. A wave of villagers—not just more warriors, but teens, pregnant women, children, elders—poured through the orchard and onto the field of battle. Ahead of them raced Zabu, Ka-Zar's sabretooth cat. Shanna had ordered him to stay and guard little Matthew, but the feline knew where he was needed most.

Sauron hissed and took flight. His squadron of raiders scattered. They vanished toward the clouds. A few arrows raced after them, but fell far short. They were gone. The growing twilight would soon swallow every trace of them.

Zabu sent a blood-curdling roar after them. Shanna bellowed even louder. It did nothing to slow the enemies down, but the outburst restored Shanna to full equilibrium. If those murderers returned. . . .

Tongah rose from the disrupted corn and bent over Ka-Zar. Zabu nosed in, rolled the fallen man over, and began licking his face. By the time Shanna arrived, her husband was stirring.

"He lives," Tongah said.

"Oh, my love," Shanna said. She leaned down and kissed him, wishing him awake.

To her joy, he did open his eyes. He stared vacantly for an instant, then focused on her features and smiled faintly. "I am a husk," he groaned. "I'm like a fly after the spider has sucked out its juices." The smile collapsed.

"He feasted on your energies," she said. "But we chased him away before he could take too much."

Ka-Zar tried to raise his head to check on his fallen comrades. "How bad?"

"Some were struck by the first hail of weapons," Tongah

declared sadly. Still crouched beside Ka-Zar, the chief surveyed the battle site. "An axe caved in Mhogo's skull. The others may have a chance, except . . . oh, no."

Shanna saw where he was looking. An entire mountain of heavy stone settled upon her heart. Fighting back the tears, she raised Ka-Zar to a sitting position so that he could see.

Immono lay crumpled in the corn furrows, his head twisted at an impossible angle. He had freed himself from the claws of the flying reptile, but not before he had gained too much altitude to land well. He was staring sightlessly at the darkening sky.

"Shanna . . ." Ka-Zar murmured.

"I know, I know," she said. "We need help. I'll make the call."

CHAPTER 2

N ear the idyllic, thickly wooded community of Salem Center in upstate New York, the summer night lay gently upon the Xavier Institute for Higher Learning, a latter-day incarnation of what had once been called Professor Charles Xavier's School for Gifted Youngsters. The day's mugginess had dissipated. Mild breezes caressed beds of petunias and wafted the leaves of trees that had just thickened into the full bounty of the season. A few puffy clouds rolled by beneath the dome of stars and moon. A passerby on Greymalkin Lane would have every reason to think of the facility as the epitome of quiet, contemplative study.

It's amazing what good soundproofing can do.

Deep beneath the visible portion of the building, bodies careened off the walls of the Danger Room. No silent contemplation here. Anyone treading across its threshold dared not relax their guard for a moment. If they did, they might have to pay a heavy price, in spite of the safety protocols.

Sailing through the air came two heavily muscled men known to the world as Wolverine and the Beast. Anyone would have labelled them hairy, particularly the Beast with his thick coat of blue fur, but at the moment they seemed even more so. Behind them raced six metal tentacles crackling with enough voltage to stun an elephant. The charged corona that extended from the devices was tugging each and every whisker, curl, and eyelash within reach straight out from the follicles. The two men were haloed in fuzz.

A feminine laugh echoed off the walls. The pair looked ridiculous. It didn't change the fact that the situation was serious. Nothing the Danger Room threw at its occupants was intended for their amusement. For many years, the chamber had been the key training site of the X-Men. If any group of super heroes had gone to greater measures to regularly challenge their powers, reflexes, and determination, they had probably swiped the idea from this mightiest of obstacle courses.

"Don't slow down now, Cornball!" Wolverine shouted.

He was speaking to the youngest occupant of the room. Sam Guthrie, or Cannonball—Cornball only to a certain rough, gruff, mannerless elder X-Man—was rocketing across the room. The Beast and Wolverine were his passengers, surfing atop the kinetic envelope that surrounded the youth. He had just saved them from the initial thrust of the tentacles.

In fact, Cannonball *was* slowing down. He hadn't much choice. The added weight was not the problem. The other wall was. If he sped up any more, he wouldn't be able to stop in time. They were safe enough inside his bubble of power, but the impact of the wall would likely knock him for a loop and give the Danger Room another chance to nail them.

"Now, Bishop!" Cannonball yelled.

The tall, broad, dark-skinned X-Man on the floor to Cannonball's right thrust out his arm. Out zoomed a burst of energy just like one of Sam's own explosions. In fact, it *was* one of Cannonball's blasts, absorbed a few moments earlier and saved until it was needed. The wave slammed against the tentacles, twisting them into pretzels.

LAW OF THE JUNGLE

The electrical charge in the mechanisms vanished. The metal arms scooted back into the wall like parts of one very sore octopus.

Cannonball throttled back, lighting deftly in a standing position. The Beast and Wolverine sailed on into the wall, but by the time they arrived, their speed was manageable. They struck feetfirst, spun, and landed adroitly on the floor next to a buxom, almond-eyed vixen in a skintight costume.

"Game's still live, Betts!" Wolverine said, extending his claws from the backs of his hands and swiping at her.

Elisabeth Braddock, also known as Psylocke, yelped and sprang back. Wolverine's slash—as light as it was quick—didn't come near her costume but she made a frantic unnecessary leap to "safety," which put her squarely on her rump.

"That, my blessed Ms. Braddock," stated the Beast, "is what ladies who laugh at fuzzy men deserve."

Psylocke's expression blackened. Rolling gracefully into a ninja stance, she sent a blistering telepathic comment straight into the skull of everyone in the room.

"My stars and garters!" the Beast blurted. "I take back the term *lady*. It does *not* apply."

Betsy opened her mouth to append a comment with her actual voice, but never got the words out. A panel slid open in the nearest wall. The muzzles of an entire row of laser cannons jutted forward.

Everyone ducked. Beams sizzled past just overhead. Everyone went back to work. Psylocke sent out the telepathic code phrase that would let them know which of dozens of rehearsed counterstrategies they would use. Each of the five X-Men rolled toward their designated position.

The cannons ceased firing.

"Hey—" Cannonball said. "Who aborted the session?"

Wolverine drew back his hands, ready to slash the nearest muzzle anyway should it resume firing. No one relaxed until the room's intercom crackled and Storm's voice came through the speakers. "My apologies for the interruption, my friends, but something has come up. Please meet me in the War Room."

Cannonball, Psylocke, and Bishop spared a few moments to grab towels and wipe off some of the sweat of the workout. The Beast combed down his disarrayed fur. Wolverine was Wolverine. They did not dawdle. Only an urgent matter would have prompted Storm to shut down the Danger Room sequence.

Still, the session had served its purpose. The Danger Room had gone through numerous upgrades over the years. The most recent ones had come from the Shi'ar Empire, as a gift from the Shi'ar empress Lilandra Neramani, friend to the X-Men and lover to the X-Men's founder, Charles Xavier. Unfortunately, the latest upgrades were telepathic circuits that had the Danger Room respond directly to the thoughts of the person running the session. None of the X-Men had been entirely comfortable with this particular upgrade, and so the Beast and Cyclops had removed it and reinstalled the previous version. This morning's workout was as much a test of that reinstallation as it was a test of the X-Men's fighting ability.

The five mutants marched through the building and filed into a huge room containing a ring of swivel chairs flanked by various monitors, arrayed around a huge central holographic display unit. A mere fraction of the chairs were occupied. The chamber could seat the entire X-Men roster, along with Professor X and whatever allies, super powered or otherwise, might be in residence at the mansion at any given time. But only Storm, Iceman, and Archangel were there to greet them, making eight in all.

"Thank you for coming," said Storm. She motioned them toward their seats. She herself remained upright, pacing the room in the broodingly serious way that characterized an African goddess of weather. "We've received a plea for help from Shanna O'Hara, on behalf of herself and Ka-Zar. With the Professor on Muir Island and Scott in Alaska visiting his grandparents' estate with Jean, I'm stepping up as co-leader and authorizing a mission to the Savage Land."

"How bad is it, Ororo?" asked Iceman. He had fetched a glass of water and was getting rid of nervous energy by manipulating the size and shape of the ice cubes he'd formed in the liquid. He was in human form and in street clothes. He had been planning to go into town to sample microbrews at Harry's Hideaway. Pretending to be an ordinary guy out for a laid-back evening, not a mutant with a certain amount of uneasy personal history behind him.

Storm taped a computer mouse, which caused a holographic display in the center of their circle to awake. Within it formed a green-skinned creature with the head, wings, and tail of a pteranodon, but a body somewhat like that of a human. Even in simulation, his eyes seemed to bore right through whatever he gazed at.

"Sauron has recovered," Storm stated almost unnecessarily. Everyone in the room recognized the figure. "He has been leading groups of savages, sometimes mounted on pterosaurs, in raids upon the villages of the United Tribes. Taking captives to feed his vampiric needs, no doubt, and killing those that get in the way. Tongah's Fall People have borne the brunt of the latest attacks. Ka-Zar was hurt, ambushed by Sauron himself."

"Last I heard, he was completely loco," Wolverine said. "Hardly knew which talon to pick his nose with."

"Or perhaps even burned to death inside the Pangean relic where Ka-Zar last encountered him," Storm confirmed. "He was not a serious threat. Something has happened to improve his condition. He is mentally coherent again. In fact, from the summary that Shanna forwarded to us through our private link, he is more capable of strategy and analysis than ever."

"Woulda been better if I'd finished 'im off last time I tangled with 'im—or if we did it a couple years back." Wolverine had recently faced Sauron, and only let him go due to Sauron's powers of hypnosis.

"It wasn't our place to be his executioners, Logan," Storm said patiently. This was an old argument, but she needed to make clear her position. "Certainly not after Professor X successfully purged the virus that turned Karl Lykos into Sauron. He was cured. He deserved his chance for happiness as much as anyone else. For a brief interval, he was able to carry on a legitimate medical practice. He helped people. He had the love of a brave and good woman."

Wolverine did not give in. "Emphasis on the word *brief*, 'Roro. The Toad nabbed 'im and made 'im as dangerous as ever. You forgettin' that pretty little lady is history, killed by her man himself?"

"That was unfortunate, but if we followed your argument to the extreme of its logic, you might as well say we should travel back in time and suffocate any infant who is destined to become a killer."

At the mention of time travel, Bishop's face clouded. "Logan," he told Wolverine, "you do not mean what you say."

Wolverine's eyes flickered beneath his bushy eyebrows. "I always mean what I say. This time around, could be the best thing if we forget about the cure angle."

"We will have to accept every possibility," Storm said. "The certainty is that he must be stopped. You will *not* kill him if we can safely take him alive. If there is any shred of Karl Lykos remaining within him, it deserves a chance to be restored."

"You can count on me," Logan said. "An' I'll follow your lead no matter what—you know that. But you also know in your gut that sooner or later, it'll come down to blood. Always does."

Bishop combed his fingers through the narrow shred of beard on his chin. "I saw him only once, from a distance, when Storm and I fetched Rogue, Jubilee, and Wolverine from the Savage Land. I know him otherwise only from the archives and from conversations with some of you. He has often been associated with the mutates of the Savage Land, am I correct? The group from which Vertigo sprang?"

"Yes. Some of the mutates have put in appearances," Storm replied. "Barbarus, Gaza, Lupo, and Amphibius have all taken part in at least one village raid. It is probably safe to assume that Brainchild is assisting them, somewhere in the background."

She prodded the holographic display. Sauron's image vanished, replaced by five smaller representations. Gaza was a giant, muscular savage, with eyes that had obviously never known sight. Barbarus was not quite as large but appeared just as strong, with an extra pair of arms. Amphibius resembled a giant, humanoid frog, Lupo a wolfish man with pointed ears. Brainchild's body was scrawny and small, but his cranium bulged out to twice the diameter of a normal person's.

"These five are seldom far apart, and tend not to leave the Savage Land as some of their brood do. They may be the cause of Sauron's resurgence. They were originally created by Magneto to be subservient to his desires. They have depended on masters to focus their ambitions. Sauron has played that role when Zaladane wasn't available. Perhaps they found him and somehow resurrected him so that they would have a commander once more.''

''What about the others?'' Bishop asked. ''Whiteout and Worm?''

Psylocke shuddered. She was the one X-Man in the room who had been part of the mission to the Savage Land in which Worm had first been encountered. She telepathically shared a memory of how the mutate had seized control over the bodies of herself, Colossus, and Dazzler.

''Fortunately those two have not surfaced,'' Storm said. ''They were more Zaladane's pets. Which isn't to say that we shouldn't be on the alert for them.''

''Still enough of a zoo to make this a *real* fun trip,'' Iceman muttered.

''When do we leave?'' Bishop asked.

''We leave in the morning,'' Storm said.

Wolverine squinted. ''Why the delay?''

''Ka-Zar and Shanna have beaten off the most recent attack. It sounds as though Sauron has enough victims to sustain him another day or two. We won't indulge in any unwarranted delays, but it's only prudent to take what remains of this evening to outfit ourselves properly and get some sleep. It's going to be a long trip to the southern polar regions and a potentially exhausting ordeal once we're there.''

Bishop asked, ''Is there any particular reason why you emphasized *we* so heavily?''

''Yes—I'd like you to remain behind. I'm not comfortable leaving the mansion completely empty with so many of us so distant, especially with Cyclops, Phoenix, and the Professor also away.''

Nodding, Bishop said, ''Understood.'' Storm was grateful that the time-travelling X-Man didn't argue. But then, Bishop was a soldier first, and knew when to follow orders.

Storm looked around the table. Everyone looked ready to go now.

With one exception. Archangel kept his eyes on the table, his blue-skinned face grim.

''Warren?'' Storm asked. ''Is everything all right?''

Archangel looked up. ''Yes. Yes, I'm fine.'' He hesitated. ''Sorry. I was just lost in thought for a moment there.''

''See you bright and early for takeoff,'' Ororo concluded.

Archangel lingered behind after the others slipped out the doorway.

''You truly did not wish to go,'' Storm said. ''If that's how you feel—''

Warren grimaced. ''No, no, I have to go. Even if it was just me by myself, I'd have to go.''

''But you don't have to like it, is what you're saying.''

''Brings up a lot of history, Ororo.''

''I know it does.'' She ambled toward the door, pausing to squeeze his blue arm. ''Try not to agonize, my friend.''

''Oh, I'll just lay back on my pillow tonight and dream of beaches on Maui. Palm trees swaying, foxy chicks in bikinis near the water. Life's a breeze.''

Creatures roamed in Warren Worthington's nightmares. They gibbered, shrieked, and worst of all, laughed. Those visions were the easy ones, because even in sleep, he recognized them as unreal. They were the traces of hallucinations thrust into his brain by a master of hypnotism. The hard part came as the dreams turned toward his original reaction to those chimeras.

I was spineless, Warren thought. *I was terrified.*

His eyes. His eyes.

Sauron gazed at Warren and it was as if his unnatural, reptilian orbs filled the sky. Shudders coursed along Angel's wings—his old, feathered wings, not the mechanical appendages he wore now—rendering them so nerveless he could barely stay aloft.

So much fear. It churned his intestines. He was willing to do anything to stem it. Sauron turned him against his friends. He obeyed. The fear still rooted deep in his bones, but as long as he obeyed, it didn't grow worse. Even that slight blessing kept him a faithful slave.

More memories. Fleeing those eyes again, racing up from a jungle and through mists into stark, freezing air. The prospect of death from the cold appealed to him more than turning and facing that green, winged demon.

Somehow, he had gone back and fought. Ka-Zar had *made* him go back and fight. For a few short minutes, Warren had endured the quivering muscles, the looseness in his bowels, the chatter of his teeth. But those eyes had locked upon him again.

And Sauron spoke the words that would echo for years thereafter:

"I long ago took your measure . . . and found you wanting."

Archangel lurched to a sitting position, flinging the top sheet and blanket off the bed. He almost cried out before he completely woke and saw where he was.

Psylocke regarded him silently, mouth drawn into a thin line.

Archangel winced. "You read any of that?"

She bent her head. "Your mind was in such turmoil, I couldn't help but reach inside to try to calm you. Yes, I glimpsed what you were dreaming of. I'm sorry. I had no right."

"It's . . . all right," he said forlornly. "We should have talked before we fell asleep. It's just that I still haven't come to terms with how useless I was those times against Sauron. I was—"

"Wanting?"

"Yes. Wanting. Inadequate."

"Sweetheart," Betsy said, leaning over and kissing him firmly, "you are not the same person you were then. I've taken your measure, too, you know. Trust me, Sauron doesn't know what he's talking about. You have proven yourself a brave and complete hero. You're *my* hero."

"Thank you," Warren said. He let himself be drawn into an eyes-to-eyes moment of connectedness. Betsy's body was warm beside him, chasing away some of the chill he felt within. "Keep sending me that thought. If I can see half of what you see in me, I'll be fine. But I'm not there yet. This came to a head in the Savage Land. The circle won't close until that jungle is back under my wings."

A wren chirped on a branch out the window, composing a tune to mark the paling of the sky. The radio alarm clock on the nightstand clicked and out poured an old Credence Clearwater Revival tune.

Warren pressed the button and the song broke off. Ninety minutes until departure time. He reached for his lover.

"Be careful what you ask for, young man," said Psylocke with a smile. "You might get it."

CHAPTER 3

The first time that Storm had come to the Savage Land, she, Cyclops, Nightcrawler, Colossus, Banshee, and Wolverine had tunneled through solid rock while she froze an avalanche of hot lava that was trying to incinerate them. For all her brave attempts to fight her deep-rooted claustrophobia, she had emerged into the open air of the jungle as limp as the porridge she had often eaten as a child-thief in Cairo. She had been so in need of calm and recuperation that she proved a pathetically easy target for Karl Lykos, providing him with the mutant lifeforce required to fuel the rebirth of Sauron.

The second time she had come to the Savage Land, the X-Men had landed their *Blackbird* at Deep Ice Station Alpha, one of the U.S./UN military bases that guarded the perimeter of the prehistoric biosphere. An earthquake—triggered by ancient technologies that Brainchild, under the direction of Sauron, had activated—had brought the underground complex down around them. Rubble had pressed suffocatingly around Ororo, as it had when she had been buried alive in the bombing that killed her parents.

Good had come of both those ordeals. After the first trip, the X-Men returned home to find that Phoenix and the Beast had not been killed in the volcanic event, as feared. Furthermore, the team had preserved the Savage Land from the destruction being wrought by the god Garokk, the Petrified Man. The second trip, they had beaten Sauron, returned him to New York, and cured him—a happy ending for Karl Lykos and his beloved Tanya Anderssen, had not the Toad and the Brotherhood of Evil Mutants come along years later and rewritten it.

Yes, good had come, but if Storm had to endure another dark, ominous trip beneath a mountain of collapsing rock, then by the Goddess, she would surely turn catatonic and wish to die.

At the moment, she was confronted by more immediate worries. The X-Men's supersonic transport bucked and rattled, caught in the fierce weather that afflicted the Drake Passage between South America and Antarctica. Driving snow pelted the windows. If not for Archangel's piloting skills and Ororo's constant tempering of the storm's fury, they would never be able to reach, much less land upon, the mountain shelf that Shanna's communiqué had directed them to.

A surge of turbulence pushed them up a hundred meters and down two hundred in the span of three seconds.

I think I'm going to be sick, Psylocke reported telepathically.

"Ororo!" Archangel barked. "Can you do something about that wind shear? I'm starting our final approach. We won't have enough altitude to tolerate that sort of abuse anymore."

"I'm trying, Warren. That one would have been much worse if I'd been idle."

The screen in front of Archangel acquired a blip. "There," he said. "That's the beacon." Ka-Zar had installed it a year earlier, and Shanna had provided the code sequence of nonsinusoidal wave emissions that would render it visible to their equipment.

The plane shuddered as Warren dropped the landing gear.

The blip wavered and hopped from one side of the screen to another. It was supposed to remain steady between the cross-hairs.

"Controls don't respond like they should," Archangel reported. "Too much ice and wind."

Ororo opened her mouth and thought, *Hear me, sister wind. Be calm. Let us ride the sky gently, happy in each other's presence.* The mantra helped her focus her weather-manipulation powers.

Gusts whipped up the nose of the jet. Archangel roared an unintelligible curse and forced the stick back into its proper position. *Calm, sister*, Storm begged. *Be at peace.*

Snowbound cliffs rose to starboard. A dark wall of mountain loomed ahead. Somewhere down there was a spot flat enough to land, but the swirling ice and snow concealed it.

"Oh, God," Psylocke said.

Storm felt a warm caress deep inside, behind her heart, at the core of her weather sense. The attunement came, so clear that it truly was as if she were communicating with an entity. Be it a wind sister or Mother Nature, she smiled at the vivid familiarity. She reached upward.

The winds steadied. They were still blowing hard, but only from one direction and at a consistent rate. The snow seemed to lose its animosity. The view ahead cleared. A narrow strip of level mountainside appeared straight ahead. The beacon confirmed it as the landing site.

Sweat poured down Archangel's blue forehead. His arm muscles quivered from the strain of holding the controls firm. He was murmuring to himself. Still, for the others, it seemed to be a quick, safe touchdown on the slab of rock and snow. Only the final, sharp bump showed that anything was less than optimal.

"Goddess, that was close." Storm heaved a deep sigh,

unbuckled, and stood up. Something crunched beneath her booted feet.

"What are these yellow-green crystals on the floor?" the windrider asked.

Psylocke groaned.

"Betts wasn't kidding about throwing up," Iceman explained. "But don't worry. As you can see, I froze it before it touched anything."

"Super heroes don't dribble-vomit," the Beast declared. "Strictly projectile all the way. Very impressive, Ms. Braddock."

"I warned you not t'take that last stack o' pancakes this mornin'," Cannonball added.

"Be quiet now," Betsy said in a voice so tiny it resembled thoughtspeak. "Or next time I'll take aim."

Warren stood up from his pilot's chair. "She was probably reading my mind as we landed, and knew how little control I actually had over the aircraft."

"I was calming your thoughts, helping to keep you focused," Psylocke said. "I forgot to do the same for myself."

"I vote that we debark before anything thaws, and remember to set the self-cleaning cycle," Hank said. "And let's not forget to think well of Forge for making our vehicle so entirely user-friendly."

"Everybody for the exit," Logan called. "Don't forget to zip up your parkas."

Bone-cracking cold, made all the worse by the region's katabatic winds, assaulted them as they descended the ramp. Storm deflected as much of the blizzard as she could, but the temperature was beyond her ability to mitigate. They needed every last bit of the insulation afforded by their clothing.

The ramp retreated as they walked away, and the exit portal sealed itself shut. The outside lights blinked out. Their transport had not gone idle, however. In addition to the cleaning apparatus, power continued to flow through several major systems, keeping the polar air from crippling it, maintaining its readiness to fly the moment the X-Men returned. And all the while it would remain invisible to the detection equipment of the various UN bases hidden elsewhere in the icy desolation.

Storm had been deprived of the sight of snow for many years during her childhood. In the warrens of the Nile delta, imprisoned by the desert tones of ochre, tan, and rust, she could only dream of its cold, ivory purity. One of her first weatherworking tricks had been to chill a cloud and stand beneath it, letting the icy flakes fall on her outstretched tongue. Now it was the desert she missed, with its blessed heat. She rejoiced when they slipped beneath an overhang of rock and out of the gale. At last, she could cease expending energy just to make conditions manageable.

Before her stood a cavern.

"Goddess," she whispered.

This is not a tomb, she reminded herself. The cavern had survived for millennia; it was stable. At the other end, they would emerge through a waterfall into the Savage Land. No traps. For most of its length, the walls did not crowd any closer than a hallway in the Xavier Institute. Knowing her phobia, Ka-Zar would not have let Shanna suggest a route that would have her screaming for the open sky.

She drew in a deep breath, braced herself, and continued forward.

Storm did not need to announce to the group precisely when they crossed into the influence of the weather nexus that contained the Savage Land. Everyone could feel it. On one side of a passageway laced with stalactites and stalagmites, the frosty breath of Antarctica nipped at their extremities. On the other side, a moist, tropical draft warmed the cave walls, eradicating any trace of ice. The threshold was that distinct.

They shucked off their cold-weather gear and left it piled neatly on a ledge to slip into on the return hike.

The roar of the waterfall filtered down the twists and turns, becoming thunderous as they approached. Muted light appeared. Soon they were able to douse their flashlights. One final turn, and they faced a cascade of warm water.

"Last one through's an ankylosaurus," Hank shouted, and leapt into the spray.

The others flung themselves after him, falling a mere ten feet or so into a broad, deep pool. With the cool, refreshing liquid around her, Storm's burden sailed from her shoulders. No more walls. She kicked exuberantly, surfacing into an atmosphere as warm as her homeland.

Wolverine gave her a hand onto the bank. She summoned a zephyr to dry her uniform, regarded the verdant foliage on every side, and sighed gratefully.

"Bright as an equatorial afternoon," Hank said, scratching his pointy ears. "I've always wondered how the Savage Land manages that. It must be four P.M. by now. At this latitude, at this time of year, the sun's already below the horizon. Manipulating the climate is a feat in itself, but where does the place get its light?"

"It's made from ozone," Iceman joked. "That accounts for the hole in the ozone layer over the South Pole."

Hank chuckled. "What you don't realize, Mr. Drake, is that you could be *right*."

"Let's take a look around, Warren," Storm said.

He nodded, spread his intimidating biometallic wings, and flapped aloft. She summoned winds to follow, but found herself nearly colliding with a cypress tree on the way up.

LAW OF THE JUNGLE

"You okay, Ororo?" Archangel called.

"Fine now," she said. "I had forgotten how unusual the wind is here. I have to 'speak' to it carefully."

The terrain sprawled beneath them. Warren whistled. "Oh, man, what a sight!"

Ororo had no words for it. The Savage Land filled a huge valley rimmed by the Eternity Mountains. Above, a glorious umbrella of mists held in the tropical air. At times, the cloud bottoms whirled and puffed into phantasmagorical shapes, brushed with the tones of sunset and rainbows. All without, as Hank had pointed out, an actual sun to generate the colors.

Though the highest ridges were lost to the inversion layer, foothills and lesser peaks thrust up from the jungles, some so distant the humid air rendered their slopes indistinct and almost illusory, like the creation of some faery artist. On the valley floor spread a carpet of green, green, and more green. Cycads, ferns, palms and other relics of the Mesozoic Era filled dells where dinosaurs and protomammals reigned. Elsewhere, flowering plants, broadleaf trees, and elephant grass hid a riot of other animal species.

Humans were here, too. Tendrils of smoke from wood fires rose from river banks and clearings, marking the sites of the villages of the United Tribes—the Fall People, the Lake People, the Sky People, and others under the guidance of Nereel. Storm hoped to see Nereel, recalling wistfully the smile that used to light up Colossus's face whenever he spent time with the warrior woman.

Aside from the smoke, the traces of the indigenous people were well hidden. Just a few scattered fields, a watchtower on stilts, or the carved points of a log stockade. No paved roads, no buildings of concrete and steel, only the most primitive dams and bridges. The residents of the Savage Land lived close to nature. The rare outsider that came to live here, such as Ka-Zar and Shanna—even Karl Lykos, when he had been able to maintain his human shape—observed that covenant as well.

Not a trivial thing, Storm knew. Many times the land had withstood attempts at exploitation, from within and from without. There, down on an island in the center of a vast lake, stood a remnant of one such blasphemy—a citadel created by Sauron and his mutates, in imitation of one built by Magneto. Only a shell was left, but it was a reminder that the Earth, for all its size, had no wildernesses left that were unscarred.

"There's the village of the Fall People," Warren shouted. "Right where Shanna said to look."

Storm spotted it, near the banks of the crystalline stream that flowed from the waterfall through thick jungle on its way toward the lake. It was not in the same locale as last time. The Fall People were largely hunter-gatherers, and moved between several different sites as game grew scarce.

"Good," Ororo said. "Let's start transporting the others."

She and Archangel swooped back to the pool. Warren, not surprisingly, chose Psylocke as his passenger. Storm wrapped her palms around Wolverine's wrists and vaulted skyward. Cannonball prepared to follow with the Beast, and Iceman generated an ice slide to follow along on. In this humidity, Bobby Drake would have plenty of moisture to convert to ice.

No pausing to admire the scenery this time. She raced in Warren's wake. She couldn't catch him. Once Archangel hit his cruising speed, she would have to whip up a gale force wind in order to keep up. Disturbing the environment to such a degree would be irresponsible.

"One of these days you have to learn to fly," she told Logan.

LAW OF THE JUNGLE

"Hope not. Yer the cutest taxi I know, 'Roro."

"Thank you, old friend," she said with a smile. The banter reassured her that, despite their disagreements over how to deal with Sauron, Logan wouldn't let it get in the way of his performance as an X-Man. More importantly, he wouldn't let it interfere with their friendship.

Ororo glided beyond a towering stand of eucalyptus trees and suddenly found herself over the fields and community grounds of the village. She dipped toward the center of a ring of bamboo-and-grass huts and teepees, where Psylocke was already engaged in conversation. Storm recognized Shanna by her lithe body and long blonde tresses, and Tongah by his remarkably tall body and Mohawk haircut, a style not unlike the one she had affected for a time, though hers was never cropped as closely.

A well-muscled blond man was ambling gingerly toward the group. Beside him walked a huge sabretooth cat.

"Ka-Zar's still hurtin'," Logan said. "He usually moves as smoothly as Zabu."

As if he had heard his name, the great feline lifted his head and coughed a greeting.

Storm dipped between the crowns of the huts and dropped Wolverine the last few feet to the ground. Compact as his body was, she murmured thanks that she was free of the weight. Unburdened, she was able to flutter to a dignified landing.

Cannonball roared down with the Beast, Iceman bringing his ice slide down behind them.

Shanna and Psylocke slipped off to the side, into a knot of village women, babies, and toddlers. Wolverine strode between the huts, obviously needing to assess the village's security before he could endure standing and talking. Ororo chose to remain on the packed-dirt storytelling circle where

Ka-Zar, Zabu, and Tongah stood. Iceman, Archangel, Beast, and Cannonball shadowed her.

"Welcome, wind-rider," stated Tongah. As chieftain, he was the official host. Etiquette required that he speak first.

"I am happy to see you looking well, my friend," Ororo replied. He was looking particularly healthy considering that he had been dead prior to the High Evolutionary's resurrection of the Savage Land. "We are grateful for your hospitality."

Ororo was acutely conscious that the native and his people were the true custodians of the Savage Land. It was all too easy to ignore their contribution, as if Ka-Zar, Shanna, and those born in the outside world were somehow inherently superior. She vowed not to fall into that habit. It resembled too much the way European colonists had treated her beloved Kenyans, barely two generations ago. She wished she could have answered in his own tongue—he had used English in honor of his guests.

"As we are grateful for your aid," he said. He clasped one of her hands between his palms, bowed, and released her.

Only then did Ka-Zar step forward, with his faithful sabretooth at his side. "On behalf of Shanna and our little family, hello to you all." He reached out and patted the head of a small boy who had climbed on Zabu's back.

"He has your nose," Ororo said, smiling at the child.

"And Shanna's temper," Ka-Zar chuckled. He checked behind to see if his wife was listening, but luckily she was still to the side next to Psylocke, who appeared to be conversing with the cluster of tribeswomen.

"You are well?"

He winced. "Bruised from the fight. I'm hoping another long night's sleep will wipe out some of the fatigue. There's nothing quite like having an energy vampire suck half the life out of you. It's early to bed for me tonight, dosed with another of the tribe shaman's herbal remedies. It worked wonders last night, and I can't afford to be below par at a time of crisis like this.''

"What happened to the Ka-Zar of old who always charged into danger, without an ounce of caution in his skull?" she said with a laugh. "Always pushing past the limit?"

"I'm an old married man now. A dad. I've had to get smarter." Ka-Zar looked around. "Seven of you?" he asked.

"Yes."

"I will miss saying hello to Scott and Jean and the others. But seven is a good number.''

Storm cocked an eyebrow. "Why do you say that?"

He cleared his throat. "Perhaps you've heard some of what the Savage Land has gone through lately?"

"You have my sympathies. The incursions from the civilized world have, from all I've read, been outrageous.''

"And devastating. We've had a record number of births among the village women this season, but it will take many more like that to bring the population back to old levels. Too many dead, Ororo. Sauron, Terminus, Zaladane, Garokk, Stegron—it's becoming hard to count the number of ravagers who've tried to destroy the habitat or its inhabitants. You heard about Roxxon Corporation trying to flood us out in order to come in and drill for oil?"

"Yes. I'm told their lawyers have convinced the courts the floods were all the work of a renegade employee. A man conveniently deceased, of course.''

"Yeah. The corporate board of directors covered their tracks. That incursion made me particularly angry, Ororo. I can't do much to stop gods and aliens from turning up, but Roxxon's agents were human. They were just one more example of outsider prospectors trying to get at the gold or the oil or the vibranium in our soil. I can and will see that their kind find the door to the Savage Land bolted shut in their faces. In the past few months the only people we've let in have been journalists, and that was only so that the plight of the Savage Land remains in the news back in the developed world. Shanna says we should go so far as to kick out the anthropologists. We have only five of them in the whole habitat, keeping a low profile and living right with the indigenous tribes, as adopted members.''

''The policy of 'no outsiders' has long been in force,'' Storm commented.

''More or less. We eased off more than we should have. We now follow the restrictions to the letter wherever possible. We could have asked the UN for help this time, but if we let S.H.I.E.L.D. agents crawl around here, it would set a precedent of intrusion we'd never be able to back away from. They'd bring in armored vehicles and helicopters, they'd need roads and causeways to get around. Before long they'd be rolling right over burial grounds without even the decency to say, 'Oops'.''

''Peace, my friend,'' Ororo said, stepping back from the vehemence in Ka-Zar's tone.

''Sorry.'' He relaxed his fists. ''The X-Men are old allies. Friends. We've been through a lot. But right now, Shanna and I didn't want to have to call anybody from outside. You could say inviting you was a compromise. No bulldozers and corps of engineers. Just a few super heroes, keeping the damage to a minimum.''

''I . . .'' Storm struggled to think of the correct response.

''Hey, bub, you did *ask* us to come.'' Logan was suddenly standing beside Storm, having slipped forward in his inimitable, quiet way. He had acquired a tobacco leaf from the drying racks at the end of the row of tee-pees and had rolled it into a makeshift cigar. He lit it, puffed, and raised his eyebrow at Ka-Zar.

Storm, murmured Psylocke telepathically. Storm glanced back to the other female X-Man, who was still with the group of tribal women. Shanna had turned away and was approaching.

Yes, Psylocke? Storm asked silently.

Serious turf issues here, Psylocke sent.

So I've noticed.

I'm not reading all that much ambivalence from Ka-Zar, actually. It's our She-Devil over here. She doesn't like it that I've already established a rapport with the villagers.

Leave it to Psylocke to be digging up dirt mere minutes after arriving on scene, Storm mused. *Why on Earth not?*

I think it's more a general paranoia about outsiders than anything personal toward us. Also, I think Shanna figured they were "safe" from us "interlopers" because, aside from Tongah, they don't speak English. She wasn't taking into account that my telepathy enables me to communicate with them directly.

Storm answered, *Thank you for the warning.*

The psychic conversation had whisked by in a fraction of the span it would have taken to say the words aloud. Shanna was just now joining them. Wolverine and Ka-Zar were still gazing at one another in the manner of decisive warriors.

Interlopers. Storm resented that designation, but she was resolved to be diplomatic. Everyone was tired and edgy. Half a day fighting on the same side and the friction should—she hoped—evaporate.

"I can see your concern," Storm told Ka-Zar. "Rest assured, the X-Men will abide by your wishes. Let's not let this get between us. We came for a reason. Has there been any more news in regard to Sauron?''

''No. But Shanna is better able to bring you up to date. I've been flat on my back much of these last twenty-four hours.''

Shanna crooked her arm inside Ka-Zar's elbow, her stance not unlike a mother leopard guarding an injured cub. ''We have heard of no new raids. That's the pattern. A quick ambush, and the attackers fade into the jungle.''

''Or they fly off on their leatherwings,'' Tongah added, in the outraged tone of a warrior whose opponent will not stand and fight.

''The fact is,'' Shanna said bitterly, ''we have no idea where Sauron's base of operation lies.''

''That . . . isn't like Sauron,'' Ororo said. ''Every time he's emerged from hiding, he's carried on like a pharaoh in his palace.''

''Or,'' rumbled the Beast, who had walked up while Archangel joined Psylocke, ''like Tolkien's arch-villain in *The Lord of the Rings*, from whence Lykos pilfered his alias.''

''He isn't behaving that way this time,'' Shanna explained. ''We not only don't know where his Barad-Dûr lies, we don't even know which part of the Savage Land serves as his Mordor. On the occasions when we've been able to observe where the pterosaur riders have gone, they've found temporary havens on islands or hilltops, and moved on to their final destination under cover of darkness.''

''Oh, great, we come all this way to square off against him, and we don't know where to find him?'' Iceman asked.

''No,'' Shanna said. ''That's a big reason why we needed you. If we'd had a spot to concentrate our efforts, Nereel could have ordered a gathering of the United Tribes and mounted some sort of assault.''

LAW OF THE JUNGLE

"Though that strategy would have endangered many lives," Ka-Zar admitted.

"Still," Shanna said pointedly, "we could have done *something*."

"Very well then," Storm said. "The first order of business is to locate him. I confess this guerrilla-warfare style of Sauron's troubles me. One of his great weaknesses was his tendency to make rash moves due to overconfidence. If he's curbed that handicap, we will have to be twice as ingenious to bring him down."

"Agreed," Ka-Zar said. "The only bright side is that since we don't know which way to hurry off to, we can retire to the lodge and discuss this carefully over a meal. You'll have a chance to meet some of the people you're helping, and we can all gather our strength." He waved up at the cloud layer. "There's not much left of today. Let's help you get settled in. When night arrives in the Savage Land, you appreciate good company and stockade walls around you."

Storm rubbed the tight muscles of her neck. A little R&R—not a lowering of their guard, but an acknowledgment that they had done as much, physically, as they could for the time being—would do a world of good. Some real food, not the packaged stuff that passed for victuals in modern society, that was a fringe benefit of a visit to the Savage Land that had slipped her mind completely until now.

But it would be difficult to relax enough to revitalize herself with this new concern: A cautious, hidden Sauron, who attacked at random times and locations.

Psylocke stood just outside the door of the lodge, gazing at Archangel. Warren was standing atop the guard platform near the top of the stockade wall, near the gate. The glow of the watchfires reflected off his wings, a cold, almost sinister scattering of light. She was not afraid of it, of course, but the Fall People gave the source a wide berth.

Warren had just flown a circuit around the village. Keeping an eye out for enemy activity, he said. Certainly a wise precaution, one that Storm and especially Wolverine had heartily endorsed. But Betsy saw his stiff spine and long, brooding stares into the jungle and understood that playing watchdog was not his prime motivation. Being out there meant he could be alone, working through his demons.

Time after time since they had become intimate, she had telepathically glimpsed him wrestling with the question of his own willpower. Asking himself over and over if some weakness in his fortitude allowed Apocalypse to turn him into his horseman, Death. Warren had struggled hard to regain his humanity. His shedding of Apocalypse's manipulations demonstrated to her the profound depth of his character, but somehow he wouldn't quite believe he was deserving of that internal victory, especially since he retained the cyanotic blue skin tone and biometallic wings, both "gifts" from Apocalypse.

She didn't try to reach out telepathically. He needed his privacy. All night, perhaps. If he did seek out his hammock, it would undoubtedly be long after she had entered her own dance with Morpheus. He might kiss her forehead when he joined her then, but what good was that if she were unconscious? Sometimes having a boyfriend along seemed more solitary than traveling alone.

The flaps behind her lifted. Ka-Zar ducked beneath them, stood, and acknowledged her with a nod. "Miss Elisabeth Braddock," he said, in playful imitation of the formal British speech they had both been exposed to as children. As adults, their accents had strayed far from those roots, but the bond was there, called up every time they opened their mouths to say something.

"Lord Kevin Plunder," she replied. A pleasant tingle flowed down her chest to her lower body, like the warm, alcoholic kiss of the pomegranate wine the Fall People had served an hour ago. Such a lovely curve to his muscles. And then there was that glorious blond mane.

"I'm off to my hut," he said, "before I fall over."

Even in the dim light, Psylocke made out wrinkles around his eyes. His posture lacked the fluid ease it normally possessed. But what struck her was how robust he remained at the core. Had Sauron leeched any other non-mutant human being, briefly or not, the person would be fortunate to be able to lift his eyelids the next day. This man, no matter what he claimed, had enough juice left that she found the idea of him retiring to his hut a provocative image. True, his wife was right on the other side of the hide walls of the lodge. True, her own boyfriend was perched within sight. But what was the harm in flirting?

"You'll be yourself soon," she said encouragingly.

"If I had a nurse such as you, I could probably avoid being an invalid altogether," he said.

"You have a tongue that can charm savage beasts," she said, chuckling. "No wonder Zabu follows you around." Suddenly she wondered—Zabu *was* male, wasn't he? And then even more suddenly, she had to know if Ka-Zar's flirting was just idle habit and charm, or something more . . . specific to her.

She lightly touched his mind. Not enough that he would be able to sense the probe, but a sufficient glimpse to know what was on the surface, right at that moment.

Oh, my! She whirled suddenly to hide the furiousness of

her blush. Men had such a—visceral quality to the pictures in their heads.

"What is it? Did something startle you?" he asked. The tone of frivolity was gone, replaced by concern and readiness for action.

"No. Just a telepathic comment from Warren," she lied. "Telling me not to wait up for him." *There*, she thought. *Bring up the boyfriend. Let him think you're a good girl, even if it isn't always true.*

And for goodness sake, quit feeling so pleased with yourself, Betsy Braddock.

The door flaps lifted again. Shanna stepped out. She eyed Psylocke sharply.

Whoops, thought Betsy, needing no telepathy whatsoever to read that icy expression.

"You didn't say good night," Shanna scolded her husband.

"Sorry," he said. "I gave Matthew a kiss. He was supposed to pass it on to you."

"Grounds for divorce," she stated. Then, frown melting, she pressed hands around his cheeks and pulled him forward for the kind of kiss that could never be properly conveyed through an intermediary.

"I'll just go get myself another cup of that excellent wine Tongah introduced me to," Psylocke murmured, and slipped inside the building.

In fact, Psylocke did locate her earthenware mug and poured a splash more of the beverage into it. A sip or two helped settle the fluttering of her heart. Slightly.

Zira, one of the young women Psylocke had befriended earlier, was sitting beside little Matthew, with Zabu flopped on the reed mats nearby. Zira appeared to be Matthew's governess. She possessed a bright smile and gentle movements.

LAW OF THE JUNGLE

A lovely body, too, tucked into nothing more than a loin-cloth. Psylocke envied that. It was awfully muggy in this jungle. Not the sort of place meant for clothing, even a costume as streamlined as her own.

"Almoost tookered off," Zira said, stroking the boy's head. He yawned, leaning against her.

"Almost tuckered out," Betsy repeated, slipping in a dose of corrected English before she continued in the native language. "I can see you take good care of him."

"Ka-Zar and Shanna need many eyes upon this one," Zira said cheerfully. "His legs may yet be short, but he moves like a cheetah."

"Something in the genetics."

Zira blinked. "Genetics?"

Psylocke realized she hadn't managed to translate the word. She needed to pay attention to read a language from a mind quickly enough to apply it flawlessly. Apparently she was still distracted. "I mean he takes after his mother and father."

"Oh, yes." Zira grinned at that, but then her face fell. "It is a gift and a curse. Enemies try to take Matthew hostage. Or worse."

"I—" Psylocke began. She stopped and turned.

Shanna was there, having come up as silently as a leopard. Betsy had sensed her only by the proximity of her thoughts. Her physical body was too inherently stealthy to monitor readily. Had Ms. O'Hara really been born in the civilized world? She seemed too primal for that to be possible.

"To bed with him, Zira," Shanna told the tribeswoman. "It's time, no matter how late that nap was."

She is the mother. I am only the nanny. The thought was so vivid in Zira's mind that Psylocke couldn't avoid hearing it. Some thoughts couldn't be shoved into the psychic background noise. Or had she said it aloud? No, if she had, Shanna would have reacted.

Zira stood, picked up Matthew, and tilted him so that Shanna could kiss him goodnight.

Psylocke got to her feet as well. "I'll escort them to the hut," she offered.

"Zabu can do that," Shanna said, more sharply than was warranted. And indeed, the big cat had lurched to his feet and was gazing toward the door.

"Of course. Just wanted to be helpful," Psylocke said.

"Thank you," Shanna said. "But I see that your teammates are starting to refine the plans for tomorrow." She tilted her head toward the central cluster of beeswax candles, where most of the X-Men were huddled.

Psylocke turned diplomatically and stepped toward the group while Shanna took a final few moments with her offspring.

Betsy did not, however, turn her mental focus away. Maintaining the etiquette of a telepath was one thing, but she had been provoked enough tonight. She peered beyond the crest of Shanna's surface thoughts. She wanted an accurate portrait of what the hell was going on in their hostess's consciousness.

Ah, now it makes sense.

Ka-Zar had not, after all, been opposed to the X-Men's presence. True, he was furious with the Roxxon Corporation and all the other hostile outsiders, but Ka-Zar had come in recent years to appreciate the benefits of the outside world, from knives that didn't need sharpening to pants that didn't smell like dead hide. It was Shanna who had insisted that Savage Land business be kept "in house." She had changed her mind only after Ka-Zar's wounding—in a sense, guilt had forced her to make the call. She regretted letting Ka-Zar get too exposed without enough heavy backup. Now she was a woman coping with a split in her position—on the one hand, she was sorry she hadn't issued the plea for help earlier, and on the other hand, she felt her opinion had been swept to the side.

Well, that was certainly enough internal conflict to make a person testy and even rude toward guests. Psylocke resolved to cut the She-Devil a little slack.

Except there was more. Not about the X-Men as a whole, but toward Betsy. Down a little deeper bubbled a kettle of garden-variety jealousy. Psylocke would have understood the presence of that emotion had Shanna been eavesdropping on the conversation outside, but apparently she had not heard a word of it. The feelings seemed to spring from something more basic. Say, for example, the simple competitiveness of a vibrant young woman toward any other vibrant young woman, especially when a spouse showed the bad judgment to stand next to the rival.

The law of the jungle. Fight for what's yours.

That was hardly fair. If Betsy were going to get on someone's bad side, at least let it be for something she'd actually *done*.

She wondered if Shanna came by her attitude naturally, or if this was simply the price of living hundreds of miles from the nearest flush toilet.

Whatever the cause, Psylocke found herself losing the desire to be as fully cooperative a "houseguest" as courtesy required.

"—don't think dividing into smaller units is wise," Ororo was saying as Betsy and Shanna approached. "It may be exactly what Sauron wants."

"Could be," Logan countered. "Sometimes the personal approach ain't bad. I kicked his butt last time I was here. It don't take more'n one person if it's the right one.''

''Same thing works in reverse,'' Iceman said. ''If he catches us alone, it could be it won't take more than one of him to take care of us.''

''Maybe. Roll o' the dice, junior.''

Storm shook her head. ''No, whatever we do, it must be a carefully coordinated team effort.''

''I know a way to eat our cake and have it, too,'' said the Beast.

''What did you have in mind, Henry?'' Ororo asked.

He was tinkering with a small device, his huge fingers somehow managing the finest of movements. He held it up to the candlelight. It proved to be one of the wrist radios the group sometimes used, though it had an extra, transparent case around it.

''Most radios won't work here,'' the Beast said, ''since the Savage Land generates an electromagnetic pulse that wreaks havoc with electronic devices. So the trick is to seal the equipment away from the pulses, and the circuits hold up just fine. Forge showed me how to do that to these units, and I brought along enough for the whole team.''

Storm nodded. ''Well done. But won't the pulses still distort any transmissions, even if the physical radios are protected?''

''Well, yes, but the pulses aren't actually constant. They happen five or six times per hour, and usually only last a couple of minutes. In the intervals between, we'll be able to talk. The range of these little things is not overwhelming, but it should be sufficient for our immediate needs. With Psylocke's telepathy to help, we should be able to stay in communication even if we do split into small parties.''

Psylocke nodded. Before anyone else spoke, she turned and gazed at the door. A familiar presence was approaching.

Archangel slipped through the portal and joined the gathering.

"I see," Storm said, having paused only long enough to make room for Warren and his wings. "Yes, that is better than I had hoped, but it doesn't resolve the main issue. What does it matter if the radios work if some members of the team are too far off to answer a distress call? I hate to give up the advantage of strength in numbers. That could lead to the type of setback Ka-Zar suffered. Or worse. Logan, Warren, you recall how overwhelming Sauron proved to be the time we and Kurt and Peter encountered him."

"I'm afraid I do," Warren said. Psylocke took his hand and squeezed it gently.

"Yer talkin' like we're already beat," Wolverine said. "That battle went bad because we hadn't figured out that Brainchild had installed some gizmo in Sauron's stronghold that threw a wet blanket on our powers. We'll be watchin' for that this time."

"Indeed," Hank said. "I have already been scanning for just such a suppression field. No sign of it. More's the pity. If there had been one, we would know which direction to search."

"The way I figure, if we let old green-beak rattle us, we're givin' him a step up to begin with," Logan argued.

"We're being realistic," Archangel countered. "Sauron's raw powers are not trivial. I don't expect an easy time bringing him to ground."

Logan shrugged. "It'll never work if you go in without a stiff backbone."

Warren raised his voice. "I'll do my part. Been doing it for the X-Men longer than you, pal."

"That's enough, both of you," Storm said. At her commanding tone, they both settled back. Tight-lipped, arms folded, but silent. The two of them had never gotten along very well. They had gotten into a sparring match less than twenty-four hours after Wolverine joined the team, and once Warren quit the X-Men due primarily to Logan's membership.

After an appropriate pause, Storm said, "Logan has a point. We can't let Sauron bring the battle to us, we need to take it to him. We probably can't do that as one large group of seven—or nine," she added in deference to Ka-Zar and Shanna. "I'm going to take the night to decide how many divisions I'm willing to make. It's late and we're all tired. Let's start tomorrow off right."

The gathering drifted apart, Storm conferring with Shanna.

Warren pulled Betsy aside. "I have an idea." He spoke so that no one else heard.

She looked into his mind. "Oh, good," she replied. "That's a wise move. And yes, it would work."

He nodded. "Then let's set it up." He cupped her chin tenderly in his palm. "And Betts?"

"Yes?"

"Thank you for letting me get to this point on my own."

She laughed softly. "If I'd tried to give you advice, you'd have resisted. I'm learning how you work, Warren Worthington. Next thing you know, I'll know you as well as would a wife."

He didn't fall into shock at the word *wife*. *Hmmm*, she thought. Inside the shadows beneath his eyebrows, she imagined she saw his eyes twinkle. Surely she was mistaken.

They stepped outside. Beneath the dark canopy of clouds, she summoned psychic energy and began to shape it into the construct that Warren had requested.

CHAPTER 4

Wolverine will go out alone," Storm announced.

The seven X-Men stood with Ka-Zar and Shanna just inside the open gates of the village stockade. The mutant visitors were as well rested as could be expected of a night in a land where mysterious roars and screeches tore through the jungle every five minutes. They were as ready as they were likely to get. Storm's declaration drew them up short.

"Before we hit the hammocks last night, you were insisting on groups of at least two," Iceman said.

"I've reconsidered," Storm explained. "You have no objection, do you, Logan?"

"Nope," answered the Canadian. "Suits me fine. I can produce results quicker if I don't have to worry 'bout anyone slowin' me down."

Psylocke was tempted to probe Storm's mind to confirm what the team leader was thinking, but she didn't have to. The wind-rider's decision was a perfect example why she had been chosen to command the X-Men back when Cyclops had first left the group. Betsy again did not have to be a telepath to see that Wolverine was in one of his moods. The man got on a scent like a bloodhound sometimes and couldn't be dragged back to the kennel. Had Storm ordered it, he would have been a team player and stayed with whomever she assigned, but he wanted to charge ahead this time on his own.

Was it the jungle? He liked it here. Was it calling him?

The best thing was just to get out of his way. Storm had not only done so, but made it seem like her idea. Ororo had taken a situation that could have exacerbated tensions, and used it to reinforce her authority.

Pretty smooth, Betsy told Ororo mentally. *You saw which way the wind was blowing.*

Storm didn't reply, but did smile a small smile before continuing. "I'll drop you in deep jungle, then, where your tracking ability will do the most good," Ororo told Logan. "Ka-Zar just reported that a clan of the Lake People have located signs of recent enemy presence. Perhaps you can see a pattern to the comings and goings."

"You and me are thinkin' alike," Logan replied. "It's a go. Sooner the better."

Storm inclined her head.

"As for the other teams," the wind-rider continued, "Archangel and I are a natural tandem. We'll reconnoiter the valley by air, covering as much terrain as possible both quickly and quietly. We'll pursue Sauron or pterosaur riders should they appear, and fetch the rest of you if we should locate anything resembling a stronghold."

"Ye olde mutant air force," the Beast quipped.

"Yes."

"Ka-Zar and I will be coordinating searches by the Fall People and the Swamp People," Shanna said.

Ororo nodded. "Which leaves four X-Men to pair off into two more teams."

"Actually, it doesn't," Psylocke said. "I was talking with Zira at breakfast. She mentioned that there are two people in the village who survived an early raid by Sauron. And, of course, there are scores of witnesses to the attack upon Ka-Zar. I think it might prove fruitful if I probe the minds of some of these individuals. I may uncover useful information that would help us against Sauron. Something in their memories they don't realize is important, so they haven't mentioned it.''

Ka-Zar murmured appreciatively. ''That's a great idea. I'll round up some volunteers.''

''Some of Tongah's people won't care to have someone playing Peeping Tom with their minds,'' Shanna interjected.

''But others will,'' Ka-Zar said. ''Especially if they think it will help put an end to the raids.''

''It does sound like an efficient use of Betsy's talents,'' Storm admitted. ''Very well. She'll stay here, at least for today.''

''Which leaves us with an odd number,'' commented the Beast, settling his hairy paws on the shoulders of Iceman and Cannonball.

Storm frowned. ''It does. So be it. Let's keep the three of you as a unit. While Archangel and I visit places like Garokk's old city and other farflung locales Sauron frequented in the past, you can serve not only as a search party, but provide firepower along the lake near the villages in the event of new attacks. Cannonball can airlift you if you need to hop from place to place quickly.''

''As you command, fair lady,'' Hank said. Iceman and Cannonball nodded.

Storm held up her wrist radio. ''Everyone linked up? Good. Then let's do it.''

Logan bent down and gazed closely at the footprints in the mud of the clearing.

''Four of 'em,'' he muttered aloud. ''All men, by the depth

of the impressions.'' The two Lake People warriors that crouched beside him did not respond. They didn't understand English. Logan pointed at the spoor, and counted off four on his fingers.

The warriors nodded, and then pointed at an additional set that did not match the others.

"Yeah. Lupo." The prints resembled those of a human only to a degree. The claw marks and toes looked canine.

"Lupo," said the older warrior with the velociraptor-tooth necklace around his throat. He gave a tiny howl like a wolf.

It had rained just before dawn, but no drops had rinsed away the tracks. They were as fresh as the warriors had promised when they rendezvoused with Wolverine just outside the village where Storm had delivered him.

So far, so good.

The older warrior, whose name seemed to be Gelm, gestured at the rock outcropping ahead and the pterosaur droppings upon it.

"Yeah, they took to the air, looks like, not too long ago," Wolverine said. "You think so, Aben?" he asked, winking at the younger tribesman.

Aben nodded, flapping his arms like wings.

"If they're gone, why'd you bring me here?" Wolverine pointed to himself and shrugged.

The pair tilted their heads back. Their nostrils quivered.

"You guys're good, y'know that?" Wolverine was impressed. They had noticed the scent of wolf lingered in the air. Nothing as definite as a trail. The mutate and his party definitely had taken to the air. But he was still somewhere in the vicinity, or had been very recently. The flight had been short, perhaps designed only to interrupt the trail and make things difficult for a tracker.

This was a lead he could work with. Lupo and his group

were probably setting up for a raid on Gelm and Aben's camp. It was inhabited by only twenty or so natives—just one clan, and therefore a prime target.

Wouldn't it just be too bad if their plan developed a few rips and slices?

"C'mon," Logan said, pointing at the thick jungle beyond the clearing. "Keep up if you can."

Logan crept carefully along the animal track, nostrils flaring at the panoply of aromas here in the jungle. He had jogged, climbed, and slashed his way through at least four miles of verdant growth—how many species had he seen?

Such a place. True, it was not the conifer wilds of the Canadian taiga, but it still felt like home in so many ways. The more he gave in to the untamed energies of the land, the more natural it felt. He'd had to go solo. Instinct. Not that he'd wanted to offend his teammates' abilities, but he'd known how it had to be. He couldn't have explained why in words. Not to worry, though. Storm, perceptive as ever, had figured it out, and let him out of the harness.

He silently brushed aside a frond bigger than his torso. A few feet away, a small, deerlike creature was sipping from the rivulet that dribbled along between the giant trees. A dikdik, perhaps. One of the most timid of herbivores, the sort that bounded away at the first hint of danger.

It hadn't detected Wolverine, so furtive had been his approach. He reached out with his hand and gently nudged the animal's tail.

Viiiippp.

The dikdik, its throat fluttering and its eyes wide as saucers, bounded into the undergrowth, so quickly it seemed to overtake its own little squeak of alarm.

Wolverine chuckled. He bent and sipped from the same narrow stream.

There in the soft earth beside the water was another wolf-like print.

Wolverine narrowed his eyes. *Good.* The scent had been growing stronger and easier to detect, but now he had a physical trail to follow again. He sketched a big ''X'' in the soil beside the track, so that Gelm and Aben would immediately know he had come this way. He had long since outpaced them, but there was no reason to make their lives difficult.

He moved even faster than before, nose and eyes picking up the signs of where Lupo had gone. His hands began to twitch, aching to extrude his claws and feel the pitch of battle.

It was a jungle out there. It was a jungle within. Life had a way of balancing out just right sometimes.

Psylocke shaded her eyes as she emerged from the dim light of the lodge into the overcast-but-brilliant Savage Land day. Sweat poured down her sides, and her hair was matted. It was bad enough spending the morning in hard psi labor. To do so without a morning shower and coffee, that was duty above and beyond the call.

As a tough preteen, Betsy Braddock, sister of the future Captain Britain, had always longed for adventure. As an adult with adventures galore in her résumé, she understood that her childhood fantasies had somehow glossed over the possibility of missions to places with no softsoap, no corner pharmacies, not even a decent mirror.

But then, she had changed in so many ways since that spoiled, rich English upbringing. Right down to the body— no longer blonde and a trifle on the frail side, but long, dark-tressed, Asian, and powerful. A bizarre body-switch with a woman named Kwannon—now deceased—had seen to that. To this day, she had yet to fully adjust to the change.

Her latest probe subject, one of the warriors wounded in the melée that had brought down Ka-Zar and killed young Immono—Psylocke shivered at the shared memory of the youth's neck bent so grotesquely from the fall—lifted the flaps and came out into the open as well.

"Thank you, Ushatch," Psylocke said. "My apologies for the dizziness. It will pass by the end of the day."

"No matter. It is good to be able to help." The warrior, as Psylocke now knew from having seen inside him, was the kind of man who hated being an invalid. Luckily, his injuries were the sort that would cease to hamper him by the next feastnight, the every-thirty-days ritual the Fall People used as one of their key measures of time, having no moon to observe. He would eventually heal completely. "You found something?"

"I don't know," she said. "I hope so."

He nodded optimistically.

As Ushatch limped back to the medicine man's hut, Betsy stretched out the kinks in her joints and performed a slow-motion version of a white crane kung fu form she had been honing lately. Her ninja-trained muscles complained about the minimal level of physical activity she had endured these past few hours. Another price of losing her birth body.

She awakened the psychic tendril she had woven the night before, at Archangel's request. Along its length came Warren's soothing presence, though he was way out over the southern hills, ordinarily far enough to require more effort to make contact. Reassured, she let the connection fade once more into the background.

She heard footfalls, and opened her eyes. Ka-Zar and Zabu were ambling toward her. The jungle lord shrugged. "Learn anything? Shanna and I have little to show for our morning's work, I'm afraid.''

"Not much here," Psylocke admitted. She scratched Zabu behind his ears. "Just one little aberration I noticed in a couple of the accounts."

"And that is?"

Psylocke liked the way he hovered so near, within an arm's reach, able to share the aromas of body and breath. That was the insular, private way talking was done among the indigenous peoples. An American or a Brit would have felt their personal space was being invaded, but Betsy found it no intrusion when the other individual was Ka-Zar. That was even more true now that he seemed to have sloughed off most of his fatigue. He brimmed with some of the vigor he'd shown on her first visit to the Savage Land, when he'd literally snapped the chains Zaladane had placed around his wrists.

"Ushatch has traveled with you for years," she stated as she started to stroll around the village, Ka-Zar matching her stride next to her. "He was with you back when Karl Lykos was part of your entourage."

"Yes. That's right." Ka-Zar winced. His surface reveries, too "loud" for Psylocke to avoid reading, swam with images of the good man Lykos had been then, fighting hard for the welfare of the tribes, putting his medical knowledge to good use whenever he could fend off the jealous interference of the native shamans.

"In spite of his pteranodon shape, Sauron still speaks with a voice that is recognizably that of Karl Lykos," Betsy added.

"Yes. It's always been that way." Ka-Zar shivered. "It's a bit like hearing the voice of a friend coming out of a crocodile, as if he's been eaten whole."

"You heard him speak when you were attacked. Ushatch heard it, also. Same voice, right?"

"Without a doubt. Right down to the accent. It has a trace of Greek in it from his father. Also some Spanish influence, the result of childhood years spent in southern Chile and Argentina. Not a standard mixture."

"Ushatch doesn't speak English."

"Only a smattering. Shanna and I have, uh, 'contaminated' quite a few of the Fall People, but he's not among them."

Psylocke hadn't needed the confirmation, since she knew Ushatch's background thoroughly as a result of the psi scan. "What all this means," she said, "is that Ushatch didn't listen to the content of Sauron's words during the attack, nor to the accent. It was just gibberish to him."

"That makes sense," Ka-Zar said. "So?"

"So he was able to pick up on a discrepancy you might have ignored. Sauron's voice wasn't modulated the same way as in years past. Everyone alive speaks with a characteristic tone and stress to their sentences. A flavor. Think of Lennon and McCartney back in their salad days. You've seen documentaries, or heard the songs?"

"Lennon and McCartney? Of course. I haven't spent *all* my life in this jungle, Ms. Braddock. Let's see. I'd describe their voices back then as young, jocular, full of their Liverpudlian origins. Both of them—all four Beatles, actually—sounded remarkably similar."

"Right. But even when their visual image wasn't on screen, you always knew when John Lennon was speaking. There was always the hint of a second meaning, a subtext. Paul's 'flavor' was on-the-surface, more honest, perhaps less sophisticated."

"Oh, my God," Ka-Zar murmured softly. His thoughts

were tumbling through the memories of the battle. "Now I see. At no time in the past did Sauron ever speak so . . . so . . . Hell, how do I put it?"

"He was gleeful."

"Yes. That's it." Ka-Zar snapped his fingers. "Karl was always serious. Sauron was dismissive, arrogant, even sadistic. Neither of them ever sounded like what I heard two days ago."

"Your attacker had a lightheartedness to his speech. I looked at that piece of Ushatch's memory several times. The creature definitely had an evil quality. He was as boastful as ever. But he also spoke like a man thoroughly enjoying the advantage he had over you."

"Impossible," Ka-Zar said. "Neither Karl Lykos nor Sauron is acquainted with the concept of 'fun'."

"The flavor of one's speech reflects the personality within. The ability to derive mirthful satisfaction from one's own success requires an inner stability neither Lykos nor Sauron has ever demonstrated. Could we be facing a new Sauron? A stranger?"

"What are you saying? That someone else was transformed into that half-pteranodon body? Someone who just happens to have Karl Lykos's voice? He knew me, Betsy. I acknowledge the difference in his tone, but there's too much about him that's the same for him to be an imposter."

"You think."

"Well, yes. I think. It's an opinion. We'll have to mention this to the others and see whether it gives us any insights."

"I'll bring it up when everyone reports back in tonight. I could use the afternoon to probe a few more witnesses, see if I come up with anything better." She rubbed her gritty scalp. "Meanwhile, is there any place around here that a lady could take a bath?"

"As a matter of fact," he said brightly, "we have quite remarkable facilities. Let me show you the way."

He directed her toward a small side gate in the stockade.

Wolverine leapt. The beetle-browed warrior at the end of the group below never knew what hit him.

The sound of the impact caused Lupo and the remaining three renegades to turn, but not fast enough. Wolverine hopped off his victim's back, extended the claws of his right hand, and charged. His swipe divided the nearest enemy's club into quarters. Before the raider could react, Logan jabbed him with his left, currently declawed fist. The man staggered back, asleep on his feet.

Logan couldn't bring himself to kill if he could avoid it. The raiders might be hypnotic slaves of Sauron, and not responsible for their actions.

The falling body was in the way. Logan leapt over, but the obstacle cost him his best angle of attack. Lupo and the remaining two men jumped to the side.

The advantage of surprise was gone. Too bad. Logan had decided the risk was worth it. He could have waited for Gelm and Aben to back him up, or radioed for reinforcements, but this felt like the right moment. Two down. That was enough, if he didn't screw up.

The two warriors lowered their spears and thrust, forcing Logan to duck and roll between them. One of his claws sliced the shin of the enemy on the left. The man leapt back, yelping. A painful wound, but not crippling.

Lupo held back. Momentarily free of the chaos, he lifted his head and howled.

More howls answered him from the jungle shadows.

The pack had been downwind. Logan hadn't detected

them earlier. He'd hoped the two-legged enemies would be the only ones involved in the fight. *Oh, well.* This just made it more interesting. He'd just have to be efficient.

The man with the wounded leg was still stumbling back. Logan went for the other one.

The bugger was fast, he had to give him credit. The spear tip came straight at his guts too quickly to avoid getting poked.

So Logan didn't even try to evade. He twisted just enough to take the impact in his side, where his adamantium-laced ribs deflected the spear. The maneuver brought him inside of his attacker's guard. One punch to the solar plexus took him out.

Logan whirled. The gash in his side burned. Blood poured down, a streak of crimson from ribs to knee. He'd survived much worse, and his mutant healing ability would take care of the wound soon enough. Without slowing down, he charged the final savage.

This man wasn't as fast. His spear thrust missed. He was stronger, though. His punch to Logan's jaw landed like a sledgehammer. Logan returned the favor. His opponent's jaw, not being enhanced with unbreakable metal, didn't hold up as well as the X-Man's had. Logan kicked him away. Four down.

His skull still rang. Stars twinkled across his field of vision. Lupo raced in, knocked Logan down, and chomped his forearm. Before Logan could jab, the mutate was rolling past, into the clear.

"Afraid to dance up close?" Wolverine taunted. He shut out the pain of the bite as he had the spear wound, though both were still costing him blood. He pretended the blow to his head hadn't happened.

LAW OF THE JUNGLE

"I will serve your flesh to my pets for dinner," Lupo snarled. He pranced through the ferns, just out of Wolverine's range, eyes glittering.

Logan paused, expecting another charge, and realized his error. Lupo wasn't intending to follow up. He was stalling for time.

The wolves! Vines and shrubbery erupted. Four huge dire wolves vaulted toward the X-Man.

Logan went to ground, covering his exposed face and elbows. Sharp canine teeth savaged him, seldom penetrating thanks to his uniform, but subjecting him to a world of hurt.

The beasts were fast, and accustomed to taking down creatures larger than humans. Logan entered an eye-of-the-hurricane calm—the clarity of pitched battle. Decisions came to him so instantaneously, as effective as any meticulous calculation, but without the need for self-debate.

Too many snapping jaws. Too fast. Couldn't slash at them, because they'd be somewhere else by the time his claws got there. Had to strike where they would be.

He tilted his head back, exposing his throat. Then he slashed. *Tchuk!* The animal had been unable to resist plunging into the opening. Now its side was gashed, and though the wounds were survivable, it wanted only to get away.

Logan grabbed the suffering canine and used its body to block the healthy wolf on his left. That left two on the right. He jabbed at the first, kicked at the other. They yelped and darted backward.

Another momentary opening. Logan flung the bloody one into the pair that had retreated and charged the solo animal. One, two. Blood spurted from the target's snout and from its front shoulder. It screamed and bolted.

The other two jumped Logan from behind, locking teeth into his legs. He went with the impact, rolling and lashing out with his talons. The lovely, wet sound of sharp points penetrating meat echoed off the jungle fronds.

The wolves tucked tail and ran. Red blood stained the ferns as they pelted past.

Lupo turned as if to follow, but Logan shrugged aside the disorientation of head blows and lost blood and caught him in three bounds. They tumbled over a rotting log, littering the air with fungi spores and humus.

Wolverine came up on top, knee on Lupo's stomach. He pressed a closed fist under the mutate's jaw. "Snikt," he said, mimicking the sound of his claws extending.

Lupo's feral eyes went wide. "Don't kill me!" he blurted.

His plea wasn't quite desperate enough. Without relaxing his hold, Logan glanced behind.

One of Lupo's human accomplices—the one with the pile driver punch—was charging forward, still alive despite a broken jaw and capable of delivering one last, potent spear thrust.

Before Logan could react, a tomahawk whirled in from the side, caving in the attacker's head behind his ear. His spear burrowed into the log. Logan took the impact of the stumbling body, but it didn't knock him off of Lupo. He flung away the spasming remains with a shake of his torso.

"Yer late," he called. "Y'almost missed the fun."

Gelm and Aben emerged from the vine-laced trees. Gelm picked up his hand-axe and began wiping off the blood, dirt, and brains from its edge. The two men nodded and flashed the Lake People sign of vengeance—a closed fist held inside the other palm.

"You knew him, eh?" Logan said. That eased his mind about the death. The man apparently had been doing bad things for a while—long before Sauron could possibly have coerced him. The skull crushing had been deserved.

No smiles from either tribesman, Logan noted. *Right. Gotta save the smiles for enemies who were still alive and awake to appreciate it.*

Like this dogsled whelp here.

Logan leaned down, staring eye to eye at Lupo's Lon Chaney Jr. face. "I'd love t'finish the job, but I need you alive for the time bein'. Tell me where to find green beak. The X-Men need to have a few words with 'im."

Lupo growled.

Wolverine held up his right hand with its projected claws, then twitched his left, the one under Lupo's jaw, as if to skewer his captive through both carotid arteries.

"I don't know," Lupo said through clenched teeth.

"Wrong answer," Logan said. "How couldja not know? Yer workin' for 'im, ain'tcha?"

"I meet with the master at places and times of his choosing. I am not privileged to know where he lurks the rest of the time. I stay in the jungle. He—I don't know where."

"Don't sound likely," Logan muttered. "I think you're lyin'." He pressed harder on Lupo's larynx.

"I'm not." The mutate coughed. Wolverine reduced the pressure. A little. "Only Brainchild is with him."

"Where's the next rendezvous? When?"

"I don't know!"

"Bull!" Logan spat. "How could you not know *that*?"

"The master hypnotizes me. I only know where to go, and when, after I'm there."

Logan scowled. He glanced at Gelm and Aben, who wore rapt gazes of anticipation. They probably thought they were going to witness the execution of one of their people's most infamous tormenters. Logan would have liked to accommodate them. Unfortunately, Lupo's story was believable. Sauron's powers of hypnotism were easily strong enough to do the job. The X-Man lifted his hand away.

"We'll get what we need out of you one way or another," Wolverine promised. He dragged Lupo toward a fallen tree, where the jungle canopy was open enough for his flight-capable teammates to land, and coded his wrist radio to transmit.

CHAPTER 5

The bathing facilities were everything that Ka-Zar promised. The Savage Land could pamper a woman after all, once she knew her way around.

Psylocke stood beneath a misty, ten-foot waterfall, rinsing the shampoo—no going native there, she'd brought her own—from her long, dark hair. A stone's throw away, two village women relaxed on a natural stone shelf in knee-deep water near the banks. A trio of adolescent girls were swimming in the center of the pool, giggling at the fish tickling their ankles.

Apparently midday baths were a popular custom here. A way of combating the heat of the jungle. Betsy exchanged smiles with the women from time to time, but didn't speak. To communicate would have required her to telepathically borrow knowledge of their language. For the moment, she preferred mental solitude. She wanted to partake of the loveliness of the setting as much through her own perceptions as possible.

The women were all fit and strong. The rigors of life in the Savage Land didn't encourage flabbiness. Betsy knew her ninja-trained body compared well in the buffed-and-beautiful department, but she was envious nonetheless. They could gambol about in a place such as this every day, unassailed by holier-than-thous insisting they had to sequester their loveliness inside swimsuits, denature their skin with layers of sunblock, swim only where insurance companies allowed.

The water poured down over her bare skin. Glorious. She slipped into deeper water and paddled over to a side pool. There a natural hotspring bubbled to the surface. She found the spot where the scalding water and the cool river mingled to produce just the right temperature to soothe her muscles without parboiling them. She sighed and reclined, lower body and back in the water, her head and chest floating just above the waterline.

No men around. In a way, that was peculiar. The tribeswomen didn't let modesty get in the way of mixed company in the village itself. A loincloth was apparently complete or even excessive attire for anyone but chieftains, elders, and shamans. Perhaps the center of the day was simply ladies' hour at the spa.

She would have to lure Warren here if they had a chance once the mission was over.

A figure did appear through the rhododendrons that bordered the end of the path from the village.

"You look very relaxed," Shanna declared in a critical tone. She put her hands on her hips.

Betsy sank down until the water covered her to her neck. "A little revitalization will make the afternoon's interviews go better." People who couldn't read minds never understood how draining the effort was.

"I see," Shanna said curtly. "Well, if you're done recharging your batteries, you might want to hurry back to the lodge. While you've had your wrist radio off—" she gestured with not a little irritation to the pile of garments and accouterments lying on the bank "—Wolverine called in. He's captured Lupo. Storm and Archangel are bringing them in. Ka-Zar said to tell you you're wanted to help with the interrogation."

LAW OF THE JUNGLE

"Of course. On my way."

The She-Devil vanished into the shrubbery before Psy-locke reached the pool's edge. Betsy pursed her lips, but decided it was just as well Shanna had declined to serve as escort. Betsy knew she wouldn't have been able to resist tossing a little grease on the fire of their relationship. She had glanced deeply enough into Shanna's recent memories to know that Ka-Zar had not sent his wife with the errand, as had been implied. Ka-Zar had been going to deliver it himself, until Shanna had heard that Psylocke was located at the bathing pool.

Psylocke arrived at the center of the village just as Storm landed with Wolverine. Archangel sailed in moments later, carrying the bound-and-gagged mutate.

"Quick work," Betsy complimented Logan. She winced at the bloodstains on his side and the swollen arms dotted with teeth marks. No wounds, though—they had long since healed over. "Looks like you need a breather."

Logan grinned. "Nah, I'm on a streak. Wanna go back out."

"Logan . . ." said Ororo.

"I'll stiffen up if I stop now. I'm good for the rest of the day if I get back to it."

"The drums just reported that the Swamp People spotted warriors on pterosaurs over their territory," Ka-Zar said. "They landed briefly. When they took off again, the reptiles weren't carrying as many riders."

The X-Men leader nodded her head. "Very well, old friend. I can't argue with success. I'll take you there shortly."

Psylocke leaned over Lupo. The mutate glared back. *Lord,*

what a vile mind. He was fantasizing what he would do if the tables were reversed. Especially if he had her or Storm or Shanna helpless and staked out on the ground. Beneath the bravado simmered a thick streak of fear, because he understood that the tables were not turned, and he was worried that one or more of his captors would prove as unprincipled as he.

Psylocke sent out a sharp mental whipstroke, disrupting the ugly images, reinforcing the fear, demonstrating in reduced measure what her psychic knife would feel like. Lupo yelped.

Storm turned to Psylocke and raised her eyebrows.

"He needed that," Betsy explained. "That and a lot more."

"I'm sure he did. You'll have an opportunity to, ah, 're-educate' him this afternoon. We need your telepathy to find out what he knows."

"Logan couldn't make him talk?" Betsy said wonderingly.

Wolverine shrugged. "Sure he talked. Not enough."

Storm explained. "Sauron has apparently placed a hypnotic block upon any knowledge of his hideout. Lupo can't tell us what he doesn't consciously recall. But given time, you can reach in deeper than he can himself, true?"

"I certainly can." Betsy said it forcefully, so as to intimidate her enemy. Internally she was cringing. She hated having to delve into minds as unappealing as that of the mutate.

"Good. If it turns out Lupo genuinely has no knowledge of Sauron's hideaway, he *must* know where they are next scheduled to rendezvous. We want to be able to be there at that time and place to ambush Sauron."

LAW OF THE JUNGLE

"You can depend on me," Psylocke said.

"The rest of us will continue our searching. If you learn anything, call us in by radio." Storm turned to Logan. "I'll take you to the location the Swamp People mentioned. You can search the jungle while I scout the vicinity by air to see if the pterosaur riders reappear. Warren can proceed with the broader air reconnaissance."

Ororo grasped Logan, summoned her winds, and vaulted them both aloft. Psylocke watched them shrink into the distance. Leaning back against Warren affectionately, she said to Ka-Zar and Shanna, "Logan was pushing the limit like that even when his healing factor was down to banked embers. Sometimes I think the only thing that could ever slow him down is having no pain to overcome."

"You speak as if you envy him," Shanna said. "Not enough suffering in your life?"

Betsy sighed. "That's not what I'm saying."

"Shanna knows precisely what you're saying. She's just being rude," Ka-Zar said. He ran his fingers along a pale white scar that ran down one of his forearms. "We all know there is something compelling about a life of challenges. Otherwise we'd all be lolling about on chaise lounges right now, listening to the latest Lila Cheney hit on our boomboxes and contemplating when to take the cat to the vet for a check-up."

Shanna didn't correct Ka-Zar, but she gave him one of those you-didn't-support-me-in-the-argument scowls that came so easily to her features. She took him by the elbow and drew him away. "We have to check in with some of our scouts down by the lake. Good luck with the captive."

By the time Ka-Zar, Shanna, and Zabu were out of the stockade, the villagers had finished stuffing Lupo in a cage.

They put him to one side of the circle, on packed ground, and erected a quick bamboo scaffold, placing cut palm fronds over it as a canopy.

Psylocke knew from a mental glimpse that they were going to all this trouble to secure him in the open because they didn't want the mutate in any of their huts or in the lodge. According to their beliefs, their enemy's spirit could contaminate the structures. Betsy had no objection to the arrangement. Outdoors, the sodden air didn't cling so much, thanks to the breeze.

Warren examined the junctures of the cage. "For primitives, they know how to make sturdy enclosures." He shook the scaffold. As rapidly as it had gone up, it, too, was sound. One good whack with his metal wings might chop through the bamboo, but Lupo, for all his feral strength, would not be breaking out, even assuming he freed himself from the leather bindings that enclosed his wrists and ankles, or from the muzzle over his snout.

"You needn't fret over me, lover," Betsy said, caressing his waist. "But you are welcome to stay and guard me if you like."

"No. You're safe enough here. I can't stay."

She understood. If he remained, it would reinforce Logan's suggestion that Warren lacked the backbone to face Sauron. He needed to be up in the sky, actively searching, not down in the huts with his woman.

"Take care, then," she said, and kissed him. He savored it, hugged her close, and then he was flapping his way toward the unbroken ceiling of mist.

She really loved him. She was still amazed after all these months to find that this was true. And she would keep loving him, Ka-Zar's appeal notwithstanding.

LAW OF THE JUNGLE

"Now," she said, settling down in the shade near the cage—but not so near that Lupo could reach her. "We'll see what information you have to offer."

Lupo snarled and wriggled across the packed earth, trying fruitlessly to avoid her psychic probe. He could roll himself all the way to the river and it would do him no good. His memories opened to her.

The boy's tears made muddy tracks down his cheeks. He cowered from Monom's kicks. Monom, at least thirty years old to his own eleven. Monom, heavily muscled and in his prime. And he, scrawny, undernourished, and sickly.

"She's dead, Rat-Tail. Look closely. Mama's not here to whine about me giving you what you deserve. You're an orphan now."

Rat-Tail peered out through eyelids nearly swollen shut from the blows Monom had delivered to his head. His mother, a bony, ill-groomed woman whose dirty hands and sharp tongue had rained abuse upon him nearly every day of his life, lay staring sightlessly at the entrance of the family cave, flies already buzzing around her gaping mouth.

Rat-Tail hated his mother. Not for the beatings and scoldings. For dying. Bad as she was, she was his only advocate and protector. She had found one last way to betray him to the enemy.

"On with you," Monom roared, kicking him toward the cave opening. The boy stumbled forward. He paused under the last of the overhang, shivering at the pelting thunderstorm outside.

Monom growled and stomped forward.

Don't hit Rat-Tail, *the boy murmured in his thoughts.* Don't hit Rat-Tail. *It was the plea his mother had often made*

*on his behalf. He couldn't summon the will to say it aloud.
Monom would only mock the phrase, and hit him anyway.*

*He leapt out into the storm. The rain, at least, washed his
face clean. The tears would never come again.*

Rat-Tail [Psylocke sensed another, true name somewhere
deeper down, but in these particular memories Lupo, like
many victims, viewed himself by the title his persecutor had
bestowed: Rat-Tail; Fatherless boy; Useless filth] *hovered at
the fringes of the clan grounds, nearly hidden in the elephant
grass.*

*One of the village women, a companion of his mother's
for whom he had occasionally fetched water, saw him. She
furtively checked to see if the men were watching. She picked
up a cake of acorn meal that was heating on the stones by
the campfire and flung it to the boy. Quickly the woman
scooped another bit of meal from the mortar and replaced
the missing item, the fear in her eyes reminding Rat-Tail of
how the woman's mate had pulled out an entire lock of her
hair for giving away food to the orphan a few days earlier.*

*He dug the cake out of the dust, retreated to the grass,
and gobbled it down. His stomach spasmed, more irritated
by the introduction of substance than relieved.*

*Rat-Tail braced himself for a sudden thumping or jabbing.
The clan's older boys loved to sneak up behind him and
pounce whenever he dared to approach closely enough to
beg. No ambush came. That was the way of it—sometimes
punishment, sometimes not. Sometimes food, sometimes
none. The tribe tolerated the orphan's presence just enough
to keep him dependent, denying him true sustenance, denying
him the final release from his suffering. They would not kill
him, but it would be no tragedy to them if he died—by star-*

vation, by accident, by being too slow to get away from a sabretooth cat or a woolly rhino.

The hollowness in his gut remained. He slipped away from the clan grounds, certain that he would not be lucky twice in the same day. A grasshopper twittered past. He chased it a hundred paces through the grass and finally caught it. It, too, failed to curb his hunger.

His wandering took him over a rugged spur of the foothills. His clan did not live in the jungle. That was for the prosperous, strong tribes. Instead, they skirted its edges, surviving in the savanna or in the foothills, where the herds ran. No banana trees. No prime fishing pools. Food here was gained the hard way, and one juvenile all on his own could barely acquire enough to stagger on from day to day.

Down in a gorge, he heard the growling of adult wolves, the excited yips of their cubs. Hiding behind a boulder, he gazed down and saw the pack feeding on the remains of a mastodon that they had chased to the edge of the precipice until the giant creature had fallen and broken its spine.

They feasted. They waddled away, bellies distended, licking their teeth with their long, floppy tongues.

Rat-Tail hesitated, waiting for the rush of scavengers. But the gorge had trapped the scent of the kill, and its depth had so far concealed the site from the far-seeing eyes of carrion birds, save for two parrot-sized, unintimidating vultures.

The boy rushed down. Ignoring the squawks of the vultures, he broke off a protruding rib to which clung enough meat that he could scarcely carry the load. He ran to an easily defended cleft in the rockface and gnawed at the flesh and marrow until, for the first time that he could remember, he had eaten his fill.

The next morning, when he was able to move again, he found the spoor the pack had left and began to follow it.

• • •

Wolf-Shadow, as he had renamed himself, trod tentatively along the forest trail. His companion, another outcast like himself, one of the few humans he had spoken with over the past nine years, set a grueling pace. Wolf-Shadow was used to that. He had run for hours on end when the pack was chasing prey, until he was just as fast as they, with equal endurance. What he was not used to was the dim light and enclosed space beneath the green canopy of leaves.

He contemplated turning around and running back to the savanna and foothills. It had not been an easy life, but he was grown now. He was strong from raiding the carcasses left behind whenever the pack brought down prey too large for them to devour completely—a mammoth, a giant sloth, a musk ox. The pack accepted him, letting him remain near and help warn them of dinosaurs passing or alert them to new game to hunt, as long as he did not try to mingle close enough to touch a cub. They were his benefactors in a way his own people had never been.

His nostrils quivered at the dank, alien aromas. He tipped a pitcher plant and cried out as the acidic nectar stung him. No, he did not like this place, but he remembered his companion's promise: The Creator knows what it is to be an outcast. The Creator can give you power.

The wolves had not removed the loneliness from his existence, not entirely. He had no woman. No person or people who had to listen to him, be they his female or his children or his clansmen. He no longer possessed the tiny reservoir of purpose that had kept him alive throughout his teenage years. His birth clan had been attacked by a sortie of River People warriors. Some victims had been taken captive. Many more had been killed, including his stepfather, Monom. De-

prived of the hope of eventual revenge for childhood mistreatment, Wolf-Shadow's life had no direction.

He was, so he'd been told, just the sort of individual the Creator was looking for.

The jungle parted. There it was—a structure such as Wolf-Shadow had never seen. Within a palisade of logs, a stone tower climbed as high as ten men. His companion called to the guards, who stepped back from the gates and permitted them to enter. The interior of the tower daunted Wolf-Shadow even more. Strange mounds of metal and glass hummed, blinking with colored lights.

"Welcome," called a voice. The word was part of the common language of the Savage Land, but had been rendered with an accent unlike any of the tribes Wolf-Shadow had ever encountered.

A tall, powerfully built man stepped to the edge of the bright podium near the center of the chamber, emerging from silhouette. Wolf-Shadow's eyes widened. The stranger's hair was white, but he seemed as strong and healthy as Wolf-Shadow himself. He wore a strange, thin garment, not an animal skin, and accouterments of glistening metal. He was as near a god as Wolf-Shadow had ever pictured.

"I am the Creator," he said.

[Psylocke halted the progress of the memory and gazed intently at the figure on the podium. She knew him as Magneto. How severe his expression was, tempered with no hint of mercy or doubt toward any who would stand in his way. At that point in his life he was very much still the scourge who had founded the original Brotherhood of Evil Mutants, showing only the faintest glimmer of the sincere man of conscience he would later become.]

Wolf-Shadow prostrated himself on the floor, and did not look up until the man walked forward and lifted him up. He held a metal object toward his guest's body. A little black needle twitched from side to side within a niche covered by some sort of clear substance. A light blinked.

"You have within you the quality I seek," the Creator said. "Prepare to discover a new destiny."

Throughout the process of transformation, the Creator hovered near, always checking, always murmuring reassurances, explaining when he could. The latter process grew easier after sessions inside one of the Creator's secondary apparatuses. Suddenly the Creator's language was no longer a jumble of sounds. Terms such as electricity, nations, philosophy, *and most of all,* mutation, *settled into his knowledge base.* [Telepathy, Psylocke realized. Magneto built a device that let him teach the mutates telepathically. It was a laborious and inefficient method, a pale shadow of the tutoring Professor Xavier could manage. It forever erased some of the subjects' initiative. But it permitted him to advance his underlings far beyond the levels they could have reached through traditional instruction.]

The Creator provided the sort of nurturance and attention of a parent. He became the father Wolf-Shadow/Rat-Tail had never had.

The physical alterations were agonizing that first time. His limbs stretched and reformed. His ears stiffened and stood straight upright. His body hair thickened. But the pain meant nothing once the voices began to murmur deep in his brain. The wolf pack howled, and he understood. Bats and monkeys and boars—all spoke in languages he could understand as easily as he now understood the German and English the Creator favored. And he could speak to them in return, in such a way that they were forced to listen.

"Go out among them, my son," the Creator said. "Win

them to our cause. I name you Lupo, master of beasts."

Lupo had his purpose now. He grinned and did as his benefactor requested. He would fight for him. If the Monoms of the world or any other enemy stood in his way, they would regret it deeply.

The memories came thick and fast now, fueled by Psylocke's knowledge of how they should progress. She shared Lupo's glee as he harassed the tribes of the Savage Land, taking captives for Magneto's experiments from the Water People, the River People, or whomever they wished to teach a lesson to. She witnessed his rage when Ka-Zar managed to thwart some of their raids.

His form remained largely human at first, more like his compatriots Gaza or Equilibrius or Piper, unlike Amphibius, but he willingly accepted the Creator's decree that it would become more feral as time passed. He had a place, and others like himself to join with. He had a reason to exist.

Then came the interlopers. His master's old enemies. First the one with wings, then the other four. [Psylocke was drawn to the images of Archangel (then simply the Angel), Cyclops, the Beast (before he had mutated to his current furry form), Iceman, and Phoenix (then going by the name of Marvel Girl). How young they were. Still teenagers. Heroes, in a persecuted sort of way, while Betsy Braddock, her powers still latent, could only fantasize about the life they led, envying it in the way only someone who has never endured the trauma would.] *They and Ka-Zar struck the Creator down.*

Lupo survived, but it hardly seemed like survival. The changes the Creator had made were still dependent on his devices. When the machines no longer functioned, Lupo and the others reverted. He was once again no more than a tribal outcast, retaining only a smattering of his affinity with the pack. The lack of initiative, the need for guidance, was the only true inheritance he brought away from the collapsed citadel.

Then came Zaladane. She gave them a focus once more. She set Brainchild to recreate the genetic transformer, and he not only restored them, but found a way to plant the seed of new transformations deep inside, so that even if they should lose their powers, they would recover on their own.

Zaladane suffered defeats, both at the hands of Ka-Zar and a changing cast of X-Men. But Brainchild found Karl Lykos and raised him up as Sauron to be their new leader. And again, the X-Men and Ka-Zar and that accursed She-Devil had thwarted them, devolved them, stolen the meaning from their lives. No matter how much stronger their powers grew—in Lupo's case, making him truly beastlike in physical form—no matter that their group grew to include such potent members as Vertigo, Whiteout, and Worm, the battles ended in defeat.

As for the Creator, he betrayed his promises. In the end, he personally fought his creations and destroyed Zaladane. Now they had only Sauron to turn to, and he was not himself. He wandered the corners of the Savage Land, gibbering mindlessly, flying off whenever he or Barbarus or Brainchild tried to lure him.

Ah, but that was over now. They had found him, and . . .

Psylocke withdrew. She shuddered. Lupo's was not the most abhorrent soul she had touched in her career. The Shadow King merited that distinction. Lupo was venal, but was to be pitied more than reviled. That didn't remove the distasteful-ness from the process. Looking into memories, even those of a stranger, could be an intimate, comforting experience, like putting her feet into a favorite pair of bedroom slippers. This, however, was like finding that those same slippers were full of maggots. She wanted only to be done, so that she could restore the distance between the two of them, the separateness.

Not yet. The first plunge had, by necessity, been imprecise. She had to gain a sense of the totality of his life before she could look for something specific. This time she could highlight recent experiences. On her way out, she had seen the threads of the hypnotic overlay that Sauron had installed. That would be the focus of her second probing.

She took a deep breath. She could do what needed to be done.

The final memory she had glimpsed had been the most tantilizing. The last the X-Men knew, after the battle with Havok, Polaris, Cyclops, and Phoenix, Sauron had been driven into an unresolvable internal battle between his evil self and the part of him that was still Karl Lykos. It was as if someone had posted a sign, NO ONE HOME. Lupo seemed to have some idea how the monster had been restored to sanity.

She began to unravel the skeins, only to find a knot. Peculiar. And obviously intentional. Someone had taken precautions against a telepathic probe. The barriers were ingenious. Professor Xavier or Phoenix could manage this sort of work, as could Psylocke herself, but not easily. If this was an indication of the depth of Sauron's mental prowess, it didn't bode well. The only clear image was that of Brainchild pouring over books and computer screens, but though Lupo had looked over his comrade's shoulder on many occasions, the text was blurry. Psylocke couldn't read it, even though Lupo had been able to at the time.

There. She freed another image from the tangle. Sauron

was strapped on a table, wings folded, his gaze directed aimlessly at the ceiling of a cave. Suddenly it was later—hours later, days later, or weeks, she couldn't sift the information out of Lupo yet—but Sauron was still there, on the table. The difference was that his gaze was steady and his beak curved in one of his hideous smiles.

Psylocke gasped. This new face was not like the Sauron further back in Lupo's memory. As with Ushatch's recall of the ambush, she saw a relaxed, almost mirthful Sauron. Gaza came forward and released the straps. Sauron stood, stretched his wings toward the natural stone walls, and turned to greet his mutates as they approached. First Brainchild, then Lupo, then Barbarus, then . . .

Then he turned back. He gazed straight at Lupo.

No, she thought. He's not looking at Lupo, though that had been whose eyes she was viewing the scene through. He was looking—

—at *her!*

Psylocke jerked back, but she was caught. For an instant, she felt herself back in her physical body. She heard the shouts of villagers, thuds of bodies impacting the ground, the screeches of pterosaurs. Then the psychic snare closed completely, taking her astral form, and her awareness, down into a deep, lightless place.

Psylocke woke blind and deaf. Oh, her eyes functioned, showing her a cavern full of elaborate devices, lit by fluorescent fixtures in the ceiling. Her ears worked, bringing her the noises of machinery whirring and gutteral conversation echoing out of the tunnel to her left. But the murmur and images from other minds had vanished. Inside was only blackness and silence.

She moaned and tried to lift her head. But it, like the rest of her body, was strapped tightly against a tilted platform. She wore a heavy, unfamiliar collar.

A furry, lupine form that she had come to know too well leaned over her and grinned. "Tell me, do you feel . . . vulnerable?"

Her hand twitched. She longed to form her psychic knife and drive it into his brain. Not a single pulse of psychic energy flowed down her arm. Her powers had been thoroughly neutralized.

No. More than neutralized. Drained. She realized that she had so little strength left, she might not have been able to stand on her feet if she were released from the platform.

"How could I feel vulnerable?" she shot back. "I have seen into your soul. You barely know how to blink without a lord to instruct you."

Lupo reached out and dragged his paw slowly down her body from neck to navel. His blunt claws left long red marks, though to her relief, they did not break the skin. He leaned down and . . . sniffed her.

A leather-winged monstrosity stepped out from behind the platform. Lupo backed away.

"I have ordered him not to damage you," the chimera said. "But I would say you are very fortunate that Lupo must be leaving for the jungle very shortly. I didn't free him from that cage only to see him amuse himself. He still has work to do."

"Sauron," she hissed.

"New and improved, and yet very much my old self," the pterohuman quipped. "I see you found my little booby trap. I set them in all of my main raiders' minds, you see, in case Ka-Zar was so rude as to summon a telepathic ally.

Truth be told, I was expecting Jean Grey, but you are just as tasty.'' He lifted Lupo's paw away, and brushed one talon softly along her thigh. "Though I prefer blondes.''

"Like Tanya Anderssen. You tasted *her*, you pig. To death.''

He shrugged.

That shook her. Sauron *shrugging* at the death of Karl Lykos's beloved? According to all X-Men records, Sauron had often expressed no remorse that she was dead, but he had never been casual about it. It was the first and strongest attack she could think of to faze him, given that he had siphoned off all her super powers for the time being.

"I never consume more than I need," he said matter-of-factly. "On that occasion, I simply needed every bit she had. None of you mutants had offered yourselves in her place.'' He rubbed his green hands together. "It's not my fault Tanya was not as nourishing as you were just now, or the way your companions will be, once I have them strapped to these tables.''

Out of the corners of her eyes, Psylocke saw a row of platforms. Ten or more. He had prepared well. Astoundingly well, she saw to her regret.

He stroked her one last time and let her be, as if to say she was not even a worthy object of lust, but merely food. "You remember Brainchild?" he asked.

The mutate stepped forward into her limited range of vision. He slicked back the fringe of hair on the side of his huge cranium, as if preening for a girlfriend. He smiled.

"As you can see, my servant has assembled quite an array of ingenious equipment," Sauron cackled. "As long as you remain in this cavern, an inhibitor field will be generated through that collar you're wearing. You won't be able to use your abilities even after they begin to reawaken. By the time you're strong enough to break free, I'll have feasted upon you again.''

"You really think you're going to defeat all of us as easily as you took me? The others won't be unconscious when you kidnap them.''

"I think I have an excellent chance," he stated. "You were the critical obstacle. But even if I overestimate my advantage, I have no choice but to make the attempt, don't you see? I had to lure the X-Men to the Savage Land. True mutants are the only sustainable source of the fuel I require to be all that I am meant to be. I knew from the first that you would come. I only regret that Havok is not among you. His particular power configuration is suited to me better than any other.''

Psylocke refused to show any sign of how daunted she was, but she was definitely intimidated. She and the X-Men had played right into Sauron's designs. It chilled her to hear how calmly he assessed his situation. He did not boast like the Sauron of old; he was decisive and controlled, without irrationality.

She strained to probe him. A whisper came. A misty image. Behind it, a shadow. Sauron the monster, enslaving Karl Lykos the man. His selves were still divided, but somehow the disharmony no longer impaired him.

"Come, Lupo," he said cheerfully. "I have to return you to your haunts and rendezvous with Amphibius if our schemes are to unfold correctly. Farewell, telepath. I do hope I can provide you with suitable company soon. It would be a shame if I am forced to kill some of your friends. They are not as useful to me dead.''

Sauron and his bestial mutate marched away down a corridor hewn from native rock. Brainchild remained.

"This was your doing," she said. "You changed him, somehow."

Brainchild sniggered. "I tell no secrets. Sauron is as he always should have been. My brood and I have a master to focus our efforts once more. Not that fool Zaladane, always driving us to do too much. Not the Creator who betrayed us. Sauron is one of us. A mutate."

"And just as ugly as the rest of you," she growled. She heaved against the straps, but the leather only dug into her skin.

Brainchild licked his lips. He reached down and picked up a loose eyelash that had fallen on her cheek. He kissed it. "Such a beauty you are. And here you are, all strapped down. Perhaps I should unbuckle you. It would make it easier to . . . reposition you."

She narrowed her gaze. A taunt. Yet she couldn't stop the flood of images that came to her of all the ways she might win her freedom, if his lust should prove unmanageable and he gave her the freedom he had just suggested.

He laughed deeply. "Your expression betrays you, woman. No, I am not going to be tricked. Storm did that to me once. Besides," he waved at the exit. A pair of burly, hirsute guards had emerged to assume posts there, now that Sauron had departed. "Even if I released you, the inhibitor collar would still work. I doubt your martial arts skills are enough to deal with the dozens like them you would have to go through to win free of the cavern. Even at your full strength they would overwhelm you, and at the moment you are so, so weak."

Her muscles shook from the temporary effort she had mounted against the straps. Weak as a kitten. No. A kitten was stronger. Weak as a potato.

"I have work to do to prepare this facility for the other guests," Brainchild whispered, his mouth no more than a finger's width from her ear. "But as I do, I will be watching you."

CHAPTER 6

Shanna saw the smoke signals rising and heard the pounding drums. "Matthew!" she cried. Her feet left divots in the grass as she accelerated.

Maternal alarm flooded her so thoroughly that she whipped past two bends of the trail before she recovered her ability to think. *Calm down*, she scolded herself. *Hysteria won't help him.*

The self-lecture worked. Legs still pumping hard, she settled into the strategic composure she had developed in her earliest days in Africa and India, when her leopards ran with her. She raised her wrist to her mouth, activating the device Hank McCoy had given her.

"Attack on the Fall People village," she blurted.

Storm's voice crackled out of the tiny speaker. "How bad?"

"Don't know, I'm not there yet," Shanna puffed. "The drums just say trouble, all warriors come quick. I'll be at the gates in two minutes."

"We're on our way," Storm replied. "Archangel, Cannonball."

"I heard," Archangel replied. "I'm way out by Garokk's ruined city, but I'll be there as soon I can."

"An' I'll be—" Cannonball's transmission drowned in a wave of static. Another EMP. The radios would be out for a bit. No matter. The important part of the communication had already taken place.

The community watchtower swung into view. The juvenile boys stationed on the platform saw her and waved vigorously. She gave them a quick gesture of acknowledgment.

The tower was intact, the boys unhurt. The stockade walls loomed through the trees, unharmed. Whatever the crisis, it was not as widespread as it could be.

She bounded through the gateway. Her first glance darted straight toward the hut she and Ka-Zar were inhabiting while the X-Men were based here. Zira was standing just outside the entrance, clutching little Matthew protectively in her long arms.

He's safe. Shanna's heart ceased jumping like a cricket from one side of her chest cavity to another. Her son was safe.

She spun to the right through the meat-drying racks and the tanning hoops to the packed circle of ground at the village center, where the mutate had been imprisoned.

The cage hatch was wide open, the occupant gone. A group of warriors was clustered around the scaffold that had been under construction when Shanna had left for the rendezvous by the lake. They were gazing ruefully at the scuff marks on the ground near the cage—marks made by shoes, not bare feet.

"What happened?" she demanded.

"The woman who looks into minds was taken," stated Bral, an elder. "She cried out and collapsed. Before anyone could rush to her side, the monster appeared from the sky, swooped down, and seized her. We—"

"He clouded our minds," added Nyo, Bral's younger brother. "It was only for a moment, but it made every one of us pause."

"During that time, he launched back into the air," Bral continued, pointing upriver. "Two riders on leatherwings swooped down in his wake. They freed the wolf-brother and carried him away as well. My arrow struck the saddle of the second rider, but I fear it drew no blood. The attackers escaped. We are sorry, sister-warrior.''

Shanna blanched. Psylocke taken? The She-Devil immediately regretted all the petty things she had been thinking about the telepath. Despite her annoyingly flirtatious demeanor, she was an ally—and a valuable one. No one deserved to fall into Sauron's clutches, particularly not when she had been put in danger as the result of an invitation Shanna herself had extended.

Dust and particles of grass whirled as Storm landed in the village circle. Shanna rushed toward her.

''Sauron kidnapped Psylocke. They went that way. They might still be in view if you fly high enough.''

''If they are, I will stop him,'' the wind-rider vowed. She lofted upward, summoning a jet of air so strong the treetops roiled like tentacles and the watchtower rocked back and forth. Even a pterodactyl in full dive into the lake could not cut the Savage Land atmosphere so swiftly.

To the awe of the villagers, Archangel raced toward them even faster than Storm had left, seeming to be only an azure blur until he braked for his landing. He jogged the last few paces, halting the last of his momentum with his legs.

He saw the opened cage and the empty spot where his lover had sat and let out an inarticulate yell. Shanna told him what had happened.

''I'm on it,'' he barked toward Shanna. Then he was in flight, crying out Betsy's name.

He's as hot-headed as I about his mate, Shanna thought. She hoped Warren wasn't rushing headlong into more than he could handle.

● ● ●

"One down, without even a fight," Logan muttered as the last of twilight faded from purple to black over the village of the Fall People. "Got mud on our faces, people."

"Y'hand out compliments like Cable, Wolvie," Cannonball said, referring to his former mentor in the New Mutants and X-Force. "I think we're feelin' bad enough as it is."

Sam waited for Wolverine's comeback, but Logan merely paced stiffly back and forth, rubbing the nearly healed scar on his side, shadows deep beneath his bushy brows. *He's gnawing his foot off,* Sam thought. *He pushed himself hard all day, caught a bad guy, and now he has nothing positive to show for it.*

Sam recalled all the times he'd seen Psylocke and Wolverine tumbling around the gym or the lawns of the Xavier Institute. Kicking, jabbing, rolling. Delighting in the chance to practice lethal moves with a partner who could withstand the intensity. It had been their ritual ever since Betsy had acquired her ninja skills. Though her romantic involvement with Warren had curtailed the frequency of such practices, Sam suspected Logan was remembering them now.

Sam had his own memories to cope with. Such as his first encounter with Sauron. His protective blast envelope disrupted by Phantazia, Sauron's teammate on that roster of the Brotherhood of Evil Mutants, Sam had proven vulnerable at just the wrong time. The horror of Sauron's spearlike wingtip thrusting completely through his body still made him shudder. There he'd been, skewered like a cube of lamb at one of his family's backyard barbecues.

That was the sort of stuff Sauron was made of. That was the type of freak who had Psylocke now.

Sam tried to distract himself by nabbing a strip of dinosaur jerky from a basketful that a lithe young village woman was offering the visitors. Didn't work. If he'd been capable of distraction, then the mere sight of the all-but-naked server would have done the job. Still, the meat soothed his gullet going down. He had not eaten in many hours.

Ororo was sitting, finally, on the chieftain's stool Tongah's aides had brought from the lodge for her. Deep lines etched her usually smooth brown forehead. She, Warren, and Sam had flown from one end of the valley and back again countless times in the hope of spotting Sauron. She hadn't even taken a break to carry the flightless X-Men back to camp at dusk, leaving that to Sam.

"No telepathic contact whatsoever," Ororo was saying to Hank and Bobby as Logan and Sam joined them. "She's disappeared both physically and psychically. Sauron must have a way of dampening her powers."

" 'Twould seem so," the Beast said. "Not surprising. He's done that before, with the help of Brainchild. The mystery is how he surprised her. The villagers say she was unconscious before Sauron ever swooped down to abduct her."

"She wouldn't've been taken like that if she'd been awake," Logan said. "Hell, she probably wouldn't have been taken, period. Green-beak's hypnotic powers wouldn't have meant squat against Betts."

"I'm not certain who would have prevailed in a telepathic melée," Storm said. "However, it does seem likely that if Psylocke had her shields up, she would have been able to stalemate him for a considerable time. She appears not to have had the opportunity to erect those defenses."

"He'll have drained her by now," Iceman said. "He'll be stronger and harder to beat."

"We've lost several advantages," Storm declared. "Including our radios. Sauron has one now. He can listen if we continue to use them."

"Not to worry," Hank said. "I set them so that they'll

only work for a day unless I enter a code I've prepared. By midnight the circuits in Psylocke's unit will fuse themselves together. Once that happens even Brainchild won't be able to restore it to functional capability.'' As he spoke, he went to each person, raised their wrists, and punched in the necessary code. "Of course, it also means we cannot track her down via the radio signal."

Cannonball lifted his radio to his mouth. "Hey, Warren. Time for dinner, fella. Y'can't do much more right now."

"Negative," Archangel replied. "Save the leftovers. I'm staying out here awhile."

Ororo nodded at the young X-Man. "I appreciate the attempt, Sam, but I already tried. As long as Betsy is in danger, Warren will obsess. He'll stay out all night even if I order otherwise. I won't force the issue yet. He has the stamina. My hope is he'll wear down enough to get some useful sleep before dawn."

"Okay," Cannonball responded. "How about the rest of us? What can we do? Do we just rest and try out the same strategy tomorrow?"

"In the absence of new information, I'm afraid that may be all we can do."

They paused, keening their ears. From far off came the sound of native drums. Ka-Zar soon trotted up.

"Message from the Swamp People," he said. "It's old news, but it may help. Not long after the attack here, one of their scouts witnessed Sauron cruising by carrying a woman in a costume. Doesn't mean the monster stayed in the vicinity, but that does add up to more sightings of him or his riders in that piece of the Savage Land than any other."

"It may not be as solid a lead as we would like," Storm said, "but we'll take it. Tomorrow we'll devote a squad to that region. Meanwhile I'll go up after supper. I'm tired, but it's worth a look right away as long as I know where to concentrate my efforts.''

Sam said, "I'll help."

"No. If you go up at night, our enemies will see the glow of your kinetic envelope. Probably hear you as well, no matter how silent you've learned to be these past couple of years."

Cannonball looked up into the shrouded heavens. He could barely see the bats swooping over the village in pursuit of insects or fruit-bearing trees. It was a witch's cauldron up there. In a way, he was glad not to be journeying up into *that*.

Ororo soared through the blackness. The mist layer was an oppressive weight somewhere above her, depriving her of the starlight she had come to love on her night flights over the Great Rift Valley of Africa, back when she was worshipped as a goddess. Still, the night was the night. The darkness stole away the distractions of color and contrast and movement, leaving her head clear and sharp. A gift.

Below, lights twinkled. The absolute blanking of the heavens made each source vivid. They were fires, mostly, blazing in the villages and camps of the United Tribes. Fires to keep away the wildlife, and fires around which to gather for storytelling. Otherwise the only illumination came from the lava fields on a mountainside to the north—a dull, emberish glower—and from the phosphorescent fish and squid down in the depths of the lake—darting, ghostly streaks.

A warm gust buffeted her hair. She redirected it, using its vigor to sustain the artificial currents that held her at this altitude. Warm. Tropical. Yet a few thousand feet up, beyond the mists, frigid air was roaring past on its way to the Transantarctic Range, further chilling an ice pack that had not melted for thousands, perhaps millions, of years.

Though it was one of the most stunning natural sights Ororo had ever seen, the entire climate of the Savage Land was, in fact, artificial. She reached out with her power and tried, as she had on previous visits, to grasp the scheme behind the magic. It was a work of genius and cosmic technology. Clearly, some of the ancient infrastructure that had warded this place for so many years still operated. The ring of mountains, the geothermal sources, the inversion layer—those all helped, but they didn't explain it all. She could see it, could revise it here and there the way she did the climate elsewhere on Earth, but she couldn't have originated it so completely and, once done, expected it to continue without her active guidance. If she were younger and could ever bear to submit herself to an apprenticeship, she would want to study with a weather sorcerer who could fashion a masterpiece such as this.

What was that?

Her gaze locked on the swamp below. Tiny witchfires danced across its dank waters—methane gas, bubbling up from the putrefying lower layers, the sort of phenomenon sometimes mistaken for UFOs. The glimmers were not significant in themselves, but she was certain that for an instant, something large had passed between her and them.

A flying creature? It would have to have been as large as the flying reptiles she had shared the skies with that day. But wild pterosaurs didn't fly at night. That meant the being near her was either one of Sauron's riders on a tamed mount, or Sauron himself.

"Archangel," she said into her wrist radio. "Meet me over the swamp southeast of the lake."

"On my way."

Good. He had heard her. She had feared that this would

be one of those unlucky times when the EMPs would be masking radio contact. No need to stall, then. She took a deep breath. Time for—

Lightning!

The bolts split the sky as she asked, illuminating the whole area. She glimpsed a dark, winged silhouette cruising low over the bog. It suddenly wheeled and started to climb.

Sauron. And he was alone.

I have you now, murderer, she thought.

She formed sleet and more lightning, funneling it toward the speeding figure. The gale pelted him sideways, but he ducked and circled into quieter air in a stunning example of flying agility. The draining of Psylocke had charged him with such vigor he was as fast as a swooping eagle, but as maneuverable as a swallow.

The initial burst of lightning faded, plunging Ororo into gloom. She called up another round.

Sauron was no longer fleeing clockwise as she had anticipated. She had to hurriedly scan about in order to locate him.

He was coming straight for her.

She commanded a thermal current to form and rocketed herself upward. When Sauron plunged into the updraft, she twisted it around like a funnel, intending to disorient him.

To her amazement, he kept his equilibrium. Though he was racing in tight circles, he was apparently avoiding dizziness. All her effort only made it easier for him to catch up to her altitude.

''Goddess!'' she blurted.

Look into my eyes, mutant. The voice in her mind was sneering, insistent, penetrating. She clutched her temples, trying to block the mental intrusion. A cold squirt of fear bathed her intestines. She had miscalculated. His hypnotic powers had greater range than when last she had fought him. Had he always been this strong, or was it a temporary advantage gained by draining the energy of a telepath?

Ororo abandoned the offensive. She needed to guard herself, allow time for Warren to reach the battle site. She released the lightning, letting the Savage Land skies fall once more into deep blackness. If she couldn't see Sauron's eyes, she couldn't be hypnotized completely. A wind rose to her call and whisked her northward.

Slow down. Slow down. Let me hold you in my grasp, called Sauron.

To her horror, she did slow down. She called rain, hoping its pelting spray would knock him downward, but she couldn't get herself to move faster.

Dry the rain. Don't try to stop me. Turn around.

She tried to change the rain into sleet as before, but the effort failed. The best she could do was maintain a steady drizzle.

Turn around? No, she must not.

Lightning! he demanded. *Give me light!*

"No!" she yelled. Yet, each time she disobeyed, waves of agony pulsed through her skull. She spun, dismissing the drizzle. She refused to let him rule her. If he wanted lightning, she would give it to him, but her way. Down his throat.

In the suddenly rainless, silent night, the flapping of his wings revealed his location. She propelled herself toward him, and when the gap closed to mere dozens of meters, she struck at him with a lightning bolt.

The jagged snake of electricity vaulted across the gap. It struck Sauron at belt level.

Then, before the light faded, she realized the bolt had not struck his body, but an odd belt he wore. A nimbus of energy surrounded the belt, consisting of the energy with which she had attacked him. It had been absorbed. Neutralized, as by a lightning rod.

One of Brainchild's toys, she realized. Sauron had not come out tonight bereft of countermeasures to her power. He had been ready for her.

The continued glow from the belt kept Sauron illuminated. She could see right into his huge, baleful eyes.

Now you are mine. Cease your struggles.

She pulled up, maintaining only enough wind to keep her at her current altitude and coordinates.

"Good, my pretty cloud nymph," Sauron cackled aloud. "Now stay still. I deserve a taste of you right away for all the abuse you levelled at me tonight, wouldn't you agree?"

"You . . . haven't . . . defeated . . . me . . ." she hissed between clenched teeth.

"A detail I'll remedy immediately," he said. He reached her and, wings flapping hard in order to maintain position, reached out to grasp her.

She cringed backward. Closing her eyes would reduce his hypnotic effect by at least half, but she found she couldn't even do that. His eyes seemed to grow until they filled her field of vision. Nothing remained in the universe but those orbs and his raucous, mocking voice.

Silvery fragments of metal whisked between them. Blood fanned from a slit that sprouted in one of her enemy's wings. A few drops struck her face, jolting her back to a state of control.

She cut the wind that supported her and dropped like a bomb right out of Sauron's reach. The talons on his left foot grazed her head, tearing loose a lock of her white tresses.

He let her go. She looked up to see him whirl sideways. A moment later another winged shape crossed between her and the fading glow of his lightning-swallowing belt.

Bless you, Warren, she thought.

"Greetings, Archangel," Sauron shouted. "Too bad you couldn't fling more blades at me while I was preoccupied, but then you might have killed your teammate. Never willing to do what it takes to win, are you, my old friend?"

Storm halted her plunge fifty meters below Sauron. Her hands were trembling. The wind obeyed her fitfully. The urge to continue fleeing was powerful, but she overruled the desire. Warren had broken Sauron's hypnotic control over her, not to pave the road of her retreat, but to assist her in winning the battle.

In the agonizingly sluggish moments necessary to take a breath, shake off her disorientation, and initiate a new offensive, she puzzled over what was happening above. Warren had not yet followed through on his surprise attack. She couldn't see him in the darkness. The only thing she could truly make out was the tiny blur of light that clung to Sauron's midsection.

Why was Archangel letting their enemy babble on?

Goddess. Is he afraid to engage?

"Always the most weak-willed of all the X-Men," Sauron taunted. "Your metal wings haven't changed the man inside. Give up now, child. I will let you live."

Fipp-fipp-fipp-fipp.

Sauron squawked and whirled around. Another barrage of Warren's blades raced past him, just missing. The monster pumped his wings hard, presenting as difficult a target as possible.

Storm finally comprehended. Warren was not afraid to fight. He was playing it smart, gliding in circles out in the darkness where Sauron couldn't see him and at a distance that would minimize the hypnotic effect. In fact, he had been less rattled than she by the villain's incredible strength.

LAW OF THE JUNGLE

The last of the glow from the belt vanished. Now everyone was flying blind again.

No advantage then, to keeping the night dark. Storm called forth more lightning. A continuous round of small bursts, to give herself and Warren a clear shot.

Sauron blinked and covered his eyes. The discharges painted the cloud layer with a steely tone, and turned the jungle to a palate of shadow, charcoal, and ash. Between this ceiling and floor hung the three of them, mutants and mutate snared in a lethal aerial dance.

"There you are," Sauron screeched at Archangel. "Come to me. Surrender yourself."

Archangel came, but not passively. He raced directly toward Sauron. "Storm!" he shouted. "Wing-and-Prayer maneuver!"

Ororo smiled and initiated the first move of a strategy she and Warren had practiced time and again in the Danger Room. She hurled gale-force blasts at their enemy, timing it so that Archangel would arrive immediately after they ceased.

Sauron was knocked from his stable glide and sent flailing. Unable to control his trajectory, he tumbled pointed tail over beak toward the terrain below.

Archangel hit him hard with a double kick. Only a last-instant twist saved Sauron from taking the impact on his spine.

"Striking to maim," the villain screeched. "You want me to suffer, don't you, Worthington? What a sinister blue creature you've become. Your fear of me has stolen your battle ethics."

Storm was unnerved to hear how composed Sauron still was. He was still able to snatch at ugly truths to use as psychological weapons. First he had implied Warren too ret-

icent to fight hard; now, too eager. But his voice had qua-
vered. Warren had hurt him. In spite of the smug words, the
mutate was retreating.

Warren circled and came back strong again. He truly
seemed to be intending to inflict the maximum amount of
pain. And why not? It was the only thing that might daunt
Sauron.

"You did me a favor," Archangel growled as he closed
the gap. "Those other times we fought showed me I needed
to work on my willpower. Now eat metal, you—"

Ororo didn't hear exactly what Warren called their opponent. The slur was buried beneath the noise of wingtip blades
erupting like rounds from a machine gun.

Sauron hung in place. The projectiles whisked past. Storm
gasped. Warren had missed! At that range, with such a clear
shot and a hovering target, that could only have happened . . .

If Sauron had hypnotized him into missing.

Then Sauron folded his wings and dropped. Droplets of
blood—dark specks against the lightning glow—scattered in
his wake. Warren had not entirely missed. He had nicked the
monster in at least two spots, and this time deep enough that
the nerve-disruption side effect of the metal properly stunned
the villain.

Warren shook his head, swerved, and kept dogging Sauron
as he fled. The hypnotic effect was dazing him, but it wasn't
stopping him, and Sauron knew it. The mutate was trying to
escape.

Hear me. The voice blossomed in Ororo's mind, but she
forced it out. She wouldn't be his victim. They had him on
the run. He'd given them an ordeal, but the tide had turned.
If Archangel didn't take him down, she would.

The X-Men had defeated Sauron in these very skies. He
had tried to escape at the end of that encounter, but she had

thwarted him. The memory of it surfaced strong and fresh. She had opened up the cloud layer and shunted the polar air directly at him, until he was so chilled his muscles refused to obey his commands.

What had worked once, would work again. She beseeched the forces of this strange land to heed her.

And they did. The clouds parted, revealing the stark filigin cloth of the Antarctic sky, dotted with the stars so rarely glimpsed by Savage Land natives. The frigid current plunged down.

A wall of air pounded her. She reeled, flipped upside down, and began flailing. *What?*

A tempest filled the atmosphere. She lost sight of her target, couldn't find Archangel. She tried to calm the storm with her powers, but the sleet and gusts only intensified. She concentrated harder.

And the disruption grew.

Suddenly she understood. It was her own power that assaulted her. Her body wasn't doing what her mind commanded at all. She was executing commands thrust covertly into her mind from outside.

Focusing in the manner that Professor Xavier, Phoenix, and Psylocke had taught her over the years, she identified the precise spot where the alien influence had taken hold. She unravelled the noose.

But the skies still flung her about. She was still falling fast, incapable of directing a breeze to keep her aloft. The crisis she had spawned had taken on a life of its own far beyond her capacity to simply abort.

No equilibrium. She struggled to stay conscious. Perhaps, given a few moments, she could at least aim for a landing in the lake. But at her speed, even striking water would be fatal, and the denizens of the waters were not hospitable to guests.

Strong hands gripped her wrists. Her trajectory levelled off.

"Hang on!" Warren shouted. "It's going to be a rough ride!"

Archangel had a good hold on her, and needed it. The gale whipped him from a different direction every few moments, ridiculing his command of the air. His bionic wings meant little in such unpredictable conditions. He was pumping hard to make landfall somewhere—anywhere—where they could take shelter.

The only consolation, Storm thought grimly, was that Sauron would be struggling against all this as well.

"Did you get him?" she yelled.

"No," Warren yelled back. "It was all I could do to notice that you were going down. He went the other way."

Suddenly the jungle rose up beneath them, revealed by the latest bolt of lightning. A low cliff loomed to their left. Warren leaned to port and aimed them beneath an overhang. They landed hard, rolled, but came up intact and bruised more in spirit than in body.

Even beneath the shelter of the rock, rain whipped in, striking Ororo's face, muddying the dirt in which she sat.

Another flash illuminated the ruptured heavens. No sign of any flying creature, much less a humanoid pterosaur. Sauron had escaped.

CHAPTER 7

In the morning, the rupture in the cloud layer remained, revealing, in bizarre contrast to the brightness below, the dark winter Antarctic sky. To Ororo, it was as if the demons of Kenyan myth had torn out a piece of the sky god's flesh.

She glided above and beyond the village, surveying the nearby region. At least the winds obeyed her that much now, though she was still buffeted at unexpected moments. Rain continued to thrash the grass-and-bamboo huts of the Fall People, leaving the village children to cower in the doorways and stare in awe at the violence of the deluge.

The story was the same across the landscape. Mud slid from drenched hillsides. A drowned rhinoceros bobbed up and down in a swollen river, its bloated body adorned with one very soaked, miserable vulture. On a ridge, spurs of trees stood bereft of the limbs a violent gust had torn from them.

Ororo would have wept, but crying was not something that came easy to her after her hard years as an orphan and child thief in Cairo. She could bear to see no more right now. Reaching the far point of her latest circuit, she gave up and turned back, aiming straight for the village.

A lightning bolt crackled down, bouncing off of the protective aura Storm had woven around herself. The bolt continued to the ground, felling a hadrosaur who had been foolish enough to raise its head from the meadow to regard its herd.

"Oh, Goddess," she murmured, barely finding the energy to move her lips. She coasted unsteadily the last few miles to the village and darted beneath the none-too-intact thatch roof that extended from the eaves of the lodge. Ka-Zar, Shanna, Zabu, Hank, and Logan stood there, examining the blustery conditions.

Thunder boomed, so loudly it seemed the earth groaned in reply. Ka-Zar frowned at Storm, but said nothing. Zabu shook his mane to rid it of rain droplets and glared accusingly.

"You out-did yourself on this occasion, Ororo m'lady," the Beast commented.

Storm dipped her chin and sighed. Here she had thought she was acting to administer the *coup de grâce* to Sauron, and in fact, she had been following one of his hypnotic commands: *Ruin the weather. Do the worst thing you can think of.* How clear that sinister telepathic whisper was in her memory. At the time, she hadn't consciously heard it at all.

Ruin the weather indeed. The Savage Land climate control system, magnificent as it was, resembled a glass figurine. Tap it in the wrong spot and cracks spread everywhere.

"I can heal it," she said. "But not with the ease that I set it into chaos. The repair will take all day. Perhaps some of tomorrow."

"And if we leave things alone?" Hank asked.

"The atmosphere will heal itself, but that will take a week. Too long. Given that much opportunity, the snow and winds may have lingering ill effect on the flora and fauna. I cannot participate in the fight against Sauron today. I have to correct this."

"Yes," Shanna said tartly. "You do."

Logan raised an eyebrow. "You ain't blamin' Ororo for this mess." It was a statement, not a question.

Shanna turned and faced Wolverine squarely, holding a pose that few had the courage to maintain in front of him. "I blame Sauron, of course," she said. "I'm merely agreeing that Storm is responsible for rectifying the accident before this land suffers any more abuse."

"Fine," Logan said. "I just wouldn't wantcha gettin' the idea that green-beak doesn't know how to be real sneaky with that hypnotism of his. He'll catch you off-guard even when you think you have him dead to rights. *I* know."

"We've all learned that lesson," Shanna agreed. "Ka-Zar and I know that Ororo treasures this place as much as we do. We can't help it if it's difficult to endure the devastation while we're in the midst of it. We've had too many tastes of what happens when our climate mechanisms are corrupted."

Ororo could not have been more sorry. She had already apologized profusely when she and Archangel had dragged into camp, but she wanted to beg forgiveness again and again. What Wolverine said was true—Sauron's powers were insidious and devastatingly powerful when he had a source of mutant energy to feed upon. Even so, it was she who had failed last night. She had possessed the strength of will to defy him, if only she had been attentive enough to notice his trickery.

"I will leave the rescue of Psylocke to the rest of you then," Storm said. "By now enough of the maelstrom's fury is spent that I can initiate the repair. If you'll excuse me, it will take a great deal of concentration."

She stepped out of the shelter into the pelting rain and reached upward with her powers, found a zephyr of polar air, and turned it back toward the vent in the clouds. Then another, and another. Next, she strengthened a pulse of warm air rising from the geysers near the swamp, one of the many sources of heat that supported the tropical, prehistoric environment of the Savage Land. After that, she evaporated a small snow cloud that was assaulting the heat-loving foliage on a hill upriver, not far from the waterfall where the X-Men had emerged when they first arrived.

That was how it would be. One little bit at a time, like sopping up a bucketload of overturned syrup with a single paper towel.

Warren Worthington III saw the rift above him begin to draw shut, one puff of cloud at a time, restricting the blasts of snow and subzero gusts that had been pummeling the ground for hours. The turbulence lessened until it no longer took every bit of his might and skill just to keep flying. He headed back toward the Fall People village. His early morning search had produced no sign of Sauron or any of the mutates. *Might as well stop for now, and eat something*, he thought—he'd had no lunch or supper the day before—*and help ferry everyone to their patrol sites.*

As he descended, he spotted Ororo out in the open. She was shuddering. Her teeth were clenched. Her eyes fluttered open at irregular intervals, remaining tightly shut at all other moments. Such effort.

She looked glorious, though. She was brimming with the aura of a goddess. Long, lean brown arms beckoned the forces of cloud and wind.

Preoccupied with the spectacular sight, he nearly bumped into Wolverine on his way into the lodge.

"Something I can do for you?" Warren asked when Logan didn't step aside.

"You smell different," Logan said.

"You're no rose yourself," Warren retorted. He lifted a

white-gloved hand to push on through. Only then did he notice that his teammate wore a tiny, but friendly, grin.

"I mean," said Wolverine, "you smell *right*. Less doubt in you today, Worthington. You proved somethin' to yourself up there last night."

Warren cocked his head. "You complimenting me, Logan?"

"Don't let it go to yer head," the other replied. "Just keep this attitude goin'. You didn't let old green-beak tug yer strings after all. That's the edge you gotta keep. None of that second-guessing crap you were wallowing in before."

Spoken like a man who could trust his instincts, Warren thought. He never dared do that, for fear his instincts would turn out to be some vestige of Apocalypse still contaminating him, urging him to be the horseman of Death. "Of course there are other ways," he snapped. Last night, he had struck in a rage, without self-control. It turned out okay, but that was luck, not design. He had to insist on higher standards for himself. "Maybe if I'd thought of some alternative attacks, he wouldn't have had the chance to trick Ororo."

"Believe that if you want, flyboy," Logan said. "But don't let it slow you down."

"I'll give that advice the full consideration it deserves," Warren responded.

Wolverine stepped past, out into the downpour. He tilted his head up toward the clouds as if daring them to wash him away. Archangel watched him for a moment, then slipped inside the structure.

Logan was right about some things. Warren's state of mind had improved. He no longer agonized over how he would act when he faced Sauron; he had already shown that he would not repeat old mistakes. But the knowledge gave him only a scrap of peace. Sauron was still at large. Betsy was still a prisoner. Closure had not been achieved.

Iceman, the Beast, Cannonball, Ka-Zar, and Shanna sat cross-legged in a circle around platters of fruit, bowls of porridge, a pot of steaming tea, and more. Warren rubbed his belly and savored the aroma. It might be a Stone Age breakfast, but right now it beckoned him more than any at the five-star restaurants he frequented in his spoiled rich-boy days, before his skin turned blue.

And what's Betsy eating this morning? Would she be fed at all? The thought ruined the first taste of the biscuit he raised to his mouth.

"Today Shanna and I will stay near the village," Ka-Zar told Warren when he'd taken the edge off his hunger. "Storm is obviously devoting every bit of her attention to the skies. We can't let her fall victim to the same sort of ambush that claimed Betsy."

"That's one reason Wolverine is out there now," the Beast added.

Warren mentioned the calmer conditions, and offered to help in the transport. "Wolvie going to join you three?"

"No, he wants to go out alone again," Iceman said.

"The man is crazy. It'll make him a target," Warren declared.

"Our comrade of the Great White North perceives that eventuality," Hank said. "He embraces it."

"In other words," Cannonball said, "he's daring Sauron to come get him so he can get a shot at him."

"Wasn't that what I said?" Hank asked.

"I'll say this for Wolvie, he's the only one of us that won a fight yesterday," Bobby interjected. "What's wrong with letting him try again? It's not like he'd let any of us tell him not to.''

"It's more than a little inconvenient that Ororo is so thoroughly diverted.'' Hank popped an entire kiwifruit into his mouth and swallowed it almost without chewing. "We could benefit from her active leadership today.''

"We'll just have to muddle through, Hank,'' Archangel said. "I was there the first few months Ororo served as leader of the X-Men. She's come a long way, but we've been in plenty of tough situations without her or Scott or the Professor to give orders.''

"I know, old comrade,'' Hank said. "It's not orders I was referring to. There is a synergy that happens when we operate as a team. I am troubled at the way Sauron has managed to disrupt it.''

"It bugs me, too, Hank,'' Warren replied. He washed down the last gulp of porridge with a dose of tea—blinking at the jolt of caffeine and wondering what sort of herbs the Fall People had steeped—and stretched out his wings from one bamboo rafter to another. "Who wants to ride with me?''

"I need to go,'' Ka-Zar said unexpectedly. "I should speak with the Swamp People scout. I'll need to serve as translator when he gives his report. Once that's done, you can bring me back to help Shanna guard Ororo.''

"Very well,'' Archangel said, clapping Ka-Zar on the shoulder and heading for the exit. "Grab your barf bag and let's go. I plan to make it a quick trip.''

Because, Warren thought, *I'll go crazy unless I get back up into the atmosphere, where I can at least pretend I'm doing something to rescue Betsy.*

• • •

Hank McCoy shaded his eyes, watching as Archangel sailed upward, hauling Ka-Zar back to the village. Warren had been awfully efficient and businesslike about the transport, as if his mind were elsewhere.

'Twas a strange and wonderous phenomenon to behold, Warren so deeply in love. There had been a time when the Beast's blond teammate had been the quintessential playboy. Not that he had tarnished the reputations of an inordinate number of ladies—after all, one could hardly accumulate a Cassanova-level romantic résumé when faced with such awkward impediments as disrobing in a lovely young thing's boudoir and suddenly having to explain why one possessed a set of feathered appendages sprouting from one's back—but Warren had broken his share of hearts. Never committing, always on the move, a rich and handsome bachelor always slightly out of reach. How Hank had envied him.

Hank did not envy him now.

The light across the landscape flickered and grew stronger. He looked up at the clouds. "Ah. Excellent work, my dear Ms. Munroe," he murmured. Storm had finished sewing shut the rip in the Savage Land's inversion layer. The last of the autumn crispness dissipated, restoring the clinging mugginess characteristic of the valley.

She still had plenty of work to do. Though it wasn't raining on Hank, Bobby, and Sam here at the edge of the great swamp, thunderheads and funnel clouds still loomed in almost every direction.

Behind the Beast, Iceman and Cannonball were entertaining the scout of the Swamp People that Ka-Zar had just interviewed. Iceman formed a snowball and tossed it toward his teammate, who ducked it, allowing the missle to splatter against the hut wall. When Bobby formed another, the native gestured that they should pause. The burly, loincloth-attired hunter took the snowball from Bobby and lifted it to his cheek, marveling at its cold, soft texture.

"It's all yours, Gaibanee," Bobby said.

Hank grinned and led his two companions off along the wide dinosaur track that led into the elephant grass and cypress trees at the border of the marsh. Gaibanee waved farewell.

The native hadn't been able to tell them much. The previous afternoon, the man had been sitting in a tall tree, waiting for a herd of triceratops to clomp past, when he had observed Sauron carrying Psylocke away. The mutate had disappeared behind a stand of huge camphor trees. When Gaibanee had later ventured to the site, he saw a few pteranodonlike footprints. Nothing more.

Had Sauron merely been taking a short rest, or hiding as Storm, Archangel, or Cannonball cruised past? Or was he headquartered somewhere in this mucky tangle of vegetation? The latter was a distinct possibility. Even the Swamp People didn't venture very far into its depths. A group of ne'er-do-wells could operate in secret for months before any of Ka-Zar and Shanna's allies stumbled across them. And it was this very swamp over which he'd been surprised last night by Storm and Archangel.

They came to a stream of sluggish water choked by lily pads. Hank noticed Sam frown and sigh. The youth wanted to vault across it with his power. Hank shook his head. That's how they had operated throughout much of the previous day—using Cannonball's projectile flying and carrying ability to move efficiently from place to place. The problem was, that style of searching had yielded absolutely no results. It was a noisy and attention-grabbing way to travel. Today they would try stealthier tactics, à la Wolverine.

That meant a great deal of walking.

Iceman extended his hand. A bridge of ice formed. The trio trotted across. They slid into a grove of huge rhododendrons. The clouds opened up again, prompting a pitter-patter through the canopies of foliage above them. It would take half an hour or more to reach the spot Gaibanee had described.

"You know what the worst thing is about not knowing where to find Sauron?" Hank murmured to Bobby.

"No," Iceman replied. "It's too hard to figure out which one is worst. Too many candidates."

"More than anything, I don't like that *he* always has a pretty good idea where to find *us*."

"Now that you mention it, that's true. What are you suggesting? Should we hide?"

"Hide? Probably not. I'll give myself a few more hours to mull it over. I don't have enough pieces of the puzzle yet to know if we can do anything that would come to any good. But aren't you feeling the urge to turn the tables on our vexatious nemesis?"

"Amen to that. Keep that brain working, Dr. McCoy," Bobby said as he froze a patch of quicksand up ahead.

Ororo dissipated the thunderhead out over the lake. She glided unsteadily over the great body of water, searching for further corruptions of the normal weather patterns. She sensed disquiet. A funnel cloud spun in the roiling air in one of the side valleys, but it had not touched ground and she could sense that it was weakening. Turbulence flogged the waves in the lake to whitecaps, dismaying pelicans and small pterosaurs. The winged predators were out in force despite the conditions, vying for the fish that swam just beneath the surface, feeding off storm debris. Flashes of lightning still coiled over the foothills, but started no fires in the drenched grass.

At last, the situation was stable enough that she could justify a breather. Long hours of study and minor tweaking would be necessary to reverse the subtle, hard-to-isolate flaws in the atmosphere, but the rift was thoroughly closed. Even if she were to stop now, the snow would not return and the flooding would grow no worse.

Despite the friction of the air as she flew, perspiration trickled down her chest, and her hair was a mop against her back. Her spine ached as though she had been practicing weightlifting with the entire planet upon her. As for her general level of energy, she half-believed that Sauron had succeeded in catching her already and had drained her strength with his usual brutal aplomb.

She wobbled toward the village, her flight as tipsy and haphazard as a butterfly's. Coming to rest on the packed ground, her knees abruptly folded. She collapsed forward between the rain puddles, scuffing her elbows and chin. It took her several heartbeats just to find the vigor to roll over.

Gentle hands rinsed her muddied jawline with a moistened scrap of soft doeskin. Ororo gazed up to find Shanna kneeling over her.

To the X-Men leader's amazement, she beheld sympathy and gratitude in her hostess's countenance. Her surprise must have been blatant, because Shanna chuckled.

"I'm not always a she-devil," she said. "You should see me when I get all mushy and maternal with my little boy." She helped Ororo sit upright and held out a stalk of some sort of plant.

"What is it?" Storm asked.

"Sugar cane. You looked like you needed a quick carbohydrate fix. This is nature's own sugar rush. Sorry, but we're out of Jolt.''

"This will do nicely. Thank you," Ororo said, putting the juicy pulp to her mouth and sucking a sweet burst.

Shanna guided her weary guest to a bamboo platform where they could be get out of the mud, and rinsed her off with gourd dippers of collected rainwater. "That's the handy part about dressing native," Shanna said. "No laundry to worry about. It's the main reason I moved here, you know."

Ororo laughed.

Shanna's smile turned back to the comradely expression she had worn prior. "I'm sorry I snapped at you this morning. The Savage Land couldn't have a better warden than people like you."

"But it does," Ororo said. "It has you and Ka-Zar."

"I believe that's what I said," Shanna added cheerfully. "You are like us. Giving two hundred percent to make things right for this land."

It felt more like three hundred percent, thought Ororo, lowering herself laboriously to one of the log stools that bordered the wash area. She noticed several of the tribe's older women nodding at her. Apparently stepping up on the platform and being rinsed of mud by a respected local figure was a sign of deep respect. Perhaps she should mention that to some of her inhibited male teammates.

Her head swirled. Good thing she was sitting. Shanna frowned and gestured for a pair of tribeswomen to hurry with the soup and flat bread and vegetables they were bringing. "Eat," she said. "Get back your strength."

Ororo did not realize she had kept her eyes closed until she opened them and saw the wicker tray of food right under her nose. "Oh, how wonderful!" she said as she smelled the slightly fermented bread. "This looks like *injera*. The Ethiopian staple. Do you know it?"

"I've tried every kind of African cuisine except raw monkey brains and live dung beetles," Shanna said. "Yes, this is just like *injera*." She tore off a shred of the spongy loaf and tasted it. Her eyelids closed in pleasure. "And no one in the village makes it better than Refira."

Refira, a short, bosomy woman of obvious strength but little of the hard leanness of other villagers—perhaps she enjoyed her own cooking as much as others did—smiled as she set down the tray, recognizing her name and the complimentary lilt in Shanna's voice, if not the actual words.

Ororo used a scrap of the bread to scoop up a swallow of curry-fortified beans and hungrily downed it. The Goddess's blessing that everything was soft and required so little chewing. At the moment, even working her jaw required undue strain.

She was just as weak as a villain would wish her to be.

CHAPTER 8

One of the things Sam Guthrie didn't miss about leaving his boyhood home was the odor of the dairy ranch just down the road. As far as he was concerned, Professor Xavier could have included that incentive on the recruiting poster for his School for Gifted Youngsters: *Be a mutant. Wear a costume. Travel to exciting places and meet famous people. Get away from fresh cow pies steaming in muddy corrals on summer afternoons, day after day after day.*

Looming in front of Cannonball was the carcass of a brachiosaurus. It was half-immersed in tepid, yellowish swamp water, adorned by flies and scavenger insects, its vertebrae protruding from the collapsing hide on its back. It stank worse than anything back in Kentucky.

"Better radio Storm," he drawled. "Tell her we found Sauron's secret headquarters."

"Droll and perspicacious as ever, my dear Sam," the Beast declared.

Cannonball enjoyed the chance to joke. As the senior member and field leader of X-Force, he had had to stifle his playfulness more than he liked. Now that he was a junior teammate of the adult squad, he didn't have to set such a careful example.

"Bobby, my friend," the Beast said, "do something about that thing before my nose withers and falls off."

Iceman nodded. He froze the hulk from crest to below

water surface, flies and all. The odor diminished until it was only a few times more potent than the fetid, stagnant pools they had been traversing for hours.

Hours. Cannonball grimaced. The problem wasn't so much the rigors and unpleasantness of the terrain, it was that they had so little to show for it. They had found no trail, even though they had succeeded in locating the spot Gaibanee had described. Hank's keen eyes had discovered a strand of long, dark human hair caught under a sliver in a log. A purple human hair. It was of the same type as Psylocke's.

A few talon marks remained on the log, though the rain had wiped out any prints that may have earlier been preserved in the mud or grass of the clearing. They had searched in a widening circle around the site, but no citadels lurked in the shadows of the cypresses and willows—just ducks, turtles, and alarmingly big crocodiles.

Hank noted the time, and lifted his radio to lips. "This is the Beast. Situation remains the same."

"Archangel. Nothing new up here."

"Wolverine. No contact."

"Base camp quiet," reported Ka-Zar. "Bird's in the nest. So far so good otherwise. No new information."

That was it for the next two hours, assuming another EMP didn't block their next status check. The circumstances had been unchanged all day. The only news of any sort was the "bird's in the nest" comment, which meant that Ororo was on the ground in the village, rather than up fiddling with the weather, and was still unavailable to help with the search.

Cannonball rounded the pool containing the dinosaur, heading for a clump of giant ferns within which to answer a call of nature in private. He'd barely stepped out of view of the others when a shape launched at him from the lower branches of the trees above the ferns.

"What?" Sam blurted. He began blasting even as he fell backward in surprise.

The shape was Amphibius. One of the smaller mutates in the employ of Sauron, he bounced impressively high when he struck Cannonball's kinetic envelope. Sam, invulnerable as ever inside the energy zone, was harmed neither by the small axe the frog man wielded, nor by the impact as he hit the ground.

Had Sam failed to notice Amphibius's leap, though, he might have acquired a canyon in his skull.

"Beast! Iceman!" Sam cried. He jumped to his feet, whirling in the direction that Amphibius had just bounded in retreat.

Hank and Bobby must have already heard the altercation, because they crashed into the fern tangle within a fraction of a second.

"Well?" Hank asked.

Cannonball was astounded. Amphibius had already vanished completely. In two quick sentences, Sam blurted what had happened.

"Quit jiggling on your feet like that," Hank commanded.

"I'm maintainin' my blast envelope," Sam explained.

"Yes, and the sizzle of it is too loud."

Cannonball cut off his power, looking every direction to be sure he wasn't ambushed again while vulnerable.

Minus the hiss and spit of Sam's power, they could hear leaves flapping aside as a sizeable creature hurtled through the vegetation. The noises came from the ten o'clock position from the direction Hank was facing.

"Go high," Hank ordered Sam. "We'll take low."

Nodding, Cannonball lit a fire under himself and vaulted above the treetops in a roar he hoped would paint a yellow stripe right down the middle of Amphibius's speckled green back. The swamp spread out below him. He scanned closely for some sign of the fugitive.

Nothing. No swaying trees branches. No wriggling grass. Amphibius was bounding somewhere near ground level, beneath two to three layers of jungle and swamp canopy. Sam gnashed his teeth. After circling three times, he gave up visual surveillance. He landed in the top of a palm tree, cutting off his power to reduce noise, and proceeded to listen.

Twigs broke in the woods on the other side of an abundant tangle of berry vines. Cannonball launched off his perch, blasting again.

He battered aside leaves and branches. Suddenly the mossy, fern-littered ground appeared. Just to his right was Amphibius, wide-eyed and squawking at the abrupt interception. Sam cut his speed, but couldn't avoid slamming into the earth.

Amphibius struck him. It didn't hurt, of course, but the mutate gained momentum from the impact. He sailed up and over a bank of thick fronds before Cannonball could turn around.

"Oh, no y'don't!" Sam shouted. "I ain't lettin' you get away!"

The X-Man hopped over the obstacle. He came down in a knee-deep puddle, scaring a pair of crocodiles. Amphibius was hopping between the tree trunks beyond, just about to vanish from view once more.

Cannonball thundered forward in a straight shot, aiming for a collision course. But the mutate apparently had anticipated that. The target folded up, dropping abruptly to the earth. Cannonball roared past and slammed into the trunk of a tree.

The trunk groaned and fell on top of him. It took three bursts of energy to get clear.

LAW OF THE JUNGLE

Amphibius was nowhere to be seen. Cannonball tossed aside splinters and looked this way and that. A laugh trickled through the vegetation. From where?

Iceman cruised over the fronds on an ice ramp and came to a stop beside his teammate. "Which way?" he demanded.

"I dunno," Sam replied. "I'm going up again to have a look. He was headed thataway." He pointed in the direction Amphibius had seemed to be fleeing.

Bobby raced into the forest, flinging a few icicle darts ahead for good measure. Sam rocketed into the sky.

The canopies again interfered. Cannonball spotted the Beast leaping past the site of the recent altercation, and glimpsed Iceman streaking on ahead, but there were just too many leaves. He came to roost on a smooth wide branch, cut his power, and keened his ears. He could hear nothing over the racket of the parrots and other birds fleeing from Bobby's strange, frigid appearance.

A splash.

Cannonball thundered off, this time cutting under the uppermost canopy, frightening still more parrots as well as a troop of monkeys. He soon reached a deep channel of water that he hadn't been able to spot from higher up. Crocs were thrashing about, as if they had taken down prey.

Worth a closer look, Sam decided. He cut his speed and ricocheted from tree trunk to tree trunk, gazing at the panorama of jaws and scaly bodies in the water.

It was not Amphibius. The crocs were subduing an anaconda. The huge snake was a meal that would feed a whole crocodilian family, and they weren't about to let it escape. Sam's brows rose. *Lord, that's primeval*—a sight to gawk at from beginning to end, if not for the urgency of his mission.

Iceman burst through the cycads on the bank and reined

up, whistling at the reptilian battle splashing the front end of his ramp. "Well?" he asked Sam.

Sam shrugged. Then he frowned and looked at the water. The channel was one of many winding through the trees here. Muddy, interconnected, deeply shaded, a lot could hide in under the surface.

"I think Amphibius is swimmin' away from us," Sam said.

The Beast, huffing slightly, sprinted to the bank and joined Iceman on his chill perch. "Swimming, did you say? I was afraid of that. He's custom designed for this landscape. He wouldn't have dared attack us alone if he hadn't had the ability to hit and run."

"Are you saying we should give up chasing him?" Iceman asked.

"*Au contraire,*" Hank replied. "He wouldn't just be out here for no reason. There's something in this vicinity he's protecting. We'll take up residence, look for signs of him, but also investigate whatever it is he doesn't want us to discover. If we get close enough to it, he'll come to us."

Sam clenched his fingers together, as if he had them wrapped around a fat, slimy neck. He'd done enough waiting. Time to make life difficult for the bad guys.

Logan knelt down, studying the tracks in the soft clay of the jungle floor. This deep beneath the galleries of branches, the plants grew in scattered clumps, deprived of the light they needed to be profuse. The spoor was easy to follow.

It took an experienced tracker to read the confusion of toe marks, however. He identified the deep, large impressions of the pack leader, the nearly-as-large but more graceful marks of a dominant female, the shallow and smaller holes left by a juvenile with a limp. And more. Still eight of the beasts.

LAW OF THE JUNGLE

He had come across the trail shortly before the report by radio that Hank, Bobby, and the kid had encountered Amphibius and were trying to corner him. He would have called for Archangel to airlift him to the swamp to add to that effort, but he had decided he might find more fun and games nearby. After all, wolves shouldn't be traipsing through deep jungle. They liked open terrain or forests like the taiga lands of the Great White North, which Logan had called home in what seemed like the distant past. Ka-Zar said some packs had even ventured out of the Savage Land entirely into the snow fields. The jungle lord had assisted UN environmentalists to barricade a ravine so that the animals wouldn't find their way down to the penguin rookeries. *Talk about banquets in tuxedoes.*

No, wolves shouldn't be here. Unless they were Lupo's wolves, summoned to help in one poisonous scheme or another. Maybe the animals were guarding something. Either way, Wolverine longed to put a claw or two between them and their intention.

It raised his hackles that Lupo had escaped so quickly. Worse yet that Betts had been snared in the process.

He sniffed. The scent had intensified. It lacked the pungency of the actual beast, being only a vestige rising from the print, but he guessed the pack had travelled across the patch of ground no more than half an hour earlier. They had been traveling at a leisurely trot. If they kept that pace, he could probably catch up to them faster than his buddies in the swamp could round up old frog-face.

He stood and jogged onward. The spoor led across through a thicket, down a slope to a small creek—burbling with the runoff of the storms Ororo had been quenching all morning— and up the much steeper bank on the other side.

Logan was just reaching the top of the incline when he

heard a rush of movement in the viny, flowering plants to which he was clinging. A cascade of wolves rained down on him. More than eight. Twenty. Twenty-five, perhaps. He had no time to actually count.

He crashed spinefirst onto the cobblestones of the creek-bed. A groan tried to burst from his lips, but he swallowed it. His adamantium blades flashed, thudding into wolf ribs. The big male atop his chest yelped and jumped away.

Even as he slashed at the ones continuing to land on his upper body or belly, others sank teeth into whatever parts they could—his knees, his groin, his underarms. Some tried for his throat. His healing factor would deal with it in time, but it still hurt.

He kicked, winning enough clear space to roll to his feet. The wolves hounded him from all sides. Blood dotted their teeth, adding to their frenzy. His blood. They held back only when his claws were actually swiping or thrusting toward them.

"Twenty of you to one of me. I gotcha outnumbered," Wolverine growled. He strode forward over the slick rock, carrying the battle to his furry opponents.

"Wrong!" shouted a voice. Abruptly Wolverine was tumbling heels over head into the deeper part of the stream, jawbone singing. If not for his unbreakable bones, he would be spitting out teeth.

The wolves leapt in again, but not before Logan glimpsed the hulking, four-armed figure at the base of the creek bank.

"Howdy, Barbarus," the X-Man taunted. "You hit me with one fist or four? Whatever it was, didn't do the job." He struggled for footing in the thigh-deep current, nearly overwhelmed by the onslaught of lupine weight, but grinning.

Barbarus shrugged. "I'll try again. No rush." He lifted both his right arms and snapped fingers.

The wolves backed away. They paced five to six feet away from Wolverine, snarling, their eyes full of bloodlust, barely held in check.

"You did that almost as good as Lupo. Didn't know his critters would listen to you, too."

"They don't." Wolverine looked up. On the bank stood Lupo, with Gaza towering beside him. "I ordered them back. I was indulging Barbarus. He wanted you to take a moment to contemplate the depth of your predicament." The wolfish mutate chuckled.

Wolverine just grinned back, a smile full of teeth but no mirth. "I got business to settle with you."

"Strange. That was just what I was going to say to you. You are welcome to try to do so, but I've already—how do you outsiders so cleverly put it?—'paid my dues' yesterday. To get to me today, you'll have to go through all my animals and Gaza and Barbarus, too."

As Lupo spoke, Gaza descended the bank in one mighty leap and strode forward to join Barbarus. The giant's sightless eyes seemed to twinkle in amusement.

Logan wasn't afraid. The only time he sweated it out anymore was when he was worried about someone else. Fear for his own safety had been burned out of him way back. But he had to admit the odds were lousy. Much as he liked to fight, he didn't like to lose.

He raised his wrist to his mouth to call for help, hoping an EMP wouldn't trash the signal.

His wrist was bare.

"Oh, no, no," Lupo jeered. "We can't have you calling your friends. We have a schedule to follow."

As he spoke, a wolf climbed the bank, clutching something

between its jaws. Lupơ took it, patted the animal on the head, and held up Logan's radio. "Another trinket for Brainchild's collection. He does so love to study the unique contraptions you mutants devise."

Wolverine rushed forward. Lupo howled a command, and a barrage of wolves met the X-Man's charge. He made it only as far as the shallows before he was knocked over.

Two members of the pack shifted aside, letting Gaza insert himself into the melée. The mutate hammered Wolverine. Stunned by the impact, Logan barely managed to swing his claws. Gaza avoided the razor edges with ease, able to sense their approach better than someone with sight.

A wave of dizziness pulsed through Logan's head. He hurt in a hundred places. His healing factor strained to cope with the endless series of wolf bites.

Bam! Gaza's fist came in again. Logan had been too dazed to notice it; he hadn't rolled with the punch at all.

The day had started off poorly. It had only gotten worse. Yesterday his hunches were right on the mark. But now the law of averages had come calling.

Law of the jungle. Either you go for the kill, or someone does the same to you.

Another blow above his ear. Now one to his solar plexus. With a wolf clomped onto both wrists, he could no longer summon the strength to raise his hands.

His knees buckled. Everything was hazy.

Through the fog, one huge blurry image was replaced by another, slightly smaller one with four arms. "My turn again," said Barbarus gleefully. He swung. And swung and swung.

Unconciousness was a mercy.

• • •

LAW OF THE JUNGLE

Bright, sourceless light blazed down on his eyelids, which were almost too swollen to open, but Logan did so anyway.

He was being carried on a pole. He was trussed so tightly he couldn't wiggle a finger. His hands had been carefully positioned so that even if he extended his claws, he would only be able to poke empty air.

The treetops closed in again, shadowing them. His carriers—Gaza and Barbarus—hung him between two saplings about eight feet off the ground, denying him even such small comfort as lying in the mud.

"Awake already?" Lupo leaned over him, grinning in his lupine way. "Your healing factor is truly impressive, I must say. I've heard that you had some trouble with it in the past. Pity you can't do something about your age as well. You're getting to be a pushover, old man."

"Stuff it," Logan said. His lips were so puffy and bloodied that it sounded like, "Stpppft."

Lupo grinned at the defiance and picked his teeth with a long, semihuman fingernail. "Good. So full of spunk. You'll have lots of vital lifeforce to offer the master when he arrives." The mutate tilted his head to look up at the sky. Logan saw now that they had just crossed a clearing formed by a giant fallen tree. The tree was specked with pteranodon guano. From the smell of the traces, the flying reptiles had landed here mere hours ago.

"He should be here soon," Lupo continued. "My wolves have relayed the message that we have you. He'd be here already if he didn't have to avoid being seen by that pesky Archangel."

Logan no longer wondered when or how Sauron was going to make his big move. The freak had already begun.

The question was, what the hell was he, Logan, going to do about it?

He writhed inside his bonds, but it only made the lashings cut into his skin—his costume had been removed—and even if he did manage to dislodge the poles, he would only flop to the ground amid a pack of wolves that even now were licking their lips and whining for the opportunity to sample more of his blood.

"Now don't get upset," Lupo said. "Soon you'll be feeling much, much more relaxed. Tomorrow morning you'll awaken surrounded by friends. We have such plans for you and all the other X-Men."

CHAPTER 9

Storm lay supine in a hammock, her head supported by what was surely the most unique pillow she had ever sampled—an obloid of snakeskin filled with goose feathers. The hammock was strung over the platform where Shanna had earlier rinsed her off, providing her with a roofless, unobstructed view of the clouds.

She could barely raise her hands to rub her forehead, much less rise from her bower. Her bones felt as heavy as those of a brontosaurus, her muscles as weak as a snail's.

But the sky was radiant, the breeze steady and controlled. The coming of night would probably bring more lightning. Frost might nip the highest hills. No matter. Those sorts of disturbances would play themselves out. She was at last free to turn her attention back to the reason why she had come to the Savage Land.

Shanna and Ka-Zar joined her on the platform. Zabu hopped up and nuzzled Ororo's fingers, rumbling a note of concern.

"Still no word from Wolverine," Shanna said.

Ororo lifted away from her pillow. The earth seemed to hang on to her. She set her head back down and hoped her temples would stop throbbing. "Hand me my radio, if you would," she requested.

Shanna gave her the device, which Ororo had removed while she concentrated on the climate healing.

"Better hurry," Ka-Zar said. "There's always a long EMP

at dusk. It's due any time now.'' He gestured at the lavender and orange tones along the horizon—interestingly, the hues were rising in all directions, since the Savage Land's ''sunlight'' stemmed from many sources, some having little connection to Earth's actual sun.

Ororo nodded, and entered the code to transmit. ''Beast? Do you copy?''

''You sound a little faint, my dear.'' The reply was tinged with static, and was itself below normal strength.

''Faint is exactly how I feel,'' Ororo said.

''How may I be of service, O leader mine?''

''Just a status check. Wolverine's still missing. How are all of you out there?''

''Still chasing Amphibius. We keep coming across his trail. I'd like to recommend that Iceman, Cannonball, and I remain until dark. We can keep up the effort until the last moment.''

Ororo tried to think of objections, but she found it difficult to put two coherent ideas together. She saw silver wings growing closer, heralding Warren's return. ''Very well. Archangel is returning now, emptyhanded, which means Wolverine missed their rendezvous. We'll focus on that problem. You remain and try to track Amphibius.''

''Will do. Sam will haul us back in—let's see—about an hour, I would estimate.'' In one respect, the Savage Land resembled Antarctica more than the tropics—twilight lingered, rather than clamped down like the lid of a spring-loaded trap.

Archangel walked toward the platform, folding his wings. His shoulders drooped.

''Couldn't find Logan,'' he said. ''I flew over the entire area he was supposed to patrol, but there's no sign of him.''

''That isn't good,'' Ororo said. ''I'm glad to see *you* are back, though. You've been up in the air too long without a respite."

"I couldn't even think about resting until I had something to show for the effort. Didn't happen. I thought I saw some pteranodons carrying riders a couple of hours ago, but by the time I made it through the rain to the section of jungle they were over, all I could see were wild, riderless ones."

"Sauron can't stay hidden much longer. We're covering a lot of ground. We'll stumble across something soon. Maybe Bobby and Hank and Sam already have." Storm had to say it aloud. Otherwise she would fail to believe.

Warren leaned his head back and breathed deeply. "Something smells good. It's been a long time since breakfast."

Shanna nodded. "The village women are preparing a warrior's meal in the lodge. It's light food—only a little meat—meant to sustain individuals going into combat without making them sluggish. I think you'll approve."

"By tomorrow night, Tongah hopes that he can host a victor's feast," Ka-Zar added. "That's for after the fighting, when the participants are free to gorge."

Ororo tried to smile. It was good to anticipate a victory, but until it actually arrived, she couldn't manage to get in the spirit.

"We'll bring you a tray, Ororo," Shanna said.

"No. Help me up," she replied. "If I'm going to share in a warrior's repast, I should at least carry myself there like a proper one."

Shanna supported her as she tipped toward vertical and rediscovered what it was like to balance on so small an area as the soles of her feet.

"Goddess," Ororo muttered. "This is worse than I

thought it would be.'' But she pressed Shanna's helping hands away and walked forward. She stumbled off the edge of the platform, but landed upright on the ground. After three or four hurried steps to check her momentum, she settled into a normal walk.

''Don't worry about me,'' she chided her friends, who shadowed her closely, like a parent would hover behind a child learning to ride a bicycle. ''By morning I'll be dancing on the clouds, good as new.''

The wrinkles in their foreheads said she was a liar.

They made their way over to the lodge entrance. Shanna peeked in and announced the meal was not quite ready. Ororo was content to remain standing, if only for the novelty. While Warren and Shanna listened to a scout reporting to Ka-Zar, Storm mulled over possible ways to do more for Wolverine. They couldn't be sure he had been captured, but it seemed likely. Sitting down to supper would scarcely contribute toward his rescue. But what could they do? Darkness would close in before they could find his trail and follow it.

Klaxons blared. The watchtower!

Ka-Zar, Shanna, and both X-Men whirled toward the sound. The juveniles on guard were blowing their conch shells with all their might, paying no attention to the signal codes.

A dozen riders on pteranodons suddenly careened into view. They came in low, just above the crest of jungle growth, and rushed toward the village barely high enough to clear the stockade spikes.

Archangel shot into the air, flinging wingtip blades. Blood blossomed from the chests of three of the winged reptiles. Two went down like sledgehammered slaughterhouse cattle. The third tucked its wings and crashed into a hut, scattering bamboo, wicker mats, and grass. All three riders jumped free, but all landed hard.

Warren ducked to avoid the spiked clubs of the main mass of warriors. The weapons missed him, but narrowly—he didn't have enough altitude yet for proper defensive maneuvers.

Storm tried to rise into the air. A mistake. The wind she summoned whisked her sideways—luckily out of the way of a jabbing pteranodon beak—but her control was miserable. She flopped down in the mud, using a pile of tanned hides to screen her from the view of the attackers, and put her focus where it should have been—into a counterattack.

She called upon the forces of the atmosphere and sent mini-cyclones whirling into the center of the raiders. Pteranodons squawked and spun upside down. Three riders fell.

Ororo winced. She should have been able to bowl over half the group with one sweep. Her whirlwinds were flaccid; she had succeeded only with those attackers who had already been struggling to maintain control of their nervous mounts.

Lightning, she decided. She fired a bolt at a burly, scarred rider. He screamed, but kept going, wheeling his flyer around to renew the attack. The electrical discharge had only stunned him.

She tried again. This time the bolt missed entirely. The rider finished his circle and roared down at her.

Suddenly a figure sprang from the crest of a hut, having just emerged from the smoke hole. Ka-Zar. The Lord of the Savage Land collided with the rider. Both went tumbling to the ground, while the pteranodon flapped on toward the jungle.

The backdraft knocked Storm over. She rolled and came to rest in a kneeling position. Scanning to see who to help first, she saw Ka-Zar successfully pounding his opponent,

Shanna kicking a raider who had risen from the mud to try to club an elder from behind, and Fall People warriors stringing their bows to repel the air assault.

She waved her arms and created a thermal updraft to send a pair of raiders uncontrollably skyward, but her effort had barely borne fruit when her head started to whirl. Not just the spin of weariness she had experienced earlier. This was soul-wrenching dizziness, the oh-Goddess-please-let-me-die sort that brought up her lunch of flatbread and curried beans.

"Wha . . . what?" Storm blurted, barely managing not to fall in her own vomit. She flung lightning in random directions, a reflex spawned by the deep pulse of threat overwhelming her. The bolts were the weakest yet, barely more than filaments of static dancing no higher than the eaves of the huts. One happened to strike a pterosaur as it swooped low; it did no more than cause the beast's foot to twitch.

Storm writhed, but forced her eyes to stay open and focused. All around her villagers were twisting and flopping in the mud and puddles. Zabu staggered toward her, only to flop down and curl into a pathetic, kittenish bundle.

Two of the fallen raiders climbed to their feet and began whistling for their mounts. They appeared to be free of dizziness, and unconcerned that anyone nearby might try to thwart their escape.

Storm could hear shouts and clashes elsewhere in the stockade, proving that not all the village was hampered as was she and those near her. The explanation became clear as a young woman stepped out from between two huts, pulling off a wig to reveal hair as white as Storm's own, streaked disorientingly with green.

"Vertigo," Ororo hissed.

She had no doubt of the woman's identity, though Storm had never seen the mutate out of costume before. Vertigo was dressed in the rudimentary fashion of the Fall People. Perhaps that was how, with the wig, she was able to approach near enough to use her power so overwhelmingly.

The only mutate ever to leave the confines of the Savage Land, Vertigo had last been seen as one of Sinister's assassins, the Marauders. Apparently, Sauron, or perhaps Brainchild, had lured her back. And kept her presence secret as a surprise weapon.

Vertigo frowned at Storm. Abruptly the awful spinning inside Ororo increased. The windrider moaned and felt herself convulse. Her only satisfaction was realizing that, for all her exhaustion, she had managed to ward off some of Vertigo's initial burst—perhaps the villainess was stretching herself too thin, attacking so many individuals at once?

Storm was completely unable to fight back as a pteranodon landed atop her. Its talons closed around her. Limp and sickened, she felt herself rising into the air. Below two other raiders climbed close behind, carrying Shanna and Ka-Zar.

At that point, she blacked out.

Archangel burst up through the reptilian squadron, finding clear air just as Storm and the others began to reel from Vertigo's unexpected intrusion. He levelled off, intending to rocket down at the mutate fast enough that her power wouldn't have time to daze him. A shadow touched him. He flung himself to the side.

Just in time. An attacker hurtled past him from above. This one had no rider.

"How rude of you," Sauron cackled. "I offered you the mercy of a surprise hit. You spurned it."

"I know about your mercy, Sauron," Warren snarled as Sauron wheeled and raced in for another clash. "It's the sort that drained Tanya Anderssen of her life."

"Now is that any way to talk to an old associate? So cynical. I thought something of the sweet Angel I knew might remain, but I see you have left him entirely. Do you miss him, I wonder?"

"Miss *this*!" Warren yelled, flinging shards of metal.

The barrage whisked past Sauron, narrowly off target, but off nonetheless. "You nicked me last night," Sauron called. "No more."

Warren cursed under his breath. The spraying of the blades had won him only one small gain. In order to totally avoid them, Sauron had been forced to momentarily tuck his wings. The villain sailed beneath Archangel, too low to slash the X-Man. Warren gained a respite before the next charge in which to think. He could sense hypnotic instructions filtering into his brain. That was why his projectiles had curved away, as they had the night before.

If there was one thing he had been reminded of during that recent battle, it was that Sauron's mind-swaying power couldn't be overwhelmed, it could only be avoided or deflected. Only a potent and forewarned telepath could confront him head-on and alone. Last night, he and Storm had served as diversions for each other. But he could see Storm writhing in the dirt of the village along with Ka-Zar and Shanna, unable to assist.

He activated his radio. "Sam! Come quick! We're under attack at Tongah's village!"

The raucous static of an electromagnetic pulse answered back. The message had no way, for the moment, of getting through to Cannonball.

Archangel was on his own.

Strangely, he felt no fear. What was the worst that Sauron could do? Killing him, even making him a captive in his energy-larder—would that be worse than having his wings ripped off and his personality subsumed until he became an avatar of Death?

"No cavalry to your rescue," Sauron taunted. "Brainchild may not have been able to make your communications devices work for us, but he knew when they wouldn't work for you, either."

Fearful that another strafing run would be diverted down toward the innocent villagers, Warren gave up any plan to keep his distance. He raced toward Sauron as Sauron raced toward him. They met in the middle. He pummeled, Sauron clawed and kicked. Archangel's armored uniform spared him the gashes, but a blow to his midsection sent him fluttering backward. Sauron swooped out of range, shaking his head from the aftereffects of Warren's fist pounding his long snout.

"You X-Men know your hand-to-hand combat," Sauron acknowledged. "But you'll have to do better than that. Look at me. See how I glow? How refreshed I am? Wolverine's energies proved so fulfilling. Nor did I suffer from tapping your lovely teammate Psylocke's strength again this morning."

Warren refused to let the monster goad him. It was foul news to have it confirmed that Logan had fallen prisoner— that explained not only Sauron's vigor, but the healing of the wing wounds that Warren had given him less than twenty-four hours earlier. It was numbing to be reminded of Betsy's condition. But give in to those emotions and he would be useless to both his comrades.

Their brawl carried them beyond the village, removing the chance that the natives would be hit by friendly fire. Warren shot more projectiles. They bulleted past his target. He could *almost* aim correctly, but the cloud over his mind stole the core of his accuracy.

"Take the gift I offer," his enemy urged. "Tolkien's Sauron had his winged Nazgûl at his command. Be my Nazgûl, Warren Worthington. Serve me. Feed me."

Those eyes. Those infernal eyes. Sauron was hovering, staring intently at his opponent. Warren made the mistake of looking straight back. Once done, he couldn't look away. The first time Sauron had ever used his hypnotism against a super-powered being, Warren had been the victim. It was as if Sauron's ability had manifested specifically to combat the Angel, and fit no one else to such a profound degree.

Warren felt tentacles of outside control invade him. Within a few more moments, all Sauron would have to do was telepathically command him and he would do whatever he was asked—even fight or kill his allies. He couldn't permit that sort of perversion. He knew he had the strength to hold off long enough to implement a technique Psylocke had taught him. He turned inward and . . .

His consciousness dropped away.

"Annoying," Sauron screeched. "But either way, you're mine."

Though Sauron's influence was keeping Archangel's eyes open, blackness consumed his vision. With his last bit of awareness, he felt and heard the wind rushing past as he plummeted toward the ground.

Ka-Zar blessed the altitude, because even though he had seen Vertigo lifted aboard a pterosaur and knew she was a mere two hundred meters back among the raider squadron, the dizziness she had broadcast no longer crippled the blond-haired scion of House Plunder.

He was still dangling below a huge flying reptile, tightly confined by its calloused talons, but that was nothing alien to his experience. The creature belonged to the Savage Land. He knew its secrets.

Storm still hung limp beneath the beast just ahead. But though she seemed to be at best semiconscious, she was still fighting. Winds buffeted the pterosaurs and their riders, continually disrupting their formation. If Ororo could regain even a tenth of her strength and alertness, she could make it impossible for them to fly.

Shanna was slung beneath the winged monster just behind him. She was wide awake and her Irish eyes were flashing with a fury that made him glad they were on the same side. He winked a code at her. She nodded.

Then he screeched. The noise that emerged from his throat mimicked a call the wild pteranodons over the lake used whenever they sighted a particularly abundant cluster of their favorite food—fish.

The beast that was carrying him immediately tilted and dipped its head, searching below for a lake and the promised bounty. So did several of its kind nearby, including the gray-tinged specimen that carried Shanna. Its rider lurched forward, nearly tumbling from the saddle and momentarily losing control of the reins.

Ka-Zar was ready as the talons around him relaxed ever so slightly. He had enough wiggle room to draw his knife from his belt sheath and stab the creature in an ankle joint, so that even if it wanted to retain its hold, the pain would force its digits to open.

They did. He grabbed a handful of scaly green hide and vaulted atop the flyer's back.

The rider whirled, yelled, and swung his club at Ka-Zar. Unfortunately, the jungle lord had nowhere to go but backward. He hopped away, avoiding the club but flying off. He caught the pteranodon's tail just in time.

Pteranodons had stubby tails, not long, devilish appendages like those of rhamphorynchi or of Sauron. Ka-Zar found
almost no purchase for his clutching fingers. The best he
could do was hold on just long enough to redirect his fall—

—right onto the back of the raider who was rising up to
join in the melée.

Ka-Zar knocked away the man's club, sliced his hemp
safety cord, and shoved. The rider yelped, flailed, and lost
his balance.

"Thank you for flying Jurassic Airlines. Do try us again,"
said Ka-Zar.

The rider slid free and plummeted. The foliage below
quickly swallowed him.

Ka-Zar checked quickly to determine Shanna's status. His
wife was atop the pteranodon that had been transporting her,
but had by no means subdued its husky rider. Only an ac-
robatic swoop around the beast's neck spared her a skull-
crushing wallop.

A tinge of nausea and dizziness brushed Ka-Zar. He saw
Vertigo rushing to close in.

"May you bathe in sloth droppings," he cursed, borrowing Zira's favorite insult. He reined his flyer sharply to the
right. He would have to trust Shanna to take care of herself—
usually a safe bet. For now, what mattered most was to separate, so that Vertigo couldn't wrench both their guts at the
same time.

The reptile fought his control, but he held the reins tight.
Ordinarily, the riders controlled their pteranodons by means
of a laboriously nurtured rapport. He had no time to make
friends with his. He simply *insisted* it obey. He was Ka-Zar,
Lord of the Savage Land. He had once stopped a bull elephant's charge simply by planting his feet and staring.

Four raiders lashed their mounts, trying to catch him. They

soon would; Ka-Zar had not been lucky enough to steal the quickest member of the squadron. No matter. He had no intention of fleeing. He had waited seventy-two long hours to exact vengeance for Immono's death.

He whipped around and headed straight for a wiry, gap-toothed enemy warrior. The opponent hurriedly forced his creature to buckle its wings, dropping it below the point of collision. Ka-Zar had an instant to take in the scene around him: Shanna was wobbling. Vertigo was gliding next to her, bringing to bear the full brunt of her power. The raider Shanna was clashing was gripping her by the wrists and seemed well on the way to overcoming the last of her resistance.

Before Ka-Zar could begin to deal with that situation, the battle took him over a clearing. Below, nets hung suspended between tree trunks, about twenty feet off the ground. The pteranodon carrying Storm dropped her into the mesh. Raiders on the ground moved forward to wrap her up. A wind slapped at their hair and loincloths, and a dusting of snow pelted their faces, indicating that Ororo was still feebly trying to do what she could to save herself. Abruptly those phenomena ceased.

A rock whizzed by Ka-Zar's head. A raider had pulled up along side and was reaching in a sack for more missiles. The jungle lord banked sharply. He was nearly jabbed by a spear from above as another opponent zipped past.

Shanna was plummeting toward the cluster of nets. Ka-Zar grinned mirthlessly. His wife was proving her toughness. She wasn't going down alone. Along with her came the raider and his mount.

The nets swallowed them all. The pteranodon flapped like a headless chicken, then all at once went still.

Ka-Zar had no chance to be certain whether Shanna had

landed safely. A raider descended upon him. He slashed upward, finding flesh. Reptilian blood splattered him. The attacker rose and backed off.

A host of raiders buzzed around him. The beast carrying Vertigo was rising to join the fray. He reeled from a pulse of projected queasiness, evading further defilement only by wild swoops and sudden changes of direction. His flyer couldn't exert itself like that for long. The skies were not the place to continue the fight; he had to get to ground, find cover, and make them come after him one or two at a time.

But first, he turned and spurred his reptile toward the nets, knife held tight. He would have one chance to slash at the netting. Perhaps he could win Ororo or Shanna just enough freedom to make a difference. He leaned far over, barely keeping a grip on the saddle horn, reaching out below with the blade.

He was still in the midst of the approach swoop when his skull seemed to implode. *Let go. Let go. Let go.*

Sauron! The hypnotic command thrashed deep, unnerving his fingers. In his previous struggles with the monster, he had never felt it so loudly, so brutally.

He was Ka-Zar, Lord Kevin Plunder. He would not yield. He gritted his teeth and forced himself to drive out the foreign, repugnant influence.

Too late. His fingers were already straining too much to regain their hold. The initial, unexpected assault had done its dirty work. Ka-Zar fell.

As the net closed around him, he gazed back at the sky and saw Sauron glide serenely down in his wake. He was clutching Archangel, who hung limply. That explained the potency of Sauron's hypnotic pulse—he had just drained energy from Warren.

LAW OF THE JUNGLE

Sauron let go of Archangel, who fell like a stone toward a nearby net.

Ka-Zar wriggled an arm loose. He still had his knife. But even as he began to slash at the cords, he saw a warrior on the ground lift a blowgun. The dart stung his thigh. In moments, muscles stiffened all over his body. The rosy glow of dusk immediately faded to the blackness of deep night.

He was still semiconscious as he was bound, gagged, and tossed on the spongy moss that covered the clearing. His last perception consisted of voices, particularly that of Sauron, berating his underlings to finish up their work before anyone came along to interfere.

"Our plan is almost complete," the villain cackled. "Just a few loose ends, and my victory will be complete."

That, Ka-Zar realized grimly, could very well be the truth.

CHAPTER 10

Deep in the swamp, Cannonball gazed up at the dark sky, bidding farewell to the last shreds of daylight. "My li'l sister Joelle calls this type'a thing spook weather," he told his companions.

Auroras spun from horizon to horizon. Laser-thin, fulgurant streaks of light leapt from one clump of cloud to the next, hissing like snakes in boiling water. Standard, but remarkably potent, thunder and lightning flashed and boomed along the hills. So much static electricity hung in the atmosphere that Sam's hair would have stood on end had it not been drenched with the humidity of the jungle. He wiped another puddle of sweat from the back of his neck, where it had collected inside the collar of his uniform. *Next time I come to the Savage Land*, he thought, *I'm redesignin' my uniform first.*

"You have *this* kind of weather in Kentucky?" Iceman asked.

"We do when Storm gets a knot in her cape."

"Ho ho ho," Bobby replied sourly.

Sam's cheeks flushed. "Aw, hell. Just trying to make y'all cheerful." He cringed, wishing he knew how to purge his sense of humor of its juvenile edge. Their team leader had been awfully upset at the way Sauron had perverted her control of the weather. Not a good time to make her the butt of even the lightest of jokes.

His comrade shrugged. "Don't worry about it. I know

how it goes.'' Their glances met. They shared once again that strand of kinship that came from both having filled, at different times, the role of youngest X-Man on the team.

''This sky does remind me of home, y'know,'' Sam added. ''The clouds sweep over the Great Lakes and cover up the Appalachians from New York to Georgia. Some of those lightshows make you think y'got ghosts dancin' from haystack to barn roof.''

''You know, the aftereffects of this particular meteorological disruption provide us with unforeseen options,'' the Beast stated. He waved at the swirling iridescence reflected in the stagnant pools surrounding them. Though the daylight was no more than a lingering background whisper of deep indigo and violet, they could easily make out the shapes of fronds, trees, logs, and the occasional hump of muddy land such as the one they were standing upon. ''Do you see?''

''See what?'' Sam asked, scanning from branch to tree root, forehead wrinkling.

''I read you loud and clear,'' Bobby said, in that quick way that had Cannonball feeling too young again. ''There's enough light to keep moving around by. It's not black as a woman's heart like it usually is at night in the Savage Land.''

''Oh.'' Sam nodded. Then he raised an eyebrow. ''Black as a woman's heart?''

Bobby pursed his lips. ''Well. Black as *some* women's hearts. Hank, are you saying you want to continue the search? We haven't seen Amphibius's green derriere in hours. These tracks here aren't very fresh.'' He pointed at their feet.

''That's what I'm saying, for now,'' Hank replied. ''Another hour or two might prove a profitable investment. It was during a night search that Ororo stumbled across Sauron.

What better time to keep looking than while our enemies may be at their most active?''

Bobby sighed. ''All right. Another hour or two. Then we'll see.''

The Beast nodded, and raised his wrist radio to his mouth. ''Beast to base. Do you read?''

A muted hiss came from the radio in response. Hank repeated his statement. Again, no one replied.

''Ill portents,'' he muttered. ''The EMP has run its course. That's a clear signal coming at us. We should be hearing them.'' He checked the code he'd entered. ''Archangel? Ka-Zar? Shanna? Is there *anybody* out there?''

Cannonball grew more and more antsy watching his big blue companion. ''Somethin' ain't right. I'll hightail it to Tongah's village right now.''

''Cease and desist.'' Hank's raised voice snuffed Sam's takeoff before it began. ''Whatever happened, happened during the blackout. Stay, my young comrade. We need to consult.''

''Consult?'' Sam asked. ''I ain't in the mood t'talk, Hank. Not when buddies are in trouble.''

The Beast raised one of his pawlike hands and set it firmly on Cannonball's shoulder. ''I empathize. This is an alarming development. But I'm the eldest of our little trio. Experience tells me we shouldn't be rushing off. Do you trust me, Samuel?''

Cannonball blinked. Hank McCoy could be a serious fellow, but his question displayed an additional, almost funereal gravity.

'' 'Course I do.''

''Then trust me now. I've been getting the increasing sense we have been indulging in the wrong approach. It's time to introduce a variable.''

"Whaddaya mean?"

"If you were Sauron, where would you expect the three of us to be right now?"

Sam hated Hank's little quizzes. They reminded him of the tests Professor X used to give the New Mutants and Cable occasionally gave to the members of X-Force. Too many chances to get the answer wrong. "Uh, I guess I'd figure we'd be in one of two places: rushing back to the village, or still out here chasin' Amphibius."

"Correct."

Sam was so startled at the approval in Hank's voice that he laughed.

"We will be sure to be in neither place," Hank continued. "I believe it's already too late to help our comrades. It seems clear they've been captured. Or killed."

"That's not a conclusion I'd like to jump to, Hank," Bobby said.

"Nevertheless, a likely one," Hank said. "We can take heart in the fact that Sauron requires live mutants to feed off of, so at the very least, our teammates are probably alive, though not enjoying themselves overmuch. In any case, it also stands to reason we wouldn't find them now anymore than we could locate Psylocke earlier. Sauron probably has them tucked out of sight by now. As for Amphibius, in light of this new information, I conclude that we've searched enough for him. Methinks it is tempting fate to loiter where others might expect to find us. That's predictable. I don't wish to be predictable."

"Amen to that," Cannonball said. "Cable was always warning us to hold on to the advantage of surprise. So, where do we go, and what do we do?"

"For a start, though the bog remains treacherous to navigate, I suggest we use this convenient augmentation of our supply of illumination to find a camping location away from the trail we've been dogging." He gestured again at Amphibius's footprints. "After that, I think the prudent course is to dedicate ourselves to sustenance and recuperation."

"Wouldn't mind a bite to eat," Cannonball commented. "I'm hungry enough to eat one o' them giant centipedes I tripped over a ways back. Not sure I could fall asleep out here, though."

"True, but even a super powered mutant requires sleep to be at his best and cogitate properly," Hank added. "I, for one, feel as though we've been out-thought ever since we arrived in this primordial theme park."

"You said it," Bobby declared. "Let's go, then." He froze a causeway from their little slab of land to the next, at right angles to the direction they'd been pursuing. They squeezed through a gap in a stand of cypress trees and then through a riot of giant cycads, Iceman thawing the pathway behind so as to erase their trail. Just as they were about to emerge from the umbrella of palmlike fronds, a huge sauropod body crossed right in front of them.

They peered upward. A beast with an extremely long neck and a tail to match reached high into the treetops, nibbling the fresh leaves it found there.

"Diplodocus," Hank murmured. "Perhaps the longest dinosaur that ever trod the earth. Fourteen vertebrae in its neck. Forty-two in its tail. Not as heavy as brachiosaurus or seismosaurus, though."

"It's big enough," said Cannonball. "One swipe of that tail would knock over a bus. I say we steer clear of that sucker."

"Oh, it's not one of the species we have to be terribly concerned over. Too ponderous. We'll have abundant opportunity for evasion even if it takes an interest in us. 'Tis the velociraptors or the coelophysis packs that might take an excessive nibble out of us before we perceived we were under attack. Worse yet might be the bird-eating spiders or the bog vipers. Unique to the Savage Land, so there isn't any antivenom available, and their toxins kill in minutes. Then there's . . ."

"Y'gonna tell me about the plants, too, ain'tcha?" Sam interrupted.

"Veritably. The flora here can be just as dangerous as the fauna. There are paralyzing nettles, razor bushes . . ."

"I think I'll send up a flare and let Sauron haul my butt off to his nice, safe dungeon."

"That would be one way to find out where it is," suggested Bobby.

"See? 'Tis not so unpleasant an abode, once you adjust to its idiosyncrasies," the Beast said as Cannonball projected tiny bursts of his power at the haunch of dimetrodon that hung above their "firepit"—which contained no fire because they didn't want flames and smoke to attract unwelcome guests, be they enemies or an inquisitive Tyrannosaurus rex.

The meat steamed, wafting puffs of, Sam had to concede, downright delicious aromas into the air. Hank ripped a strip of the cooked flesh loose and bit into it.

"Mmmm. Tastes just like iguana."

Sam knelt down and cut a shred off the haunch. After the first swallow, he nodded. Not too bad. Hank was exaggerating, though. No way was this as good as iguana.

Easy to catch, though. The big, fin-backed lizard had wandered right into camp and chomped Cannonball's arm—which, because he wrapped himself in his kinetic envelope, resulted in no damage other than to the predator's teeth. Before it could scamper away, Iceman had frozen the arteries in its brain. Instant stroke.

Boy, would that tick ol' Stegron off. Cannonball hoped that ugly mini-Godzilla wasn't still stomping around the Savage Land, demanding voting rights for reptilians everywhere.

A mosquito speared Sam's cheek. He slapped, but not before the critter had done some damage. He regarded the bright spot of his own blood in his palm, mingled with the black shreds of the insect. He could feel the welt rising beside where his sideburns would be if he had any. What was that, the three hundredth insect bite tonight?

"Can y'all do something about this?" he complained.

The Beast, protected by his thick mat of blue fur, shrugged. Iceman aimed a finger and froze the three or four pests nearest Sam's face.

Dozens more took their place, whining for his hemoglobin.

"Thank you very much," Cannonball said in his most exaggerated, ya-dumb-Yankee drawl. "I could jus' blast 'em myself if I wanted to go after 'em one by one."

"Do forebear, young sir," the Beast said. "Your mutant power usually lacks the degree of silence we require."

Bobby scratched his chin thoughtfully. "We do need a solution, though. I'm going to have to give up my ice form in order to eat. As soon as I do, they'll swarm all over me as well."

"Your selflessness is an inspiration to us all," Hank declared. He waved a piece of reptile steak. "I have it. Build us an igloo, my good man."

Bobby nodded. "All right. I guess I have enough juice left. It wears a guy out having to freeze swamp water and quicksand all day long, I'll have you know." He waved his hands, fashioning blocks of ice into a domed hut. The water level of the nearby pond dropped momentarily, until replaced by brackish flows from farther out in the bog.

"Shucks, you froze some salamanders into th' walls," Sam said.

"You want perfection?" Iceman said. "Make your own ice cubes in the middle of a sweltering jungle with nothing but scummy marsh water to pour in the tray."

"Amphibians do well in suspended animation," Hank said. He picked up the cooked slab of meat and crawled into the structure. Iceman followed. Cannonball came last, covering the entrance with a blanket from his pack. A cloud of mosquitoes came in with him, but succumbed to the cold. Sam felt no remorse as he scrambled over their frosted little corpses. Salamanders, he could pity. Even dimetrodons. But blood-sucking little pests went in the same trash bin with certain evil mutants he could name.

The glow from the Beast's battery-powered camp mini-lantern turned the interior of the igloo into a cozy genie bottle. They spread their microthin all-weather blankets over the ground and things grew downright homey. Except for the cold, of course, but stoking up the thermal filaments in his uniform was enough to take care of Sam. Hank had his natural insulation, and Bobby never seemed bothered by cold even in his human form.

"Ah, the rustic life," Hank exclaimed. "Doesn't it make you gratified to be a part of this mortal existence?"

"Y'mean, happy to be alive?" Cannonball asked.

" 'Happy'? Mr. Guthrie, how can you choose such an anemic adjective? Fulfilled, replete, placated beyond measure— these are the sorts of modifiers such a venue as this deserves."

"Exactly what place are y'talkin' about? This exact patch'a frozen muck, or the Savage Land in gen'ral?"

The Beast scowled. "Don't be dense, my boy. Of course

the plot of earth on which we sit leaves a modicum to be desired. I mean all this untamed glory.'' Hank's talons almost brushed the low ceiling of the igloo, but his expansive gesture whispered of everything from the depths of the Savage Land's central lake to the ridges of the Eternity Mountains that surrounded it. ''The totality of Ka-Zar's realm.''

''*I* know what Hank means,'' Bobby said around a mouthful of food. ''He's saying a big, hairy blue guy like him feels right at home among these giant feathered theropods and dragonflies as long as his arms. He doesn't have to put up with cute society chicks refusing to go to the movies with a dude that looks like he files his teeth.''

''You slay me, old comrade,'' Hank said. ''You mock my sincere respect for this magnificent preserve. True, I experience less alienation here, but do recall, I still had my human appearance the first two times we visited. Yet I was equally enamored of the setting on both those occasions.''

''Phew, does that take me back,'' Iceman said. ''I was so young I still had zits.''

''The days of the original X-Men?'' Cannonball asked. ''No Ororo? No Logan?''

''Just the five of us. Pre-Champions, pre-Defenders, pre-X-Factor. Before Hank defected to the Avengers. Jean, Scott, Warren, Hank, and me. And Professor X, of course, but he usually stayed in the mansion.''

''He certainly did not venture to the Savage Land the way the rest of us did,'' the Beast said. ''As a matter of fact, when we made that second jaunt, the one in pursuit of Sauron, we were under the mistaken impression that the good Professor was cold in his grave.''

''Well, not all of us. Jean knew it was really the Changeling we buried in that cemetery. The Professor had a big mission that required total concentration—beating the

Z'Nox. So he left us on our own. It was our initiation, I guess. We were getting older. We'd been through some trials by fire. He wanted to see how we'd get along without him to hold our hands.''

"And y'did okay, from what I've been told," Sam said.

"Didn't feel that way to me. We got in over our heads more than once. The Sentinels really whipped our butts. Magneto gave us grief. Funny thing was, Magneto was supposed to be just as dead as Xavier.''

"Only a supposition," said the Beast. "He plummeted from an aircraft, thanks to a little 'assistance' from his sycophantic lackey, the Toad. We never saw a lifeless body as we had with what we believed to be our dear mentor.''

Bobby plucked a sliver of dimetrodon hide from between his front teeth. He chuckled. "I'm still waiting for the Changeling to turn up alive one of these days.''

"I have long pondered what course history might have taken had the Professor been available when Havok's power first manifested," Hank mused.

"Oh, that's right," Iceman said. "Alex hadn't even known he was a mutant, and then wham, he turns out to be a real keg of gunpowder. We came back from that incident with the Sentinels not knowing what the heck we could do for him. He had almost no control over his power surges. So what did we do? We took him to Karl Lykos.''

"Lykos had briefly been an associate of Xavier's," explained Hank. "He seemed to be one of the few doctors we could trust. Unfortunately I had not yet completed my own medical training.''

"We didn't know Lykos was an energy vampire, or that he'd been itching for the chance to see what happened when he got a mutant into his 'therapy couch.' When he siphoned off Havok's raw overflow, he became Sauron.''

"I remember readin' the file on that," Sam said. "I'd say y'all are taking it too much on your shoulders. Sooner or later Lykos woulda run across a mutant or two to victimize. The guy was a disaster waitin' to happen."

"Veritably," Hank said. "Nor could any value come of allowing Lykos to continue treating patients by milking them of their life force. Eventually his cravings would have mounted until he drained too much and thereby killed innocent victims—as he has since done. In any case, things transpired as they did, and we had to contend with him, then chase him all the way to Tierra del Fuego, and then here to the Savage Land."

"Chase him, yes," Bobby said. "But we didn't even figure out where he'd gone that first time."

"Indeed not."

"Now I'm confused," Cannonball interrupted. "I thought the X-Men *did* tangle with Sauron in the Savage Land."

"Eventually. Colossus, Banshee, Nightcrawler, Storm, Wolverine, and Cyclops were the team then. It was a separate journey, all mingled with the business with Zaladane and her god Garokk and so forth. Sauron had been in the Savage Land for quite some interval. But the original five of us never found him."

"We found Magneto instead, though," Bobby said.

"How could y'all lose Lykos?" Sam queried.

"We thought he had met with his demise in a fall." Beast swallowed a final chunk of lizard steak and waved his paws expressively. "We had been captured by the Sentinels, had come back with Havok and Polaris—actually, this was before Lorna was ever called Polaris—to New York to lick our wounds. Lykos drained Alex's energy, became Sauron, fought with Angel and gained hypnotic control of him. When we located Angel later I regret to say I had to, uh . . ."

"Hank knocked Warren out, to save him from the hallucinations that were still twirling around in his brain."

"So *that's* why Warren was so touchy about comin' along
on this here mission. Heck, gettin' the worst of Sauron ain't
nothin' to be ashamed of. He turned me into shish kebob the
first time I tried t'pound 'im, that time he and the Brotherhood of Evil Mutants decided to give X-Force some grief."

"Alas, it was not just on one occasion. The mysteries of
psychology being what they are, Warren has proven repeat-
edly to be especially vulnerable to Sauron's hypnotism,"
Hank explained. "In any case, the effect of the initial attack
lingered, so rendering him unconscious seemed the most convenient course of action." The Beast combed frozen mosquitoes out of his fur. "Scott, Jean, Bobby, and I left Warren
with Lorna and Alex in order to look for Lykos. Instead,
Lykos snuck into the mansion, drained energy from all three
of the group there, and went to kidnap Tanya Anderssen, the
woman he adored. We showed up just as he attacked Tanya
and her father."

"He was going to kill Mr. Anderssen," Iceman said.

The Beast nodded. "He might very well have done so if
not for our interruption. At that point, his human personality
gained a measure of control over the monster. Deeply dis-
traught that he had nearly brought such harm to his beloved,
he fled by air. With Angel still unconscious back at the mansion, we couldn't track him."

"But Tanya knew where he had gone," Iceman said.

"She wouldn't admit to that knowledge," Hank continued. "She didn't want anyone hurting him. We had to follow
her secretly. She took us all the way to Tierra del Fuego,
where Lykos's father had owned a cabin that he maintained
for adventurers who wanted to explore the rugged region. It
was long abandoned, and so isolated that Lykos knew he

would find no one from whom he could siphon the power that Sauron needed to exist. He reverted to human form and confined himself there, amid the snow drifts and the granite peaks. I believe it was his intention to starve himself to death.''

''But Tanya found him before that could happen,'' Bobby continued.

''Yes, she did. Lykos was aghast. He knew he wouldn't be able to prevent himself from vampirically harvesting her if he touched her, so he jumped off a cliff.''

''Tanya would have jumped, too, except we came around the corner just then, and I threw up an ice wall in her path.''

''That was the last we saw of either Sauron or Lykos for quite some time. Jean lowered us telekinetically into the chasm. I'm afraid we hadn't had the best view when Lykos flung himself off. We thought he had surely plummeted all the way to the bottom of the cliff.''

''Actually, he'd only fallen about twenty feet. Aside from a couple of scrapes and bruises, he wasn't hurt at all,'' Bobby said. ''We just rushed right past him on our way down. Never saw him.''

The Beast nodded. ''At the bottom of the cliff was a snow cave. It showed signs of recent entry, so we concluded Lykos had tumbled into it. We squeezed our way inside and dropped into a tremendous cavern brimming with pteranodons. The flying monstrosities undoubtedly belonged to the same mutant colony that had infected Lykos when he was a boy. One of them was flapping off carrying a bloody chunk of meat. We thought it might be the remains of our antagonist. We followed. Jean ferried us over crevices telekinetically, and Scott chased away the wildlife with optic beams. The chase led us far down a huge natural tunnel. Eventually the pteranodon stopped to feed, and we realized the meat was merely a piece of mountain goat. We decided to forge ahead. The tunnel, to our amazement, led all the way beneath the Drake Passage—''

''I like that name,'' Iceman said.

The Beast cleared his throat. ''As I was saying, the underground passage seemed endless. It brought us all the way into the Eternity Mountains. We literally dropped down into the Savage Land.''

''Lykos eventually followed us. He wasn't able to climb back up, so he ended up in the jungle, too. He lived there a long time, stealing just enough energy from animals to get by, retaining his human shape. He was a good guy for a while. Made friends with Ka-Zar and the Fall People. Helped out.''

''The irony is, Lykos fared much better than Warren making it through the tunnel. Angel had tracked us to Tierra del Fuego, and Tanya told him where we had gone. When he swooped into the midst of the pteranodon colony, they chased and harassed him all the way down the vast passageway, ultimately knocking him senseless. He plummeted into the Savage Land and was killed when he impacted the swamp—perhaps the very swamp in which we sit.''

''Say what?'' Sam asked. ''For a corpse, he was acting downright spunky earlier today. If he ain't alive, then those comments Betsy makes about his cold feet in bed take on a whole new meanin'.''

Hank grinned. ''One of many close calls, actually. A spark of life remained. Magneto, who had been hiding out in the Savage Land for some months, found Warren, took him to his sanctuary, and revived him.''

''Warren didn't know it was Magneto at first. We'd never seen him out of his costume. He was running around calling himself the Creator. He'd rigged up an apparatus that gave natives of the Savage Land altered, super-powered forms. Some of those mutates are the ones we're dealing with now, like that living pogo-stick we were chasing all day today.''

"Now that is a right fancy campfire tale," Sam concluded.

"Who would've thought a snowy chasm would lead to any region as hot as this?" Iceman hardened the dripping walls around them. "The Savage Land has got to be the weirdest place I've ever seen on this planet."

Hank's bushy brow sprang upward. "My stars and garters!" he growled excitedly. "My dear Mr. Drake, do you remember what Tanya blurted when you threw up that shield and saved her from leaping off the cliff? She pounded it with her fists and—"

"Lord, I'd never forget that. She said, 'The cold! He always hated the cold!' I tried not to take it personally."

"Yes! Karl Lykos hated cold. Sauron has always hated cold." The Beast emphasized every word. "We've even used cold as a weapon against him. That's what Storm was trying to do last night when she unleashed more than she bargained for. It's standard operating procedure against him."

"Well, of course. You use what works. I've been aching to give him a case of total-body frostbite."

"Indeed you have. And we are driven to the paradigm of frigid tactics because we naturally think of reptiles having little ability to deal with low temperatures. What if we are being too narrow-minded? Pterosaurs aren't like modern reptiles. They are at least halfway to being warm-blooded. Much like dinosaurs in that respect. If Sauron at all resembles the mutant creatures that infected him, he has ample tolerance for chill conditions, however much he might hate them. It couldn't have been more than forty degrees Fahrenheit in that cave, and the pteranodons seemed to thrive there. Otherwise why would there be such an abundance of them?"

"Dr. McCoy," stated Cannonball, "you are, without a doubt, a signed, sealed, and certified genius. I feel so dumb a mule must've kicked me upside the head. Human beings don't like cold, either, but it don't stop 'em from livin' in Alaska and places like that. They figure out a way to do it. Sauron could be wearin' thermal underwear for all we know."

"We've been looking for him in the wrong places," Bobby said, assuming his ice form in a flush of outrage.

"Let us not rush to judgment," Hank cautioned. "We may yet be chasing will-o'-the-wisps. But I suspect it is past time we considered the possibility that Sauron's hidden base of operations lies not in the heart of the Savage Land, but up along the cool fringes, in the Ice Age zone just this side of the peaks that cup the terrain."

"Remember what Scott and Jean told us about their run-in with Sauron that time Worm and Whiteout kidnapped Havok for him? His fortress was an aerie pretty high up a mountain, near the remnants of Pangea."

"Ka-Zar said he checked there. It's empty," Sam said. "But if Lykos could handle an altitude like that once, he can do it again."

"Such a location would explain a great deal," Hank added. "The natives don't care for the heights. They hazard an expedition to hunt mammoth once in a while, but most of the time there would be few possible witnesses to Sauron's comings and goings."

"I say we get out of this bog right now and get our tails to high ground."

"Not yet," Hank said. "A far more significant question remains. Namely, if Sauron is up there, why are we here?"

Iceman and Cannonball looked at him blankly. Then their eyes widened.

"Because that's where Sauron tricked us into coming," Iceman said. "Using Mr. Hippity-Hoppity to lead us on a wild frog chase."

"Or worse, into an ambush," the Beast said.

"Well, that goes unsaid. What with all that's happened, that's always been a possibility."

"A possibility, yes. Now I believe it to be a certainty. Since that is so, it's relatively transparent what sort of counter-strategy we can assemble."

"Lay it out for us, buddy," Bobby said.

"I said before it's as if Sauron has been out-thinking us all along. He had enough sense to hide his headquarters. He divided us. He seems to have prearranged each encounter he has had with us, except when Storm happened across him last night. Why were we so easily misdirected?"

"Because we're stupid?" Sam suggested.

"Hey, speak for yourself, junior," Bobby retorted.

"None of us is dimwitted, but we fell victim to a tendency any bright individual, human or mutant, is vulnerable to. We expected our nemesis to act in character."

"Hmmm," muttered Iceman. "Yeah. Sauron isn't just being a little cleverer. It's like he's a whole new dude."

"Righteo," Hank said. "In the past, we've never had to devote much energy to luring him into a confrontation. The old Sauron would have dismissed us as insects, attacked us impulsively, or surrendered to his craving for energy and become reckless. Or, as has always been his greatest handicap, his human self—the good Karl who once rescued little Tanya from the brink of death in that pteranodon roost—would have emerged to obliterate any dispassionate, carefully executed offensive Sauron mounted. Somehow in the recesses of our minds, we were depending on him to behave as he always has."

"But now we've wised up," Bobby said. "Now you're saying, let's figure out what the new Sauron behaves like, and maybe if we're lucky we can second-guess him."

"Yes."

"I see where yer gettin' at, too," Cannonball said. "If he ain't impulsive no more, we know he's got somethin' in mind for the three of us. So, do we spring the trap?"

"Yes and no," Hank replied. "Yes, in that we want him to commit resources to executing what he has so ingeniously prearranged. No, in that his ambush might be as thoroughly successful as the others, which would eliminate the last free members of the team. That would be most unfortunate."

"We'd have to call for reinforcements," Bobby said. "In fact, maybe we should."

"If we were elsewhere, that would be the obvious choice, but there's no convenient pay phone with which to call the Institute. Calling in the cavalry will take time that we don't have at present. The longer this affair lasts, the sooner Sauron is likely to kill one of us, or murder more of those unfortunate savages that live here."

"An' it's longer that he has th'others for fuel," Sam added.

"Somebody's going to have to take the bait," Iceman said. "One of us, or two?"

"Just one, methinks," Hank said.

"I'll do it," Sam declared.

"No, Sam. You're better on offense than defense. If you use your power down in the swamp, the noise and glow will reveal you instantly. Should Sauron get in range, he need only hypnotize you for an instant to get you to drop your kinetic envelope, making you all too vulnerable. I suspect we are best served by leaving Iceman to chase Amphibius. Bobby is able to make paths and get across the boggiest patches without excessive hardship. He will be a hard prey to catch, and likely to elude capture altogether amid all this treacherous footing. You and I, Cannonball, will pay a surprise visit to our enemy's stronghold, if we can find it. If we manage it soon enough, he won't realize how much we've puzzled through.''

"He'll realize it when I take that pointy tail of his and feed it to 'im.''

"I will do that," Hank said. "Your job is to pound him into a mountainside until it looks like the rock has acquired a tattoo."

"As the good book says, 'It Shall Be Done'.''

Hank leaned back and yawned. "I'll take the last guard shift. I'll wake you up at first light, and Sam and I will set out for the foothills. Recharge your batteries, my esteemed allies. Tomorrow is a day of reckoning."

CHAPTER 11

As Hank and Sam disappeared between the trunks of the cypress trees, cruising away through the dawn shadows with Cannonball muffling his roar to the stealthiest level he could achieve, Bobby Drake was reminded of all the times he had fended for himself. Quite a few. For someone who had literally grown up within the team, he had indulged in a fair share of solo adventuring.

Why then did he feel so isolated? He wasn't shivering. His powers being what they were, he *never* shivered. Yet he understood completely the apprehension of the young hobbit, Frodo Baggins, as he set out to throw the great ring of power into the volcano and thwart the Sauron of his world.

The igloo was melting fast beside him, no longer sustained by frequent refreezing. He accelerated the process, nodding as the salamanders Sam had been so concerned about thawed, flowed into the tepid swamp water, and began wriggling about.

The way back to the spot where they had diverged from Amphibius's trail barely matched his memory. Fronds that had formed deep, threatening shadows at night offered cool, green arbors in the richness of morning. The incessant twitters, screeches, and groans of the wildlife, which had been so unidentifiable and ominous hours ago, stood out now as the recognizable and appealing racket of parrots, monkeys, bullfrogs, and honeybees. Even the diplodocus, still browsing the treetops, this time with a mate, did not loom as intimidatingly nor whip its tail so brusquely.

The land was trying to lull him into a false sense of security, Bobby concluded. Setting him up for a big, bad surprise. Sort of like a quiet stroll through Central Park after curfew.

Rather rude of the Savage Land, after all he and the X-Men had done to preserve it.

In due course he came to the set of giant froggy footprints where he had seen them last. They had been obscured by bird tracks and a drizzly, predawn rain, but enough remained to be sure he had located the right patch of mud. It no longer seemed a lucky break that Cannonball had stumbled across the traces the previous evening. In retrospect, the fact that they had never quite lost the trail was glaringly convenient. Iceman had to give Amphibius credit. The mutate had consistently made it seem as though the X-Men had stumbled across a secret place he wanted to keep them away from— one that he dared not abandon even while eluding them. Bobby had wanted so much to believe he and his teammates were on the verge of a breakthrough.

No new footprints. That would have been a bit too obvious. Yet somewhere nearby he was certain he would find some sort of marker to lead him into the snare.

He marched to the top of the little knoll. A column of ice formed beneath his feet, lifting him higher and higher. Finally his upper body emerged from the treetops.

William and Maddy Drake's little boy was in a heap of trouble.

He ducked back down, hiding himself in the uppermost leaves. Cruising over the swamp were more than twenty riders on pterosaurs. Iceman keened his gaze to see if Sauron was floating among them, but he saw only pteranodons and a pair of pterodactyls carrying juveniles—messengers to travel quickly, perhaps? No Sauron, no mutates, just the locals who served their cause.

The lack of super-powered foes was of little comfort. Obviously the X-Men's antagonists no longer felt the need to operate covertly. The remaining members of the team were to be rounded up as rapidly as possible, with no concern how public the effort became.

Well, that solved Iceman's first problem, namely how to lure attention away from Cannonball and the Beast. Now he faced a more complex dilemma—how to slip through the net long enough to give his comrades a meaningful interval in which to make good on the new strategy. Fortunately none of the riders seemed to have noticed his brief emergence; their eyes were trained on the ground below their positions. If he perceived their search pattern correctly, they wouldn't pass over his location for several minutes.

He resisted forming chunks of ice around the feet of some of the closer pteranodons so that the added weight would send them crashing into the bog. That would bring too quick a response. However, as he slid down a ramp into the lower canopy, he left his ice tower intact. Eventually it would be noticed and he would have a posse hurrying after his trail of blocks of ice. But not until he had put some distance between himself and the pack.

"Hank, I've changed my mind," he murmured toward his wrist radio. "Let's trade places." He spoke without tapping in the code to open a transmission. Neither he nor the others were using the radios, because to do so would give away that the three of them had separated, in the event that Sauron's contingent had figured out how to listen.

"Just kidding," Bobby said, forming his cruising ramp as fast as he knew how. He became a blue-white blur racing through the cypress trees, a dozen feet above the misty pools of stagnant water. "I *live* for this kind of thrill."

Cold liquid struck Psylocke in the face, jolting her awake. She coughed and raised her dripping eyelids. In front of her stood a prune-faced, leathery mare of a woman wearing a loincloth, a lemur-skull pendant, and a sneer.

"Good morning to you, too, Pibah," Betsy muttered.

The jailor chuckled to herself. She lowered her gourd dipper into her primitive bamboo-and-tar wheelbarrow and flung more water at her captive's body. When the wheelbarrow trough was empty, she limped over to the well in the corner of the stone chamber to refill. The bucketsful came up icy cold from the depth of the mountain—perhaps from an aquifer outside the tropical Savage Land biosphere.

Pibah laughed louder as the frigid cascades raised goose bumps all over Betsy's body. She loved this, Betsy knew. Here Pibah was—bent, middle-aged, most of her teeth missing and whatever beauty she had once possessed sacrificed to a harsh life spent with harsh men—able to torment a woman of beauty, youth, unique talents, and an unbroken spirit.

The worst of it was, Pibah's little abuses were the least of what Psylocke had endured since her abduction. In the end, the servant did only what she was assigned. It was she who had kept Betsy fed the day before, and though she had doled out the morsels with excruciating slowness, she had not stolen any of the food nor sprinkled it with fire peppers, as Brainchild had suggested. And at least these baths did not involve harsh scrubbing or soap in the eyes. Perhaps she was still bound to a tilted slab, unable to tend to her own needs in even the most basic fashion, but at least the layers of sweat and the aromas of captivity and more were being rinsed off.

LAW OF THE JUNGLE

The overflow dribbled into the trench that ran along the base of all the slabs, vanishing from her presence. And cold as the water was, it refreshed her, in a brutal, tingling sort of way.

It could have been worse. Had been worse.

Pibah moved on and tossed water at Logan, who resided on the next slab. Beyond him Storm slept, still too drained from Sauron's last feast to awaken. The villain had drawn a huge portion of energy from her. Her just desserts, he called it, for causing him so much trouble in the night sky battle.

Across from Betsy perched Shanna and Ka-Zar. Both were unconscious, their chests rising and falling faintly, their jaws slack. As non-mutants, Sauron's feeding had hit them hard, but fortunately, with so many other sources of provision, the monster had spared them enough to preserve their lives. For now.

Beyond the two guardians of the Savage Land, intentionally placed at a distance from her to make her suffer, rested Warren. Brainchild had tilted that slab to horizontal in order to study his extraordinary wings. The mutate's swollen-headed figure blocked her view, but she knew her lover was there.

She wasn't alone anymore. Psylocke winced, wishing she weren't so glad of the companionship, and knowing full well the defeat it represented. At least there was hope, as long as the three other X-Men remained at large.

Brainchild finished his examination and wandered off. Betsy saw that Warren was awake—the first time both of them had been conscious since Sauron and his raiders had dragged in the main clump of captives during the night. He turned and looked straight at her. He spoke. Not with his mouth and vocal cords, but by a more profound means.

I remember a ride we took on a ferris wheel. I remember a moonlight swim. I remember . . .

Betsy barely managed to suppress the huge grin that tried to blossom on her face. Despite supreme effort, the corners of her mouth rose. Warren saw it, and his eyes twinkled.

I remember a walk down Greymalkin Lane, she responded effusively. *I remember writing to my brother about that ferris wheel ride. I remember telling him in that letter that I was in love.*

She was no longer headblind! The terrible, dispiriting inner silence that had plagued her for more than thirty-six hours was gone. Her mind was now brimming with the glorious, beloved "voice" of her Warren. Her angel in blue.

The bone-aching weariness from Sauron's latest leeching had not faded. Her powers had not returned in any substantive way. Her fingers twitched, but could form not a shred of her psychic knife. She was certain that she still lacked the ordinary, non-mutant physical strength necessary to stand up if the straps were removed. But that no longer discouraged her. If she continued to show the normal evidence of her defeat, Sauron would assume she was as helpless as ever.

When she had been small, her governess used to say that a rainy day was no disappointment as long as one was prepared for it. *Well, nanny*, she said to that kind old lady's ghost, *I've found my umbrella today.*

Who would have thought, she broadcast to Warren, *that in granting your request, I would benefit myself most of all?*

Warren answered not in sentences, but with images of two nights earlier, when they had sat outside the lodge in Tongah's village, watched only by the curious tribesmen up on the stockade walls, and fashioned the link that currently united them.

Psylocke and Archangel were tethered by a variation of

psionic rapport that Cyclops and Phoenix had long shared. Warren had intended the measure to serve as a crutch in his confrontation with Sauron. Betsy was so proud of him for that. Warren was a prideful man. To be able to let go of ego enough to ask for help touched her heart, because she suspected he could not have done so with anyone else. She had gladly set up the framework that would allow her to instantly send him telepathic countermeasures to the villain's hypnotism if needed, a strategy that should have worked even if Warren ventured as much as fifty miles away from her during his circuits of the Savage Land.

Ironically, when the time came, Archangel had faced Sauron unsupported, because Psylocke had herself already been taken captive. The link had not been powerful enough to let her reach him through the cavern's thick stone walls once Sauron had drained her and Brainchild had fitted her with the inhibitor. The psionic construct was not as durable as that of Scott and Jean. Nor would it be permanent. Betsy estimated it would dissipate within a week unless they chose to reinforce it. However, in the meantime, now that Warren was inside the chamber with her, the two of them needed only to be awake and alert to make it function.

We need to open the channel as widely as possible, she said. *Now that I have a telepathic anchor, I think I may be able to manage to speak to Ororo and Logan and Ka-Zar and Shanna. There's even a slight possibility I could reach Hank or Bobby or Sam.*

Go for it, he replied.

She surrendered to the delicious intimacy of the rapport. Though he had given permission, Warren resisted momentarily. An understandable reflex. She was, after all, more used to this level of psychic intensity. No matter. He was imbuing his astral armor with no greater force than a soap bubble. *Pop*. Barrier gone. She was in.

She had only to think of a memory of an occasion when she and Warren had done anything together, and she recalled not only her own impressions, but his as well. The romantic moments drew her—the walks, the intimacy, the long talks in and around the mansion or Warren's Manhattan loft—but the strongest memories consisted of crisis moments. Those were the most valuable for the purpose at hand. Sharing those riveted the two of them together more than a recalled candlelight dinner could.

She cringed as she saw herself bleeding in Boomer's arms, nearly eviscerated by Sabretooth's claws as he escaped the X-Men's custody. No direct memory of that existed in her own brain. She had been unconscious and all but dead. But Warren had been with Hank and Scott when they rushed to the chamber. He had served as witness as she breathed those shallow, ragged breaths, the rasps nearly inaudible beneath Boomer's sobs. Betsy knew now what it had been like for Warren, how he had gone blank inside, horror claiming him from the end of every strand of his blond hair to the tips of his bionic wings. His world crumbled to meaninglessness. It was the sort of memory that eradicated any doubt that he loved her.

He saw into her memories as well. She blushed as he touched an incident during the aftermath of the battle fought against Cameron Hodge in Genosha, the huge altercation that set the stage for the return of the original members of X-Men into the core team. It was the first time they had met since she had acquired her Asian body. And how that body had reacted to Warren's proximity. Though their love affair was not yet a glimmer on the horizon, she had wanted him from that moment forward. The pheromones were . . . right.

LAW OF THE JUNGLE

Could it be that she would never have been interested in Warren if she had retained her original, British-born face and form? How much of romantic love came from the right mixture of scent and other purely physical considerations?

Now Warren was pouring over her memories of . . . *oh, sweet mother of mercy, can't a girl keep any secrets?* She winced, let him share, and quickly went on to the next image.

In a generalized sense, the mingling of their souls was a pale shadow of the other night, when she had fueled it with her full, unsiphoned powers. But bit by bit, the connection regained vitality. Finally she pulled back. The doubled consciousness faded. In its place, she heard the whisper of the other minds in the room. Her telepathy had been rekindled, if at a mere one or two percent efficiency.

Much as she wished, she dared not probe Brainchild or even Pibah for information. With so faint a spark of her normal talent, she lacked the necessary finesse to get into an uncooperative subject and out without setting off alarms. For the time being, she had to approach only cooperative individuals. The circuit to Warren was firm now; even another sapping of their lifeforces would not break it. But as for the others . . . ?

Logan, she called.

Wolverine ceased staring at the floor in his usual intense, brooding way. He shook his head as if doing nothing more than flicking away the drips from the dousing Pibah had given him. *Betts?*

His reply came in faintly, but without distortion. *Yes*, she said. *Hold on. I'll see if I can bring the rest of us into the conversation.*

Next came a bigger challenge. She had had an advantage when reaching for Logan. Remnants still existed of the bond forged between them when she had undergone the process that resulted in her ninja abilities—a connection not unlike the rapport. The process resembled building a bridge after the guide cable had already been installed. To connect with Ororo required greater effort, like leaping across a raw chasm.

She tested the doorway of Storm's mind. Sweat popped from her forehead, mingling with the dew left from Pibah's anointment. There. The latch turned. She entered.

Instantly the connection with Wolverine stretched out like taffy. The middle separated. Warren's presence faded to a background whisper, insufficient for decipherable conversation. Betsy lacked the power to keep everyone linked simultaneously. One at a time then. She stayed with Ororo.

A hazy image formed of the Serengeti Plains of Africa. In the distance, snow-capped Mount Kilimanjaro jutted up and through a layer of clouds. Storm lay in the mud of a watering hole, her goddess raiment and hair lying like mop strings around her. A pair of lionesses stalked toward her. She couldn't get up to run. The most she could manage was to raise her hand and push at the air in the direction of the beasts—defiant to the end, but ineffective. Their long, sharp teeth came closer.

A nightmare. Betsy gently influenced the dreamscape. The lions froze into statues and became the guardians of an ivy-covered brick library, a building that she and Ororo had passed on excursions through Salem Center. Ororo, no longer muddy and disarrayed, rose to her feet at the base of the concrete steps.

Betsy emerged from the library foyer and smiled. *Good morning, Ororo.*

And with that, the co-leader of the X-Men awoke. She scanned the cavern, counted the captives, and sighed in frustration. Her pale eyes settled on Psylocke, but drifted away again so that the guards or Brainchild would not grow suspicious. *I see you've found some way around our enemy's slave collars*, Ororo broadcast. *Good work.*

The congratulations may be premature, Betsy replied. She filled in Ororo on her limitations.

It is a start, the wind-rider stated, refusing to be discouraged. *See how many of us you can reach, and then hoard your strength. We'll do our best to keep the attention focused in our direction to leave you as unmolested as possible.*

Betsy smiled. Barely awake and helpless on a slab, and already Ororo was composing strategy. *Bless her*, she thought.

Psylocke eased out of their contact. After informing Warren and Logan of her progress, she closed her eyes and braced herself. The next exertion would cause her pain. She thrust her awareness beyond the cavern, probing for the nearest familiar mind. *Hank? Bobby? Sam?* she called.

Nothing. It was as fruitless as yesterday, when she had tried and tried to get through to Warren.

Then something tickled her deep down. She frowned. What could it be? The emanations flowed with great strength, with a primal quality she couldn't associate with any person she knew. Even Logan did not have such an aura of untamed, animalistic sentience.

Sauron himself? No. The contact soothed her in a way no hostile presence would. She absorbed not only friendliness, but a hint that the entity had been searching for her even before she had reached out in its direction.

She opened her eyes, still grasping at the astral filaments, trying to touch enough of them to communicate with their owner. Her gaze settled on Ka-Zar's inert form. Immediately the whispers in her mind gained strength, but to her frustration, they refused to organize into true words or images. How could any telepath be transmitting so loudly and still be so mute?

But, since it seemed to be what was wanted, she continued to stare at Lord Kevin Plunder. Not an onerous chore, admittedly. She gave in to a reminiscence of their warm, almost flirting conversation outside the lodge two nights earlier. And such an excellent smile he'd worn as showed her the path that led to the hot springs. It pained her to see him slung up like a side of beef.

A throb of outrage came through from the observer inside her mind. *Good*, Psylocke thought. *Any ally of Ka-Zar is likely to be an ally of the X-Men.*

"Did you sleep well, my honored guests?" screeched a raucous voice. Suddenly the whisper of telepathic presence ceased. Betsy needed every ounce of her power to ward off the hypnotic domination as Sauron stalked into the cavern, grinning his long, toothy grin. She had nothing left to devote to conversation with a new, ethereal friend.

"Slept like a kitten, bub," Logan muttered. "Mattress was too soft, though."

Sauron fluffed back his long eyebrows with his talons, unruffled by Wolverine's sarcasm. "We're arranging a nice dungeon for all of you. For the time being, these facilities will have to do. At least until Brainchild has checked to be certain your powers will remain nullified no matter where we keep you."

Psylocke read the monster's aura, and calculated that he had lost little or none of his borrowed power overnight. That was bad in that it made him as formidable as possible, but it had one definite advantage: He would not be needing to siphon off more lifeforce from them just yet. Her recovery could proceed without interruption.

"We will escape," Storm said. "We will destroy everything you have built here."

"My dear weather deity," Sauron mocked, "you can barely lift your chin. But I am glad to see such spunk. The more vigorously you try to fight, the more energy you generate for me to feast upon."

"No matter," Storm declared. "We've beaten you before. We'll do it again."

"Perhaps, before I go out to supervise the capture of your teammates, a demonstration of your ineffectiveness is in order." Sauron danced around the room. Brainchild and the guards carefully averted their eyes, maintaining their visages of respect even while their leader acted like a fool. "Let's see. A song would be good. Something simple, not too taxing for your little intellects. Ah. I have it. A round."

He began singing "Row, row, row your boat."

The X-Men stared back at him.

"Oh, come now. That's not the spirit!" Sauron raised a hand, holding Ka-Zar's confiscated knife like a conductor's baton. "Everyone. I insist."

Psylocke sensed hypnotic commands invading her psyche. She knew how to fight, but also knew that she would lose in the end, and the effort would only deplete her. Instead, she began to sing, doing so just haltingly enough that Sauron, if he didn't check too closely, would think she was doing so against her will.

Warren joined in the chorus, aware of her reasons for cooperating, playing the part of the weak-minded opponent Sauron considered him to be.

But Storm and Wolverine pressed their mouths shut. As expected, this drew the core of the villain's anger and scrutiny down upon them. *Excellent*, Psylocke thought. She would have winked conspiratorially at them if she had dared.

"No good at all!" Sauron yelled. He stepped directly in front of Storm. She clenched her eyes shut, but he forced them open without physically touching her. He placed his huge orbs in front of her face and commanded aloud, "Sing! Sing the round!"

" 'Row your boat' into a whirlpool!" Storm snapped. The muscles of her neck stood out, denying him the surrender he was demanding, but already her words had adhered slightly to the tune. He leaned nearer. Psylocke, even with dampened powers, could see the cascade of ethereal energy pouring from Sauron into his victim.

Storm began to sing. "Row . . . row . . ." She swallowed hard. "Row your . . ." She resisted until the end of the lyric, but at the word "dream," her lips parted and refused to close. At first she mouthed the words, then they emerged in a whisper, and finally she sang at full volume. Only an occasional shift of tone betrayed the uncooperativeness seething inside her.

Sauron turned toward Wolverine. "Now, my Canadian *basso profundo*," he proclaimed, "let us hear your contribution!"

Logan opened his mouth, and belched.

Sauron glared at him. "Try again."

Logan narrowed his eyes, a feral grin forming below. "I only sing when I'm drunk, bub."

Sauron chuckled. The "bub" had echoed at the same beat as "row row row."

"Very well," the monster chirped. "Be drunk."

Wolverine limbs and body went slack. His eyes unfocused. He hiccupped.

"Row, row, row your boat," Sauron sang.

"Throw, throw, throw yer goat," Logan sang merrily in a voice Psylocke had only heard the times he and Havok had tried to drink each other under the table. Thanks to his healing factor, Logan could drink an entire fifth of that ghastly Russian vodka of his in an hour and still stand up and walk away.

"Almost," Sauron declared. "You *will* get the lyrics right. I will tell you if and when you may improvise."

Logan grimaced. Psylocke knew the pain of such prolonged resistance was excruciating; the psychic maelstrom around his head was vivid and so unstable snakes of compulsion were radiating outward. Even the guards were humming the tune now.

Gruffly and unmelodiously, he sang. Sauron nodded, wove the tendrils of command tightly into place, and turned to his remaining captives.

"Ah, my poor Lord and Lady Plunder," he trilled. "How rude to snore during our performance. Wake up, my dears."

He snapped his fingers. Ka-Zar and Shanna's eyes blinked open. They raised bleary heads and took in their surroundings, expressions hardening as they spotted their tormentor.

"Sing with us," Sauron told them.

They clenched their teeth and tried to stifle the action of their vocal cords, but they lasted mere seconds. Psylocke could see in their auras what great natural mental resistance they possessed, but it did them little good at the moment. Sauron was at his mightiest, they were at their weakest— they wouldn't even be conscious yet if he weren't propping them up psychically.

Wolverine began garbling the lyrics. Sauron whirled and stalked back to him, finally demonstrating impatience. *So*, thought Psylocke, *controlling so many at once is not the casual trick he pretends it is*. Taking advantage of the diversion, Psylocke sent out a quick telepathic burst of reassurance to Ka-Zar. She had no time or strength to get across a verbal message—a mere pulse of friendliness and presence was all she could manage.

She sensed his mind open and envelope her offering. He glanced toward her, his scowl softening into the silver-tongued-devil glance he had blessed her with back in the Fall People village. A wave of warmth blossomed between her lungs.

Reaching Shanna proved difficult. The She-Devil's mental locks were well constructed. Psylocke recognized the signs of an individual who had known tragedy at vulnerable points in life. The barriers thickened against Psylocke's probe.

Elisabeth Braddock had been a telepath too many years to batter clumsily and futilely at a volatile target. Instead, she rested her astral tendril against the wall and waited.

The rigidity of the wall did not fade. But bit by bit, as Psylocke held back and didn't push, a counterprobe emerged and tentatively nudged the tendril.

Connection. Psylocke broadcast a gentle message of greeting and all's-well. Shanna gave a little jump. Then some of the tension vanished from her posture. She darted a glance at Betsy and smiled, eyes only in order to conceal the communication from enemy observation.

Back along the link came emotions of gratitude, counter-reassurance, and camaraderie.

Well, well, well, she thought. *Not so fiery a vixen at all, if you approached her right.*

Psylocke withdrew into herself, hoarding her remaining reserves, little as they were. Any more effort right now might deplete her so much she would begin screaming from the insipidness of that ridiculous song. Brainchild, she noted, had stuffed wax into his ears. Lord, she envied him.

Sauron, having overcome Logan's latest round of defiance, was stomping gaily across the cold, rough-hewn stone floor, singing loudest of all and flapping his wings until the drenched hair of his captives dried and fluttered in the current. His eyes glittered. He wobbled as if sharing in the inebriation with which he had afflicted Wolverine.

He is still mentally unhinged, thought Psylocke. *Insanity still bubbled somewhere beneath the surface. How to uncap it and use it to the X-Men's advantage?* She didn't know yet, but it was only a matter of time until she uncovered the necessary clue.

Iceman sped through the trees beside a sluggish, ochre-tinged river. From back in the jungle growth came the crashing of savages atop ostrichlike mounts, a ground pursuit crew to go with the squadron of pterosaurs above. Bobby had kept out of their sight for a mile or more, but they had not lost his trail. If he stopped, they would catch up to him faster than he could make a pile of snowballs.

The river presented a problem. For the moment, he was hidden from the sky by lush foliage, but he would have to cross soon. Most likely the flyers would spot him in transit. If not, they would see his ice bridge before it melted.

To make matters worse, he suspected that for the past hour his pursuers had been driving him toward a specific area.

Bam! Something struck him from the left. He sailed over the low bank into the river.

Limbs clutched at him, keeping him under. He forced his eyes open. Amid the silt thrashed Amphibius. Every time Bobby started to rise toward the surface, the black-spotted green mutate gripped him and thrust him down again.

Oh, great. Even in his ice form, he needed air to breathe. Bobby was beginning to grow alarmed when his opponent's huge foot came crashing through the water into his midsection, driving out much of the dwindling contents of his lungs.

Now he was more than alarmed. The primal fear of drowning suffused him, spooking him more than several battles with Magneto and the Sentinels had done. He acted instinctively: A pillar of ice formed on the river bottom and sprouted upward. He and Amphibius climbed with it, until they were at the height of a spire twenty feet above the surface of the water.

Amphibius squawked and leapt into the river. He reappeared near the bank, beginning a hop to solid ground.

He didn't make it. Bobby froze the river edge. A slab of ice solidified around the mutate's ankles, immobilizing him.

"What an amateur," Bobby called. "A muppet could do better than that." He had saved that insult for just such an occasion.

A clamor blared above his head. He turned to see a pair of riders zooming toward him, the one in the rear sounding the alarm on a ram's horn bugle. He leapt from the pillar just in time to avoid the flying reptile's outstretched talons. No counterattack. This was his final chance to buy more time. He formed a ramp, skidded down, and sailed on an ice bridge toward the far bank.

The second rider screamed past. Iceman ducked, rolled, and flung a handful of icicles upward. Several struck the creature. It screeched from the pain and fought its rider's command to turn, earning the X-Man another minuscule breather.

Bobby checked the brightness of the cloud layer, guessing that it was noon. As he was looking upward, a half-dozen more flyers sailed around a bend in the river, flying low. The warriors yelled as they saw him.

Bobby hurried toward the willows that overhung the far bank. Suddenly his head spun. He tumbled off his ramp into the water. The shock of impact cleared his disorientation. He sat up in knee-deep water and frowned skyward, searching for some explanation.

And recognized Vertigo atop one of the pteranodons.

"Uh oh," he said. Frantically he punched in the code to allow his radio to transmit. "This is it, guys! Going down!"

A pteranodon streaked past, slashing. Bobby dived to the side. Climbing to his feet, he raised an ice shield and fended off a pair of tossed spears. He had almost regained enough balance and coherency to create a new ramp and scoot the remaining twenty yards to the bank when the willows parted. A dozen wolves gazed out at him, growling and licking their chops.

There went the fleeting hope of escape. He might be able to fend off their teeth and claws, but their howling and pursuit would prevent him from slipping away.

Another wave of nausea tumbled him down into the water. He let the current wash him downstream a few yards toward a tiny, reed-strewn islet. What he had thought was a log in the shallows turned out to be a crocodile. It lifted its head, took one step toward him, and he adorned it with a thick muzzle of ice.

The dizziness struck hard and relentlessly. Bobby flopped on his back, only to see Vertigo and her flying reptile circling closely overhead like a buzzard while other riders set up for attack glides. He tried to ice up her mount's wings, but he couldn't aim. Snow flurries erupted, scattering this way and that, dusting the swooping enemies but doing them no damage.

Talons battered his hands and arms. He was spared being seized. The creatures screeched and jerked back whenever they touched him—apparently they detested the frigidity of his body.

Iceman groaned and tried to wrap himself in a frozen

dome, but he couldn't concentrate. He barely noticed the warriors dropping into the stream and wading toward him. Two of them seemed unusually large. All seemed to have multiple heads and limbs.

No, that wasn't right. His vision was blurred. He forced himself to focus.

Wait. One of them *did* have multiple sets of arms.

Barbarus, with Gaza looming behind him. And Amphibius, freed from the trap, swimming hard toward the scene. With Vertigo above and Lupo no doubt somewhere not far behind his wolves. All the major baddies except Brainchild and Sauron himself. Obviously, this operation had been intended as the final mop-up of X-Men.

He sure hoped Hank and Sam appreciated this.

Barbarus's four fists pounded him. Gaza lifted him and slammed him back down into the reeds. When Bobby raised a hand to form an ice club, another pulse of dizziness removed any control he had over his muscles.

Gaza, Barbarus, and Amphibius took turns bashing him until, inevitably, he reverted to standard human form. One big bruise later, he slipped into unconsciousness.

CHAPTER 12

Hank McCoy emerged from a cleft between two boulders, shielded his eyes from the sourceless glare rebounding off the layer of mists above, and scanned the wildflower-dotted pastures and rocky outcroppings ahead. A small herd of eohippus darted sideways and whinnied, perhaps scenting his fragrant blue body—he wished he could have approached into the wind. A bull auroch chewed its cud by a small spring, ignoring the armadillolike glyptodont browsing in the reeds at the water's edge. Nothing out of the ordinary for this fragment of the Savage Land.

The more he thought about it, the more obvious it became that this was ideal territory for Sauron. No jungle growth to entangle his wings, far less cover to hide infiltrators. A Lear jet–sized quetzalcoatlus rode past on a thermal draft, considered the auroch and the dawn horses, and whipped upward almost to the inversion layer. Within the past hour, since emerging from the swamp, the Beast had also spotted the biggest harpy eagle he had ever seen.

Cannonball caught up with him. Sam glanced down at his wrist radio. Hank sighed.

Waiting for the right moment to act was the hardest part of strategy and tactics.

An hour had passed since they had received Bobby's blurted transmission. The lack of any followup confirmed that he had been defeated. That was bad enough. What was worse was that they still didn't know if his sacrifice had gained them any advantage.

"I could cover a lot more ground if I could coast along on a kinetic envelope," Cannonball said. His flying ability had already helped considerably in crossing the swamp and the jungle to the base of the foothills, under the cover of the trees.

"As right as a harvest moon over your farm's weather-vane, my boy. But you endeavored in precisely that man-fjner the first day we searched, and it achieved no tangible result."

"Well, no, but it felt like I was doin' somethin'." Sam sat down on a small boulder and rubbed at the grass stains on the blue knees of his costume. "Don't kid me now, Dr. McCoy—I'm sure this here 'patience' an' tip-toeing around wasn't easy for you when you was young."

"When I was young?" Hank snorted. "Do you take me for some decrepit octogenarian?"

"Nah. You ain't a day over sixty, are ya? It's hard to tell with all that hair. You could be dyein' the gray to blue."

Sam managed a hint of a smile, which Hank returned, but the jokes were wearing thin. What they needed was some luck. That had been in short supply so far on the mission.

"Look at that," Sam said. "Somethin' sure spooked them there li'l horses."

The Beast turned. The eohippus herd was clattering away up the slope. Like so many deer—they really look-ed much like fawns, complete with white spots on their rumps—though they galloped, not bounded the way deer would.

"They caught wind of some sort of predator," Hank said.

He scrutinized the little gully to their left. It contained the muddy prints of and the droppings of mammoth and other animals. The dawn horses were doing their best to avoid that trail, though it would have been the fastest route out of the little dell in which they had been grazing.

Around the shoulder of a hill came a sabretooth tiger, striding along with great purpose. The cat spared the eohippus no more than a dismissive glance.

"Hey," said Cannonball. "Ain't that . . . ?"

"Zabu!" Hank called. Not so loudly that his voice echoed over the landscape, but so that it carried to Ka-Zar's faithful animal.

Zabu paused and regarded them. He emitted a sound midway between a lion's rumble and a house cat's inquisitive meow. He remained there no longer than it took to stare at the rumps of the last few eohippus and lick his lips, then he continued up the animal track.

"That boy knows where he's goin'." Sam nodded his head firmly. "You thinkin' what I'm thinkin'?"

"Of course, my boon companion," the Beast replied. "We've been ignoring one of our most talented allies. Who better than Zabu would know where to find Ka-Zar?"

They pranced down to the trail and jogged behind the tawny feline. The animal acknowledged them with a flick of his ear. He proceeded onward at a pace meant for endurance, pausing regularly as if checking some sort of scent.

"We're an inordinately long way from Tongah's village," the Beast commented. "This must be one fatigued kitty."

"Tired or not, I wouldn't want to get on his bad side. He looks like he's mad enough to tackle a T. rex."

Fur ruffled on Zabu's back and he growled softly, as if to say, *Bring 'em on*.

"How do you suppose he knows where to go?" Sam added.

Hank scratched himself behind one of his tufted ears. "You are gazing upon the super hero of all sabretooths, my boy. His talents surpass the rest of his species the way, oh, the Hulk's strength exceeds that of yours or mine."

Zabu turned, snarled, and resumed trotting down the trail.

"You know," the junior X-Man quipped, "it makes my belly button quiver when he acts that smart."

The terrain grew rougher and more rocky. The trail dipped into a ravine and wound onward parallel to a brush-filled, frolicking brook. The air took on an alpine crispness, though it was that of the Alps in high summer.

Zabu stopped so abruptly the two X-Men nearly bumped into his haunches.

"What is it, old fellow?" whispered the Beast.

The cat grumbled in reply, abandoned the trail, and began climbing the slope, hopping from rock to rock and checking frequently to determine what he could see farther up the ravine.

Hank bounded after him, leaving Sam playing catch-up, grumbling under his breath about the steepness of the grade and the continued need to avoid flying. Near the top Zabu crept into a fissure and peeked out from the shade of overhanging rock. It was a see-without-being-seen vantage, and Hank made sure to share in the caution. Sam, bless his greenhorn soul, did not require a prompting to act accordingly.

They were finally high enough to see around a bend in the stream channel. One of the steep banks ahead was split by a tall, dim opening.

LAW OF THE JUNGLE

"A cave?" Sam whispered.

" 'Twould appear so," Hank answered in like tones. He tried to imagine how the spot would appear from above, and decided the topography was sufficient to make the gash appear to be nothing more than a shadow. It could only be seen from within the ravine, and only when quite near, as they were now. Given such natural camouflage, it was little wonder it had not been spotted during Storm or Archangel's reconnaissance flights.

The sound of voices filtered down the ravine. That and heavy footfalls gave away the arrival of a large number of men well before the party rounded a fan of scree and became visible. The newcomers trudged straight for the cave mouth.

"We have the right place," Hank said.

At the head of the procession marched Gaza, tall, broad-shouldered, and wearing an expression of proud command. A blind man, leading. Immediately behind him hopped Amphibius. Several burly warriors made up the central group. The largest two of them carried Bobby Drake on a pole suspended atop their shoulders. Vertigo hung close by, her eyes studying the unconscious captive intently—no doubt, Hank concluded, in order to daze him with her power should he demonstrate the slightest sign of awakening. After her came a few more Savage Land natives. Barbarus brought up the rear, positioned as the heavy muscle should they be pursued.

Hank winced to see Bobby jostling along, limp, his uniform torn and at least one big welt rising on his temple—a truly nasty one to be visible from such a distance—and mud spatter everywhere.

"We gotta help him," Sam said, keeping his voice down,

but imbuing his words with all the emotional force of a gutteral yell.

"No, Sam."

"But I have a clear shot. All five are out in the open, and not a one of them can stand up to me when I'm blastin'."

"That's correct only if you succeed in hitting them, and if Vertigo doesn't twist your cerebellum upside down inside your skull."

"Thanks for the vote o' confidence, old man."

The Beast clutched Cannonball by the chin and forced him to stare directly back. "Samuel Guthrie, this is not about your competence. Ordinarily I would be *pushing* you into the fray, and don't think it's easy for me holding still this way. But we can't tip our hand until we're ready to finish the job. If we attack now, maybe we'd get Bobby back, but we would lose the element of surprise as far as our other comrades are concerned."

Hank knew he wasn't saying anything Sam didn't already know, but it had to be said, merely in order to make the advice real enough to obey himself.

Sam sighed and nodded.

Hank let go and turned back to the raiding party, wishing in a way that his junior colleague had kept arguing and somehow convinced him to be impulsive. Hank's toes dug into the sand at the bottom of the fissure. He tested the springiness of his foot muscles, wanting so much to leap out of concealment and come thundering down at their enemies like the Juggernaut with a wasp under his helmet.

Before Gaza reached the cave mouth, two muscular guards stepped out of the shadows and lifted their chest axes in welcome. The mutate saluted briefly. The sentinels ducked hastily out of the way of his towering frame. Gaza proceeded inside the arch of native limestone and bat guano, an opening so generous he did not have to stoop. The other mutates and tribesmen poured after him.

Iceman vanished with them. Hank simultaneously felt the pang of lost opportunity, and relief that he no longer had to watch his dear old friend swaying from side to side like a shot and gutted three-point buck.

The guards stepped back into the gloom of the overhang, but spying carefully, Hank could make out the foot and sandal of one of them, confirming that they had been, and were, watching the vicinity for arrivals, friendly or hostile.

They were lax, Hank noted. Probably feeling like they've won. The mutates had looked less smug. Their brood had fought the X-Men several times and had probably been considerably less than enthused to realize their major offensive had failed to corral two of their targets. Were the sentries remaining alert enough to worry about? Did they have compatriots hidden in the shrubs and scree?

Hank carefully evaluated the landscape for hidden lookouts, but the only movement that caught his eye was grass swaying in the breeze, birds floating by, and the drifting of leaves and sticks along the channels of the brook. He smelled no warning aromas.

The guards probably had orders not to wander beyond the cave mouth, out of concern their movements would betray the existence of the very hiding place at which they were stationed. Well, that was something, at least—if Hank and Sam couldn't get in unobserved, at least they could operate in relative freedom while outside.

The large group of raiders had been gone only two or three minutes when Zabu stirred and clambered down the slope again.

Cannonball frowned. "You don't think he—"

"Yes, I do," the Beast replied. "He's going in after them. We have to stop him."

They hurried from rock to rock, finally catching up as the sabretooth reached the trail and turned to continue up the ravine.

Hank placed himself in the way.

Zabu grumbled. Not loudly enough to alert Sauron's guards, but rich with a threatening, *get out of my way* tone. He raised a paw, showing his huge, curved, keenly tapered nails.

"We want to help Ka-Zar," Hank said in a calm, friendly voice. "Help Ka-Zar, yes?"

Zabu put down his paw and gazed at the X-Man, blinking every few seconds and cocking his head at an angle. "Mrrrr?"

"Help Ka-Zar," Hank repeated. "Go *that* way to help Ka-Zar." He waved his hand back the way they had come.

Zabu snorted lightly, lifted up on his hind legs, put his front paws on the Beast's shoulders, and began striding toward the cave, forcing Hank to back up step by step in a bizarre imitation of a circus dance.

"I think he don't agree," Sam murmured. "He's got the veto power, Dr. McCoy, and he's usin' it."

"We could let him go ahead," Hank conceded, "but he could help us more if we planned an attack." He placed his face right up against the animal's nose. "Go that way. Help Ka-Zar more. *Pounce* on Sauron."

Zabu dropped to all fours. "Rrrr?"

"Trust me, kitty," Hank said. "We'll be back very soon. Pounce on Sauron. Pounce on Gaza. Pounce on Vertigo."

The cat turned. Growling discontentedly, he ambled downstream, in the lead as if going that way were his idea.

Sam shook his head in amazement as he and Hank sashayed along a step behind the feline's stubby tail. "I thought sure he was gonna carve you into little beast bits if you didn't get out of his way."

Hank shrugged. "I could not have perservered had I indulged in such disheartening speculation. I filled my inner being with images of our venerable smilodon as I observed him night before last, licking young Matthew's noggin and snuggling against him like a mother cat around her kitten. One uses what artifices one can to beguile one's own fear reflex. That technique, I am gratified to say, worked unusually well."

"You soothed the savage beast?"

Hank winced. "Oh, puh-lease don't use that phrase."

"Sorry. It sorta slipped out." Cannonball paused to watch a covey of chicken-sized compsognathuses as they burst from the concealment of the brush by the stream and raced across a bridge of dead branches to safety on the far bank. "So . . . now that we're goin' this way, do you mind telling me *why* we're goin' this way? You ain't plannin' to go get Tongah and the villagers to help? That would take an awful lot of time."

Hank spared a moment to admire the way the compsognathus's heads swivelled so adroitly on their necks. Their name meant *elegant jaw*. They deserved it. "Don't fret, my brave Samuel. Extended delay is the last quality I care to introduce to our strategy. We're going back to the meadows we saw earlier. If all goes well, we'll be hurrying back much better equipped to cope with our enemies' superior numbers than if you and I and Zabu rushed in right now."

"How'll we manage that?"

Hank leaned close. His tone was boisterous. "I have a cunning plan."

CHAPTER 13

T he psychic corona flared so hotly Psylocke shut her eyes and turned away. No good. The image still burned, thrusting right through her skull and bombarding the nexus of her telepathic senses. At the center of the burst hung Iceman, his head trapped between Sauron's palms, giving up life energy from every chakra of his body. Bobby's mouth was flung wide in a scream, but no sound was emerging—he had no air left in his lungs to propel through his vocal cords.

She had seen lifeforce caught in such violent outpourings many times. Usually as part of the process of death. That's what being touched by Sauron felt like—death. Except that the victim had no guarantee of release from suffering. Upon awakening, he or she might be harvested all over again.

Too much. Betsy made it a point not to cry for herself, but her resolve wasn't as unassailable in regard to the agony of comrades. Tears trickled down her cheeks. Poor Bobby. Brought in like a rag doll, fitted with the collar, trussed up, and before he could even awaken, that fiend had come in waving his devil wings, grabbed hold of him, and started to ingest his essence like a spider from hell.

Bobby was awake now. The pain had yanked him out of his merciful semicoma.

Suddenly, the waves of anguish dissipated. She opened her eyes. Sauron had stepped back from Iceman's slab, propelled by Gaza and Barbarus's vise-grip tugging.

"You dare interrupt," screeched the monster.

"I ordered them to pull you away," Brainchild hurriedly explained from his perch by his monitoring equipment. "I had to. You are nearing the limit we spoke of. Save this X-Man for later, Master. You have no real need of his energies yet."

Sauron flung off his servitors' hold. They backpedalled, flinching. He raised a wing to bat at them both, but refrained from following through. Instead, he stalked to Brainchild, whose knees began trembling.

"I do not care for underlings telling me what to do. Not even one so valuable as you, my melon-headed savant." Sauron loomed over the little mutate until the latter nearly fell back off his stool.

"For the sake of the . . . adjustment, Master, do not draw any more power." He spoke *sotto voce*, so that only his frightful lord would hear, but Psylocke "heard" him. By borrowing a little boost from each of her allies for the past several hours, her telepathy was consistently available, if feeble. Brainchild was so entangled in apprehension that he was not only psychically broadcasting everything he wanted to conceal, but doing so in such a way that he was unaware of her eavesdropping.

An adjustment, eh? Psylocke gazed carefully at Sauron. With the final boost of lifeforce, he no longer exuded the orderly, sedate mental flows she had witnessed earlier in her captivity. His aura was popping with spikes of crimson anger, swirling with brown tornadoes of confusion, and more than anything, glittering with the prismatic sheen of the two personalities within.

No. Wait.

Betsy's almond eyes opened wide. Not two layers. *Three.* The creature possessed an additional personality beyond that of Karl Lykos and Sauron. This third identity blanketed the other two the way the Angel of Death persona had once overlaid Warren's true self, back when Apocalypse had wrought his evil handiwork.

She understood fully now why this new Sauron had not moved against the X-Men until she, Psylocke, had been neutralized. Had she been able to get close and scan him before her powers had been drained, she would have understood immediately what had allowed him to stifle the insanity of his other selves and take up a fresh campaign of conquest.

Brainchild's anxiety was well-placed. The latest infusion of power had altered the balance within Sauron. The third, overlaid psyche had already siphoned as much energy as it could use; much of Iceman's strength had gone not to it, but to the dormant personas. Somewhere deep down, Karl Lykos was stirring. In the shallows, the other, manic Sauron was contaminating the calm, transcendent version that had outfought the X-Men so thoroughly these past few days.

Brainchild tapped instructions into the console in front of him. A hum emerged from a series of prongs that jutted from the ceiling, near the light fixtures. Psylocke had wondered what the devices might be; Brainchild had outfitted the chamber with so many odd accouterments that the place hardly seemed a part of the Savage Land at all, except for the natural subterranean walls and the animal-skin attire of the guards.

Sauron closed his eyes, shook his long, narrow head, and drew in a deep breath. The psychic gale around him calmed to a fitful, weakened storm. To her surprise, Psylocke began to feel soothed as well. The prongs were emitting some sort of whisper. Not the sort of thing one could hear with one's ears, but compelling to someone who possessed the mind of a psi. The murmur reminded Betsy of the white noise of a waterfall, nature's own sedative. Many was the time she had fallen asleep as a child to the lullaby of the fountain outside her bedroom window back in England.

"Very well," Sauron said. "I won't have to execute you for insolence just yet."

Brainchild gulped.

Gaza's deep voice rumbled. "You understand, do you not? We don't want you to revert to what you were when we found you this past season."

Sauron gazed at the titan with his baleful orbs. Gaza almost tripped over Amphibius while backing away.

"You think I have forgotten?" Sauron murmured.

"No, Master," Gaza said quickly. "I did not mean that at all."

"Ah," Sauron said, this time with a hint of diplomacy and forgiveness. "You were concerned for me. I see. Sometimes I forget the debt I owe you all."

Gaza visibly relaxed. The other mutates released pent-up breaths.

"Do not worry, my faithful brood," the villain said. "I have not forgotten."

Abruptly Psylocke was inundated by powerful impressions. They poured from Sauron as if he had momentarily lost control of his hypnotic ability to project thoughts. Betsy had been sucked into telepathic contact with him without intending it. Hurriedly she severed the feedback loop that would have alerted him to her conscious monitoring. Then she exited his mind. Though she wanted to probe him, this was not the time or the way. Had she not fled, he would have become aware of her within moments despite her precautions. She had to wait until the advantage was hers.

In the instant of contact, she received and memorized recollections so vivid she would sooner forget incidents from her own life. There were two scenes that stood out above all others. In the first, Karl Lykos, still a young man—and still human save for his vampiric hunger—lurked in an alley in Brooklyn. He waited until a derelict, besotted by wine, staggered through the trash heaps and flopped down on the grate of a heating vent to sleep. Lykos drained the unshaven, sour-smelling individual of energy, assuaging his addiction, but reinforcing his self-contempt.

In the other image, a pteranodon-man wandered aimlessly across the Savage Land, barely aware of his surroundings and completely unsure of his own identity. He skirmished with wild pterosaurs during attempts to scrounge food from them. He was harassed by velociraptors, lions, jackals. He sat exposed in the frequent, monsoonlike downpours, all because he had forgotten how to take shelter from inclement weather. He was tortured by fragmentary reveries of battles fought or of a blonde, vibrant lady that he had loved with all his heart. What he endured was not life; it was merely existence.

The Sauron currently sharing the cavern with Psylocke abhorred the prospect of reverting. Even more than the shame of taking up life as guilt-ridden Karl Lykos, he feared a fate like that of the drunk in the Brooklyn gutter—a victim, useless to anyone including himself. That's all he had been. A homeless automaton. The Savage Land's own version of an enfeebled psychotic who had forgotten to take his medication and could no longer recall his address.

Sauron closed his eyes, sighed, and when he opened them, he was smiling grimly, like a soldier after a firefight, who has checked himself carefully and discovered that none of the blood on his fatigues is his own, and that he truly has survived.

Betsy gritted her teeth in annoyance. The crisis had passed.

Had she possessed her powers, she was certain she could have pushed him over the edge somehow. The third personality lacked the spectral anchors typical of organic astral selves. It was artificial—truly just an overlay. Brainchild had somehow managed to make it dominant, but that did not mean it was securely attached, nor as durable as the others.

She recalled the probe she had made of Lupo's mind. Amid those glimpses she had seen Brainchild studying books and texts on computer screens that Magneto had provided. One of the book titles finally came into focus: *The Three Faces of Eve*. The tale of the very first diagnosed case of what became known as Multiple Personality Disorder. Psylocke had read it more than once. Not only was it a seminal account of that odd, rare condition, but it spoke to the nature of minds in ways telepaths needed to comprehend in order to gain proper mastery over their power. Charles Xavier had a first edition in his library. He valued it so much he had gone to the trouble of reacquiring the book when Sinister's destruction of the mansion had torched the copy he had owned prior.

Eve suffered from a Jekyll/Hyde existence, spending part of her waking hours as a meek housewife, and part as a licentious, irresponsible barfly. Her therapist had molded a third personality possessed of the moral high standards of the first, with the willpower and imagination of the second. The fusion worked, not only curing the patient, but making her happier and better adjusted than she had ever been. Dr. Leonard Samson had recently performed a similar fusion with Bruce Banner, aka the incredible Hulk—perhaps the most famous sufferer of MPD.

Brainchild had taken it upon himself to serve as Sauron's therapist, setting into motion a treatment program that mimicked what psychiatrists such as Samson had been doing for a generation. The mutate was recalling that herculean effort at that very moment, allowing Psylocke to telepathically sift the story out of him. Sauron had not been a cooperative or typical subject. The ''melon-headed savant,'' as his master had called him, had been unable to make real progress until he had rebuilt and modified Magneto's telepathic teaching devices and created an artificial prime self for Sauron via technological manipulation. The new Sauron was not a true identity at all; he was the old Sauron, playing an assigned role, with a script running constantly at the verge of awareness. Like a method actor who has rehearsed his lines a thousand times, Sauron said the right things and did the right things and, because he believed them to be functions of his own choice, he provided the will and leadership that the brood required.

As Hank would say, *Whatever works.*

Now, how to make the actor step off the stage? The inhibitor collar prevented her from attacking the construct directly. But psychic brute force wasn't the only means to victory. Psylocke dipped into her trove of battle knowledge and strategy and concocted a plan.

But did she dare set a counterattack in motion just yet? The timing seemed propitious in that Sauron was still thoroughly energized. His repressed selves were clutching more bits of vitality from the matrix with each passing minute. A nudge in the right place, and they might be able to break loose. But was that desirable? If Sauron's true self came out on top, he would be as deadly as this one, if not more so. If Karl Lykos emerged, the mutates would restrain him, and the X-Men would be no closer to liberty. If both rose up and engaged in a fight for dominance, the resulting lunatic might become so volatile and uncontrolled that he would kill the captives, either by accident or as part of some irrational, homicidal impulse he couldn't control.

Let sleeping pteranodons lie?

Betsy. Warren's mental voice interrupted her deliberation.

Yes? She glanced toward her lover, who tilted his head toward Iceman.

Bobby's been trying to tell me something, but I can't lip-read well enough, and the guards are watching us too closely to be more obvious with the attempt.

Iceman was still groggily holding his head up, spared another blackout thanks to the premature end to the energy pilferage. Betsy caught his eye, nodded at him, and eased open a telepathic channel.

My power's not completely dampened, she explained. *What is it? What can you tell us?*

The initial contact swam with impressions of pain. Betsy helped him shift the worst of that aside and generate a clear transmission. Her mind filled with the whole story of the past twenty-four hours, from the fruitless chase after Amphibius to his own capture by the main horde of mutates. Her heart leapt when she came to the part about Hank and Sam splitting off to search for Sauron in the higher elevations. She knew from scanning Brainchild that that was exactly where this prison cavern was.

Thank you, Bobby. This is excellent news.

If help was imminent, that erased her questions of when to push Sauron. The time had come. She withdrew, composed her message, and prepared to alert her comrades one by one—her weakness still did not allow large-group telepathy—so that they would be ready to do their parts.

Her fists closed.

• • •

LAW OF THE JUNGLE

Warren listened to Betsy's plan and knew exactly how to do his part. He bid her telepathic presence a fond farewell and watched the expression of the others subtly shift as she relayed her communiqué to each of them in turn.

Sauron, for his part, was not cooperating with their hopes. He turned from his consultation with Brainchild and the others and ambled back among his captives with confident, almost bouncy strides.

"Quite a refreshing development, when I stop to consider it," Sauron declared. "My larder is so abundant, I have to go on a diet."

Brainchild and Amphibius laughed with him. Stiffly, Warren thought. Like children whose abusive father has just made a joke, but who are never quite sure when the hand will rise again to slap them.

"I hardly need to capture any more of you," the villain continued. "It would only encourage me to overeat still further. Bad, very bad, for my health."

"You won't catch any more of us, bub," Wolverine said.

"Now why would you say that?" Sauron asked amiably. "When I and my fine helpers have proven so effective against the rest of you?"

"Just a hunch."

Sauron reached out with a talon and scratched the stubble on Wolverine's chin. Logan lunged. The straps around his shoulders limited his head movement to mere inches. His teeth snapped shut just shy of Sauron's retreating figure.

Sauron chuckled.

Logan spat. The glob landed squarely on his enemy's beak, right between the nostrils.

Barbarus rushed forward and raised both right fists to pummel Logan. Sauron permitted the first pair of blows to land—

one on the X-Man's jaw, the other in his midsection—before he gestured his lackey away.

"When next I am in need of a repast, I will sup upon your lifeforce," Sauron announced. "And if I do so more abruptly and painfully than usual, think of this incident."

"You know, my cheek's bleedin' inside now," Logan grunted, voice constricted by pain. Archangel estimated that Barbarus's attack would have broken Logan's jaw and three or four of his ribs, had his teammate's bones been capable of breaking. What it had done to his flesh was ugly. Sometimes Warren could not comprehend Logan's tolerance for bodily mayhem. Especially at times such as this, when his healing factor was negated. "Get in range again and what I spit will be red."

"You are pathetic," Sauron replied. His tone was still superior, his attitude generally unruffled, but Archangel sensed the first hint of impatience. A seed. Now to make it grow.

"You're as worthless as when your mind was fried, greenbeak," Logan continued. "You need crib notes to figure out which is your tail and which is your—"

"Look who's talking." Sauron cackled exuberantly. "Over the course of your life, you've learned far more about losing your mind than I. Or do I have the reports wrong? Did you have a mind to begin with?"

"I had enough brains to outsmart you last time we tangled," Wolverine said. "And—"

"Enough," Sauron snapped. "You bore me." He leaned forward, radiating hypnotic power from his eyes. "I command you to be silent!"

Wolverine shut his mouth. His Adam's apple quivered with the words he would have said, and his eyes projected a new stream of insults, but no sound leaked out of him.

Warren gnawed his inner lip, waiting for his opportunity. A little more patience. Just now, it was Ororo's turn.

"Not everything has been proceeding according to your design, has it?" Storm asked. "I saw the frustration in your servant's expressions when they brought Iceman in. You expected the Beast and Cannonball would fall with him."

Sauron's pupils glinted. "And if I did? It is of no concern that they are free. Merely a nuisance to set the trap twice. Should I be afraid? The Beast is the least super-powered of all the X-Men who came to the Savage Land. Cannonball is but a stripling. I once popped his bubble just so." The creature set the sharp, sturdy tip of a wing to Ororo's bare midsection, pressing lightly enough to avoid drawing blood, but firmly enough to inflict pain.

"All the more reason to be worried over how he feels about you now," Storm countered.

"I prefer enemies with whom I am acquainted," Sauron retorted. "Look here." He drummed his fingers along Archangel's well-muscled belly. "The more I see of our special Mr. Worthington, the more I appreciate his nature. Here he is, blue and surgically altered, and yet still the same frightened child I met all these years ago."

The villain had spared Warren the need to call attention to himself. "And you are the same old fool you've been all along. It takes two of you to make half a person."

"So says the would-be hero with a plethora of extra identities of his own. Angel of Death, carefree playboy, bench player on a multitude of teams. You are nothing, Warren Worthington, when placed against me."

The longer the conversations went on, the cockier Sau-

ron's boasts became. Like the old days. Like the enemy the
X-Men had defeated more than once.

"Try me," Warren challenged. "Here I am, drained and
collared, and you still can't take me down all the way, unless
you kill me."

"You think not?" Sauron asked ominously.

"Master," Brainchild called. "He is only trying to agitate
you. It is not . . . productive . . . to let him do so."

"Keep your place," Sauron commanded. "If you want me
to 'relax,' my friend, so I shall. In good time. When I have
concluded the day's entertainment. I am not agitated."

A lie, Warren heard Psylocke say in his mind. He didn't
need her input to know that the villain was feeling the stress.

He gave Betsy a non-corporeal hug. She would be with
him continually now, not just through the psionic link, but
with her regular telepathy as well. As much as she could
muster. What better support to inspire him to put his head
into the lion's mouth?

"I long ago took your measure," Warren quoted. "And
found you wanting."

"You have earned yourself a new dose of humiliation,"
Sauron hissed. His eyes danced with the slight wobble they
exhibited whenever he used his hypnotism.

Warren would rather have endured one of Vertigo's nau-
sea-provoking assaults than have to face those eyes again.
Spears of mental force jabbed deep into his brain. He fought
to remember to breathe. His heart kept beating only because
he concentrated on the rhythm. He couldn't feel his extremities, much less command the limbs to do anything.

But the link to Psylocke held, a bright filament around
which he could anchor his courage. He tried to send her a
message, even a single word or image, but could not. No

matter. It was enough to know she could send something to him, when the time came.

"You will do exactly as I say," Sauron said. "I am going to release you. When you are loose, stand and wait for your next instructions. Do nothing else."

"Master . . ." Brainchild began.

"Release his bindings!" Sauron insisted.

Brainchild cringed. He waved two of the guards forward. They tilted the slab to vertical and began unlatching the shackles that kept Warren trapped. As each curved metal band was lifted away, Archangel attempted to defy his instructions. He had been ordered to stand, so he would try to collapse. That was what he felt like doing anyway.

The resistance was tremendous. Warren's spine remained straight as a board. His knees did not buckle. But he knew he was making some sort of headway. Psylocke's voice murmured steadily deep down, not drowned out as he had feared would happen. He was conscious of wanting to disobey, even if he couldn't get his body to accept his directives.

During his battles with Sauron, the hypnosis had been devious, sneaking up on him and causing him to do things before he was aware of the influence. This time it was stifling and twice as powerful, but he found it easier to fight back, because he could devote his effort entirely to the mental side of the altercation. In the thick of the airborne engagements, he had been unable to make full use of the psionic countermeasures Professor X, Jean Grey, and Betsy had schooled him in over the years.

His head dropped.

"Straighten up," Sauron commanded.

Warren lifted his chin from his chest. When the guards set him on the stone floor and backed away, he remained upright, as requested. He couldn't defy one of Sauron's direct orders, but he had proved he could whittle around the edges of obedience.

"Go to the well and fetch me a dipper of water," Sauron commanded.

Warren set out for the side of the chamber where Pibah had acquired the supply with which she washed the captives. He searched for a means to resist. Ah, yes. Sauron had not said how quickly to travel. He slowed his walk to a tortoise shuffle.

"Faster!" Sauron yelled.

He sped up. But Sauron did not say by how much, so he merely doubled his pace. That was still as slow as an old man with a cane.

Sauron did not demand another increase. Repeating the order would make the villain appear as though he lacked total control over his subject, and he didn't want to fuel that impression. Warren chuckled inwardly, knowing his resistance was creating a fly buzz in the creature's pterosaurian ears.

"Be sure you fill the bucket," Sauron said. He had anticipated the X-Man's next act of defiance, which would have been to fetch only a spoonful. No matter. Warren would just have to think of something else.

Ahead lay a discarded possum rib that one of the guards had been gnawing on earlier. Warren adjusted his gait so that he would step on it—seemingly demonstrating that he was unable to direct his own actions, but actually reinforcing an advantage. The bone dug into his heel, cutting only slightly into his skin but producing a sharp twinge. The pain distracted him, thereby pulling him further from Sauron's mental whispers.

He sensed the observation of his comrades, silently cheering him on. As agreed, they were not harassing Sauron, tempting though that might be. Far better to let any failure of his hypnotic coercion seem to come entirely from a single opponent's rebuff. Assistance was only valuable if it were a secret, like Psylocke's telepathic bolstering.

Warren lowered the bucket into the well and raised it again. He left it full to the brim, so that water splashed on the limestone, the messiness serving as a metaphor for Sauron's handling of the situation.

"Fill a dipper and bring it to my lips to drink. Do so respectfully, spilling none, with a smile on your face."

You don't have any lips, Warren thought, but he did as asked. Sauron was growing careful not to leave room for sabotage in his instructions.

Sauron slurped noisily, dramatically, and turned to grin at his other captives. "You have been a dull audience, but I can't tell you how gratified I am that you have witnessed this. Think of it as a demonstration of the way things will be for the rest of your pitiful lives."

The mutates burst into applause. Warren was certain he heard a collective sigh of relief beneath all the clapping.

"Very good, Mr. Worthington," Sauron said. "Now lean yourself back against your slab and let my assistants fasten you down again."

Now, Psylocke said. Warren felt a pulse of new mental energy. It seemed to soak into his heart and grow richer.

Warren spread his wings. To do so required only an instant of control; Sauron could not possibly suppress him each and every moment. With the wings unfolded, the guards could not position him against his platform.

"Close your wings!" Sauron rasped.

He wanted to say, "No," but that required strength he didn't have. Keeping the wings apart, however, required only that he tune out.

On cue, Psylocke shut down Warren's voluntary muscle

control. It was something he could not have managed on his own, nor could she have done it without his cooperation unless she had wielded her psychic knife. But together, even as weak as they were, it worked.

It was a gamble. It risked tipping Sauron off that his enemies were commingling their efforts.

But Sauron did not pause to reflect. "Fold them! Now!" he shouted.

Warren could not have tucked his bionic appendages now even if he had wanted to. His body remained frozen even as Sauron leaned in and focussed his power to a pinpoint.

Agony. Warren recoiled mentally. The onslaught of compulsion came through in vivid, irresistible waves, unhindered by his paralysis. Within a heartbeat all he wanted to do was obey. Unable to do so, he could only suffer.

When he didn't get the result he was after, Sauron screeched maniacally. He raised his talons.

We did it, Psylocke transmitted to Storm. *He's fallen into a chaotic mental pattern. Time to break off before he suspects what we've been up to.*

Betsy released the block in Warren's hindbrain. Instantly his wings snapped shut. He flopped back against the slab. The relief was so acute he moaned.

Sauron's hand slowed as it came down. His nails dug shallow gashes down Warren's naked chest, but did not lay open his sternum as it would otherwise have done. The villain stepped back, regarded the blood on his fingertips, and scowled. His bushy eyebrows rendered the expression almost comical, but Warren wasn't prompted to laugh. His enemy was shaking, on the verge of some sort of explosion, held back only by the absolute need to believe he was in command.

Should he follow through? It would be suicide. But if that's what it took to finish the job . . .

"I long ago took—"

"*Be silent!*" Sauron shouted.

Warren's mouth closed. There was no defying the order. Had those few words been enough?

No. Sauron turned and paced down the row of victims, glaring. He jerked and mumbled in answer to inaudible conversation, but his breathing grew steadier. Brainchild's apparatuses in the ceiling were emitting a psionic lullaby again, this time strongly enough that even a non-telepath like Warren heard the hum.

"What is wrong, O high lord and master?" Ororo mocked. "Could it be that Archangel was the stronger, after all? Are you so afraid of his mere words?"

Sauron clutched for Storm's throat, only to bruise his hand against the inhibitor collar and the shackle that stood in the way. The obstacles saved her larynx from being crushed.

"So it's true?" she asked. "You *are* afraid."

"Don't listen to her, Master!" Brainchild yelled.

Sauron whirled toward his underling. "Do not use that tone with me! I am Sauron! I am the engineer of this victory! They cannot defeat me!"

"Then prove it," Ororo said. "Let Archangel speak."

Sauron closed his eyes, shuddered, and flapped his hand and wing dismissively. "Very well. Speak if you dare, Worthington. Say whatever you wish."

The manacles of the compulsion fell away. The ball of invisible cotton that had filled Warren's throat came up in a huge cough.

Warren knew exactly what he wanted to say. With his opponent finally prepared to listen, the X-Man proceeded sedately, composing his message step by step.

"I remember a woman. She was blonde and strikingly beautiful. I remember being enchanted by her bone structure. Almost elfin, I guess you would call it. Narrow chin, a soft, smooth throat, collarbones so gracile I was afraid they would break if I should shake her hand too hard. But she wasn't weak. I saw her trudging hardily along a snowbound trail that would have wearied an experienced mountaineer. I was there when she hiked across the Savage Land, being chased by giant reptiles and flung off cliffs, and still she kept going. All to find and help the man she loved."

Sauron stood rigid in front of Archangel, gazing back balefully but without applying his hypnotism. Warren had the distinct sensation his listener was attending to happenings far away, either in space or in time.

"Tanya. Yes, yes," Sauron said impatiently. "Psylocke already tried to roll that subject in like some sort of Trojan horse. Is that the best you can do?"

"She was unswervingly loyal to you, Lykos. Never stopped worshipping you from puppy love all the way up to sharing an apartment with you in Greenwich Village. In spite of all her father's opposition to the romance. In spite of all that time you hid from her down here by the South Pole. She used to drop me notes every once in a while, did you know that? In every one she would tell me how happy your lives were after the Professor managed to chase your mutate virus into remission. Seems to me she mentioned the two of you planning on having a child."

"That is past. Part of another reality," the monster said in a monotone. "I am not Karl Lykos. I never will be again."

"Why should that change your feelings for Tanya Anderssen?" Warren responded. "At first, even in your Sauron form, you craved her love. You cared for her safety."

"I spent my youth trying to be worthy of her love. Yet

when my power manifested, she refused to see how much better it made me. She wanted only that pathetic weakling. She was a fool. What does it matter if there is one less fool in the world?''

"It matters," Warren said. "I know you still love her. You try to deny it only because of the guilt you feel. If not for you, she would be alive. So much easier for you to pretend she never existed, or if her face turns up in your mental yearbook, you turn the page as fast as you can, ignoring the stains of your tears upon her picture."

"I didn't kill her," the monster said hoarsely. "The Toad captured us, made me do it. I had no choice."

At last, he was cracking. Warren licked his dry lips and kept pushing. "Oh? I thought you said you didn't care. Thought you were proud of how you sucked every last bit of lifeforce from her cells."

"I—"

"Well, which is it, Lykos? Are you glad she's dead, or do you mourn her after all?"

"I am not to blame!" he replied sharply. "If not the Toad, then it is you X-Men who opened the trapdoor through which she plunged. Your mutant energies made me Sauron in the first place. And you—Angel, Archangel, or whatever you want to call yourself—you brought Tanya here to the Savage Land when I had come to terms with my curse. You brought the two of us together that time. Her ultimate fate is a result of your actions."

"Don't think I don't lie awake at night sometimes, thinking of that," Warren said solemnly. "I tried to talk her out of conducting that search. Tanya was unstoppable. You know that, Karl. She would have come without me. The only thing that could have stopped her from being reunited with you, was you. And you stopped her, Karl. Forever."

Sauron opened his huge mouth and hissed. Warren was certain he was looking at his own demise. He suddenly felt his nakedness. One thrust of a wingtip into his viscera, one talon slash into his jugular vein, and he would be the latest X-Man to die. Sometimes the team joked at all the members who had eluded death when it seemed inevitable, but it was no joke. Warren was not the deathless horseman of the Apocalypse he had once posed as. Mutant or not, he was mortal. His time would come. Was it now?

Psylocke's voice suddenly filled his mind. *We lost the momentum,* she reported. *He started stabilizing as soon as the subject of Tanya came up. Brainchild must have realized that particular guilt was his worst weakness, and constructed some sort of extra safety net.*

Warren blinked. So prepared for a physical assault, he found it a shock to feel his future open up ahead of him once more.

Sauron turned and stalked down the row. With each step he grew more steady and composed.

"No, I will not defeat myself again," the villain said passionately. "I have come too far for that."

Brainchild whimpered with relief. Ka-Zar and Shanna and Ororo all released the breaths they had been holding. It appeared nearly everyone else in the room had been primed for the murderer's lunacy to explode into full blossom.

"I detect an odor of trickery," Sauron said. He stopped pacing when he came even with Psylocke. "Brainchild . . ." he murmured.

"Yes, Master?"

"Your inhibitor has a flaw. This witch has somehow managed to awaken a spark of her power."

The little mutate swallowed hard. He checked a display on his monitor. "It . . . is possible, Master. I did tell you last month that I couldn't be certain the inhibitor would fully dampen a telepath unless I had a telepathic ally to check my work. Whatever she may be doing is very muted, my lord.''

"But it has been enough to give this group an advantage I did not anticipate." Sauron leaned toward Betsy, tonguing the sharp edge of his lower beak. Warren was reminded of a cat grooming its fur while it contemplates pouncing on the gopher it has just cornered far from its burrow. "Hasn't it, my dear?"

"Need a toothpick?" Betsy jeered. "Oh, I forgot. You don't have teeth."

Sauron guffawed. "It gives me such pleasure to hear such gumption, and know that it gains you nothing whatsoever." Warren was discouraged to see the vivacious humor characteristic of the new Sauron surfacing once again

"Except self-respect," Psylocke replied. "But you wouldn't know anything about that."

Sauron didn't deign to respond. He placed his face directly in front of her and began generating a fresh hypnotic spell.

Betsy closed her eyes. He lifted the lids and succeeded in locking her gaze to his. Betsy's telepathic expertise and ingenuity couldn't compensate for her depleted level of power.

"You will destroy whatever mental construct you made that allowed you to circumvent Brainchild's inhibitor device," Sauron said. "Do it now."

Psylocke cried out. Lines of strain deepened on her forehead and around her eyes. Inside Warren's mind, the link to his beloved abruptly snapped. The recoil careened through him like one of Vertigo's blasts. Where there had been a comforting, constant whisper and glimmer, now there was a silent void.

Archangel fell unconscious. Awakening almost immediately—he guessed two or three seconds later—the shock was

replaced by an ache. The adjustment reminded him of the
return of the ability to see objects in a dark room after a
bright lamp has been shut off. Enough input to function, but
never enough to make up for the deprivation.

Warren filled his eyes with Betsy's face, since he could
no longer fill his mind with her presence. But that was like
looking at a photograph, instead of touching the real person.
He choked down bile. He would have wept, except that
would have given Sauron too much satisfaction.

Betsy had been knocked out as well, more profoundly. She
stirred later, and took longer to open her eyes. Her glance
darted toward Warren. Seeing that he was all right, she
turned and gave Sauron a glare full of more hatred than Warren had ever believed her capable of.

Sauron nodded, smiled, and checked the other captives.
They bore the grimaces of psychic backlash, though not as
severely as the two lovers. The villain hummed jubilantly.

"Such treachery deserves a special reward," Sauron declared. "Since it seems I have more than enough mutants to
sustain me for the indefinite future, perhaps I am better off
without the lovely Ms. Braddock. Who knows what sort of
deceit she might manage? I do not take kindly to being agitated the way I was just now. I think I shall kill her. Yes.
Quite slowly. We have the means to prolong her agony. Lupo
or Brainchild would appreciate a little . . . sport."

"No, Lykos!" Warren shouted. "If you want one of us
dead, take me."

"Stuff and nonsense," Sauron retorted. "I want to watch
your expression as your lady is whittled down, one bone or
strip of flesh per half hour." He pranced over to the group
of mutates. "Shall we begin?"

"Master," said Gaza, "shouldn't we wait until we've
caught Cannonball and the Beast?"

LAW OF THE JUNGLE

Sauron frowned. "Ah. Those two. I had almost forgotten. I see no reason not to have our fun here and take care of that loose end at the same time. That is, if for example you, Barbarus, and Vertigo want to miss this wonderful oppor—"

The cavern began shaking.

"What?" Sauron blurted.

A deep rumble cascaded down the large tunnel that led to the cave opening. Guards suddenly burst into the chamber, eyes wide, shouting. The noise of stomping feet and elephantine trumpeting drowned out their words.

A stampede of mammoths crashed into the room, sweeping aside warriors, bales of food, random pieces of equipment, and anything else in their way save the sturdy array of platforms on which the X-Men resided. Sauron squawked and shot upward so suddenly he bumped his head against the side of a stalactite. Brainchild ducked behind his console, joined by Vertigo. Amphibius hopped away, Lupo scrambling in his wake. Gaza and Barbarus tried to meet the charge head on, but even their strength paled in comparison to the beasts—they barely vaulted atop sets of tusks in time to avoid being squashed.

Warren's heart began pounding hard. "Yes!" he cried.

Logan grinned. "Incoming!"

Right behind the last mammoth, roaring and swiping at their woolly rumps to urge them to top speed, came Zabu. He broke off once the huge animals were all in the chamber, attacking guards directly. He roared at Ka-Zar.

Ka-Zar roared back.

Zabu was barely out of the way when a blue-yellow blur rocketed onto the scene.

"Over here, Cornball!" Wolverine shouted.

Cannonball had just enough time to catch sight of his

bound teammates before he rebounded off the far wall and aimed for the console. Or, more to the point, aimed for Vertigo, the mutate who could throw the biggest monkey wrench into the rescue attempt if she had a moment to apply her talents. He knocked her down just as she was starting to rise. Brainchild eluded him, but the console did not. It shut down with a flash of sparks.

"Good boy, junior," Archangel said to himself. "Got her." And he had wiped out the inhibitor field. The collar around Warren's neck ceased its subtle vibration. A whisper of power and strength awoke deep inside his body.

Sauron swooped and bashed at Sam on the next rebound. Cannonball's kinetic envelope protected him well as ever, but the impact sent him bouncing to a far corner. Sauron was thrown into a loop-de-loop.

They had to take the green-winged freak out of action, Warren knew. If he got enough of a break to apply his hypnotism, he could make Sam drop his blast aura. Warren tensed against his shackles, fervently wishing one of his teammates happened to be the Thor or the Hulk.

"Have no fear. Dr. McCoy is here!" called a gruff, wonderfully familiar voice. Warren hadn't seen the Beast race into the cavern, but there he was, bounding to the platforms. He went straight for Wolverine, freeing the Canadian's wrists to allow a certain set of adamantium claws the freedom to slash.

Snikt! The blades burst from the backs of Logan's hands. He grinned ferally. "Payback time!"

CHAPTER 14

A s Wolverine slashed away the rest of his own shackles, the Beast leapt toward Shanna's platform. A warrior who had somehow eluded the mammoth stampede was rearing back his arm to bash her with a stone axe.

"Unpleasant dreams," Hank said, and slammed both feet into the brute's chest. The opponent crashed onto the stone floor, emitting a satisfying grunt of pain and rolling into a limp pile.

Keeping alert for more such unwelcome harassment, Hank hurried to unlatch Shanna's cuffs. He had intended to free her and Ka-Zar next anyway, reasoning that they were the most helpless while trapped. Storm, Iceman, and Psylocke could use their powers even before being freed, and Warren could probably toss a wing blade or two, but the two non-mutants were sitting ducks.

"Remind me to kiss you later," Shanna said. She grinned at Hank, slid to the floor, and picked up her assailant's axe, which he had "misplaced" during his tumble. She hobbled toward the group of guards that Wolverine was bloodying. Hank was sure her feet were still asleep from being bound, but that wasn't stopping her.

"I'll collect on that, you can be sure," he called after her. As he freed Ka-Zar he murmured, "You are a lucky husband, sir."

"I know," Ka-Zar replied. Flipping loose the last shackle

around his ankle, he ran to join his mate. Hank dashed over to Archangel.

Barbarus suddenly appeared at the end of the row of slabs. Hank managed to release one of Warren's wrists—hopefully he could do the rest himself—and met the four-armed mutate's charge.

Barbarus, he knew from experience, was horrendously strong. Hank declined to meet him hand to hand. Instead, he chop-blocked him at the knees. The mutate tumbled forward, saved from striking his head on the stone only by putting out all his many palms at once. The slaps sounded like gunshots.

Hank sprang to his feet. Between one heartbeat and the next, he took in a snapshot of the situation just beyond his little battle. Bobby, his powers apparently not as depleted as the other prisoners, had assumed his ice form, turned his shackles brittle, and burst free. Ororo had managed to call up a tiny ice storm to freeze a patch of spilled water on the floor, bringing down Vertigo as she tried to wobble to her feet. With Ka-Zar joining the clash with the main fragment of guards, Logan was rushing off toward the depths of the cavern to deal with something Hank couldn't see.

From the cannon bursts and pterosaurian screeches coming from above, Sam was still managing to keep Sauron occupied. Not a bad start to the rescue. Barbarus, though, was hurtling back at Hank obnoxiously quickly.

The Beast retreated, grabbing his attacker's foremost wrist and rolling him into a somersault. The mutate slammed to the limestone again. "I borrowed that technique from the Japanese art of aikido," the Beast explained. "A logical application of the principles of leverage which—"

Barbarus bounded upright, forcing Hank to abandon an attempt to free Ororo. McCoy ducked beneath one strike, two, then was sent reeling by the third and fourth blows.

LAW OF THE JUNGLE

He saw stars. Where were the garters?

The Beast scampered backwards. "No doubt you are dissatisfied with the lack of a proper wrestling mat," he quipped through swollen lips, taunting his enemy to continue the assault rather than turn and bash Ororo or Psylocke while they were still confined to their slabs.

Barbarus closed the gap. "Yaahh!" he cried, and hammered the Beast with all four fists.

Hank deflected the blows, using his agility to compensate for the disadvantage in strength. It felt like he was knocking aside swipes of Colossus's metal limbs. A trace of panic was taking root when a giant snowball whapped Barbarus in the face. The mutate staggered back, stunned and momentarily blinded. A precise puff of wind, courtesy of Storm, tapped him behind the knees, tipping him over. Then, before Hank could leap in, down came Archangel's wing, rapping him sharply on the skull.

Hank looked up to see Warren releasing the last clamp around his ankle. The winged X-Man dropped to the floor just as Iceman trotted up. The three of them regarded Barbarus, who groaned, tried to lift his head, and passed out.

"Heave ho," Hank said. His old-time teammates reached under Barbarus and hefted their opponent onto the slab that Archangel had just vacated. They rapidly closed the cuffs around him. The shackles designed for Warren's wings took care of the extra arms.

A wave of nausea hit the group. Hank wheeled toward the spot where he had last seen Vertigo. His motion accentuated the dizziness, collapsing him to his knees.

"Oh, no, you don't," he heard an impassioned female voice call. Through blurred vision he saw Shanna leap atop Vertigo. Suddenly the nausea vanished.

But Brainchild was emerging from beneath his console,

straightening up behind Shanna with an axe handle in his grip.

Iceman tossed a rock-hard snowball at Brainchild, catching him just above the ear. He fell.

"Nice pitch," Hank told Bobby.

"No problem. That head's a big target."

Warren, shaking off the last of the aftereffects of Vertigo's interference, flapped into the upper reaches of the cavern, joining the dogfight between Cannonball and Sauron. He did so none too steadily, Hank was sorry to see. His teammates' powers seemed to be returning to full power quite slowly.

"I'll help over there," Hank said, indicating Shanna and Vertigo's tussle. "You finish liberating our fine damsels."

He reached Shanna just as she collapsed to the floor, obviously dizzy. But she took Vertigo with her. The female mutate struck the limestone hard. By the time Hank lifted away from Shanna, she was limp.

"Let's shackle and blindfold her," Hank suggested to Shanna, dropping his burden in a heap.

"Look out!" Shanna said.

The Beast instinctively bounded to the side. Brainchild's axe handle whisked by where Hank's head had been. Then Shanna was on the assailant. Her first blow struck him on the large welt left by the iceball. He yelped, clutched his head, and did a remarkably poor job of avoiding Shanna's followup punches and kicks. He sagged to the floor, dazed and temporarily harmless.

"Now, I'll shackle both of them," Shanna said.

The blaring trumpeting of mammoths echoed through the chamber again. Three of the creatures thundered out of the passageway down which they had disappeared.

"I'll be an orangutan's nephew," the Beast murmured, eyes widening.

LAW OF THE JUNGLE

Atop the lead mammoth was Lupo. Apparently his power to control certain animals had allowed him to quell the fear Zabu had instilled in these members of the stampede. He had turned them around. The barrage of tusks and tree-trunk legs sent the battling guards and Ka-Zar and his sabretooth scrambling to get out of the way.

"Hey!" Hank yelled. "That was *my* trick!"

"Heads up!" Iceman cried. Bobby was suddenly beside Hank. He threw up an ice barrier that shielded the console area, protecting himself, Hank, Shanna, Brainchild, and Vertigo.

The lead mammoth stomped past. Lupo was slapping its ears, trying to get it to obey him completely. So far his efforts appeared futile. The creature rushed on toward the exit.

The other two members of its herd followed close behind. Hank saw for the first time that one of these carried Gaza. Atop the other danced Wolverine. As Gaza swung his club at Logan, Logan swung his claws at the giant. The altercation had not resolved itself before the woolly transports vanished down the tunnel.

"I have a feeling they're going to be back," Bobby said. "We'd better wrap this up. Can't do anything with mammoths tromping through."

"That, my dear Mr. Drake, was the reason we chased the herd in here in the first place," Hank said wryly.

Ororo took charge of the defeated captives, dragging them back to the slabs for confinement. Psylocke joined Bobby and Hank as they charged into the disorganized array of guards. Thanks to Zabu and Ka-Zar—and earlier, to Wolverine, Shanna, and the mammoths—several of the enemy tribesmen already littered the cavern's rough-hewn floor. Psylocke saw to them, plunging her diluted but effective psychic knife into their skulls, ensuring that they would remain unconscious long enough to pose no threat to the outcome of the battle.

Hank pursed his lips, foregoing his usual lighthearted banter. This was the grunt work phase. He tackled a warrior who had just made it back to his feet and held him until Psylocke could minister her touch of grace. Nearby, Bobby tripped others with ice staffs and weighted them down with piles of snow, again until Ms. Braddock could pay a visit.

Killing would be too good for most of them, Hank reflected, knowing how many innocent victims had fallen to these raiders. But some might not be murderers. This way, the bad could later be sorted from the only-slightly-bad. Justice need not be hasty to be well served.

Ka-Zar's fist connected with a huge, gap-toothed warrior, who collapsed, leaving the immediate area clean of enemies. The Lord of the Savage Land sighed, turned to Hank, and shook his head. "If I hadn't been drained of strength and tied up for eighteen hours, I would have taken care of him much faster."

Zabu cornered one last resistor, a middle-aged, scowling woman with breath so disagreeable Hank could smell it from ten feet away. The cat, as ever not one to apply unnecessary violence, backed her against the cavern wall without slashing. She trembled so hard Hank thought her elbows would fall off. Then she looked up and saw Psylocke approaching, and trembled more.

"What goes around, comes around, Pibah," Betsy said, and thrust her intangible weapon between the tribeswoman's eyes. The crone gave up one small whimper and folded into a lump.

Hank nodded. He scanned around. In the lower reaches of the cavern, calm prevailed at last. Ororo had finished shackling the defeated mutates. The greatest source of danger remaining in their midst was a pile of mammoth dung a few steps away, a deposit whose slippery nature had already caused the premature defeat of one of the raiders.

Above, it was a different story. Sauron wheeled about, vigorous and agile despite constant rebounding assaults on the part of Cannonball. Sam was blasting at full speed, ricocheting off stalactites and walls faster than a pinball. The distracted look in Sauron's eyes showed the villain was growing more and more dazed, but so far he had avoided a direct hit.

Warren soared in and out of the tangle, waiting for his moment. His lack of strength prevented him from closing in. Sauron's constant changes of direction and Sam's frequent interference prevented Archangel from casting his wing knives.

Beside Hank, Iceman grimaced. "He's moving too fast. Don't know where to put my ice."

"Raise some walls and divide the cavern into smaller sections," Hank suggested. "Eventually Sauron won't have any maneuvering room."

"Okay," Bobby said. "Don't know how fast I can do that, though. I'm still awfully depleted."

"Just—"

The cavern began rumbling again.

"Here come the mammoths!" Hank cried. "Clear a path!"

The group rushed to yank inert bodies out of the center of the chamber. Iceman strained to erect guard rails, providing the stampede with a track. Hank hoped the animals would follow it.

The three behemoths roared from the tunnel as red-eyed as ever. They were moving slightly slower. Tiring at last. Lupo was firmly ensconced on the lead bull, but his yips and howls and gestures made it clear he still had no real control.

The battle atop the other two animals continued to rage. Claw marks scored Gaza's arms. Wolverine's scalp was matted with blood. Just as the combatants whisked past the huddled clump of X-Men, Logan buried his claws like skewers in Gaza's club and yanked.

Gaza let go too slowly. Unbalanced, he tumbled off the rear end of the mammoth. Wolverine stayed with his beast. He was still working the club off his claws when he disappeared once more down the passageway, a tusk-length behind Lupo.

Gaza sat up. He did not look pleased.

"How generous of our confederate to share his bounty with us," Hank declared. He charged in. His kick knocked the mutate over before he could fully straighten up.

"Whuff!" the Beast grunted. Gaza's own kick, from the ground, sent Hank ten feet into the air. The villain had tremendously good aim for someone who had been blind from birth.

Gaza rose to his feet and tried to stomp Hank, but only made it one step. Iceman put a patch of ice in his way, and Ororo buffeted him with a gust. He toppled over. He got only to his hands and knees before Zabu landed squarely on him. The cat remained aboard until Psylocke thrust her ethereal blade into the giant's skull.

Hank rose, rubbing the huge bruise Gaza had raised on his thigh, but grinning. "I like these odds."

They had only an instant to savor the victory. "Oh, no!" Ororo cried.

Hank glanced upward. Cannonball was zooming across the jagged ceiling without his kinetic envelope around him, carried by the momentum of his last ricochet. Sauron screeched in glee.

"He nailed Sam with hypnotism!" Bobby cried out. "Made him drop his blast field!"

Before the Iceman's comments were out of his mouth, Cannonball collided with a stalactite head first. He folded up and fell.

To Hank, the next two seconds happened in telescoped time, so full of incidents that it seemed a much greater span passed. As Cannonball fell, Ororo sent up a wind to catch him. Weakened as she was, all she managed was to cut the speed of his descent. Iceman simultaneously raised his hands to do something, grunted, and began creating a mound of snow on the cavern floor instead.

The Beast jumped directly beneath Sam's plummeting form. He caught him with both arms, scooping him up as expertly as a major-league outfielder catching a fly ball. The impact knocked both of them into the packed powder.

"Didn't have enough juice left to make an ice slide," Iceman reported, and sagged to his knees.

"You did enough," Hank said. He gestured at Sam, who though unconscious, was breathing evenly. "I *told* this young man he needed to wear a helmet."

Sauron's peacock-shrill shrieks pulled the Beast's attention upward. The monster swooped in on Archangel, taking advantage of Warren's spent resources. His long hind feet battered the X-Man in the head. Warren fluttered downward, blinking and clutching at a cut on his temple. He managed a fitful toss of wing blades.

One of the knives sank into Sauron's thigh. The villain screamed and began to spasm, caught in the throes of the projectile's short-circuiting effect. For an instant, Hank thought he would fall along with Warren. Clearly, the fight had drained a great deal of the energy he had stolen from his captives. But he stabilized, pulled out the knife, and cast it aside.

"You haven't won yet!" Sauron cried. The statement was so vehement Hank thought their enemy would race straight toward them. But he soared over to a high ledge and reached into a small niche.

"There's a door up there," Psylocke said.

There was. A section of the stone wall moved away. "I'll be back at a time of my choosing," Sauron taunted, and slipped into a corridor, shutting the portal.

Ororo tried to rise on her winds, but halfway up she groaned and was forced to retreat to the floor. By then, Archangel was able to stand. He launched upward, made it to the ledge, and yanked at the door.

"He's barred it somehow. It would take more firepower than we've got right now to bash through."

Hank dribbled a little snow in Cannonball's face, hoping it would nudge him awake, but the kid didn't stir. Hank regretted that Cyclops or Rogue had not come along on the mission.

"We'll get it open," Bobby said confidently.

"Not soon enough, I fear," said Hank.

The chamber was astonishingly quiet compared to a few moments earlier. Just low moans from Brainchild, an echo of mammoths stomping around somewhere deep inside the mountain, and a faint squawking filtering down a narrow passageway near the well, where he'd seen some of the raiders flee.

"I know that sound," Ka-Zar blurted. "We can still stop Sauron!" He whirled toward Betsy. "How much of your power is back?"

She winced. "Some. I was getting through to him just now. I think that's a big reason he ran away."

LAW OF THE JUNGLE

"Enough to do some damage if you get close?"

"Get me within ten meters of him and he's history," Betsy said fervently

"Come with me!" The Lord of the Savage Land grasped Psylocke by the wrist and sprinted for the small passageway. "Come on, Zabu!"

Shanna sighed. "That man. Never stops to explain. Always trying to do things himself." She took off in his wake, waving Storm and Archangel after her. "We can use anyone who can fly."

The sabretooth took the lead and plunged into the opening. The five heroes followed at their best speed.

Hank and Bobby looked at each other. At their feet, Sam groaned and began rubbing his head like a toddler trying to remember how to wake up from a nap.

"I suppose we're elected to keep things under control here," Hank groused. He gazed at Gaza's prone form. "We'd better drag him to a slab before he gives us any more bruises."

"Hope whatever Ka-Zar's got in mind works," Bobby muttered, grabbing one of Gaza's wrists. He slicked up the floor with ice and began dragging the mutate along the slippery surface.

"Nah," Hank joked. "He just wanted an excuse to run off with Betsy."

Iceman let go of Gaza to rest. "You know, I'm pooped. While the others take care of Sauron, I sure hope Lupo and Amphibius don't give us grief."

"They won't." The speaker was Wolverine, who appeared from the shadows of the cave, sans mammoths, dragging two inert bodies behind him. The captive on his left side had green, slimy skin; the one on the right had dark fur and pointed ears. Hank was surprised to see them both still breathing. He concluded they must have surrendered before Logan got in a really bad mood.

"To the slabs with them all," Hank chirped. He regarded Brainchild's smashed console. Not permanently damaged, from what he could determine at a glance. He picked up a pair of discarded inhibitor collars from the floor. "Let's see if I can get this equipment working again. This crew is over-due for a dose of their own prescription."

As they plunged down the long, twisting passageway, Psy-locke considered reading Ka-Zar's mind to learn what his plan was, but she needed to save up her psychic strength in order to defeat Sauron. She trusted that soon enough, she would know anyway.

And she did. They rounded one last curve and found them-selves in the midst of a pterosaur aerie. The chamber was huge, larger even than the one that had housed the prisoners. Pteranodons and a handful of pterodactyls hopped and flut-tered about on log perches, disturbing great piles of their own droppings. They were blindfolded—probably the only way they could be controlled in such a confined space.

On the far side air flowed in through a gap just wide enough for the largest of the creatures to fly through. The opening was angled downward—it would not have been vis-ible when the X-Men had conducted their aerial surveillance over the previous two days.

Ororo and Warren ran immediately to the slot and jumped. Psylocke's heart stopped beating until she saw Ororo loft upward, feebly but sufficiently supported by her winds.

The only human there in the roost to greet them was a wiry, gray-haired old savage, a long-time pterosaur trainer judging by the talon scars on his arms and legs. He backed up against the wall and put up empty hands when Zabu trotted up to him.

Betsy quickly scanned his mind. Not an active raider, just a devoted keeper of the flying reptiles who had refused to leave his station when his compatriots had fled. "It's all right, Zabu," she called. "He's not a problem."

Zabu flicked his ear at her and coughed a feline acknowledgment. Suddenly she was brushed by a sentient whisper she recalled sensing during her imprisonment. She smiled. Just as she had suspected, it was Zabu's mind she had touched back then. *So that's how Hank and Sam had found the cavern. What a cat.*

"Four or five raiders got away through here during the battle," she related to Ka-Zar. "And Sauron came through just moments ago." She pointed to a narrow opening halfway up one wall, the end point of the escape route the mutate leader had taken.

He nodded. "What's important is that they left some of the squadron behind." He reached up and pulled the blindfold from the sturdy pteranodon he had been soothing. He led it toward the exit. "Ready to fly?"

Betsy glanced at Shanna, who was struggling to calm down another of the flying reptiles.

"She'll come along when she gets that turkey under control. We can't wait for her," Ka-Zar said.

Betsy braced herself, hopped to the front of the saddle, and made room for Ka-Zar. With a sickening lurch, the creature leapt and spread its wings.

A gorge opened up beneath them. They soared so low she could make out individual dragonflies amid the cattails and reeds of the stream below. And those were standard dragonflies, not the monstrosities that lived in the jungle.

"Is this thing strong enough to carry two of us?" she yelled.

"I think so," Ka-Zar shouted into the wind. "We'll find out."

The pteranodon flapped its wings, gained altitude, and found a thermal updraft. Immediately it vaulted toward the roof of clouds high above. The Savage Land appeared in all its glory. Psylocke spotted Storm not far ahead, still within the pleistocene zone. Ororo was wobbling and was keeping low, where she wouldn't have as far to fall if her powers gave out.

Archangel was farther ahead, but not by much. He had barely reached the fringes of the jungle. He was pumping his wings as hard as he could manage, clearly a man with a goal. Betsy looked ahead and saw why. A green, batlike speck out over the swamp could only be Sauron.

Ka-Zar saw it, too, and spurred their mount. The wind blasted the sweat of battle right off Betsy's exposed skin. The pteranodon screeched, obviously angry to be pushed so hard. Luckily, that anger fueled it to even greater momentum. They raced right past Ororo and Warren.

Surely they couldn't catch Sauron. He had a good lead, and no one to carry. But he was merely gliding now, turning in a weary arc out over the great central lake, scattering a flock of cranes.

Ka-Zar changed direction, closing the gap as Sauron continued to follow a curve rather than get as far away as fast as he could.

A chill ran down Psylocke's spine. "He's baiting us. He wants to fight." She was as certain as if she had read Sauron's thoughts.

"If that's so, he's doing us a favor," Ka-Zar declared.

Great minds think alike, Betsy thought. Ka-Zar's breath

was strong against the nape of her neck. She could read his passion and commitment. Victory or death. The clarity of the emotion was like a drug, coursing from his veins to hers and back again.

As they reached the shore of the lake, placing them past the last convenient source of cover, Sauron turned directly at them and began flapping hard. Ka-Zar eased off on the reins of the pteranodon. Psylocke knew he was saving energy and calculating the best evasive maneuver, but she ceased paying attention. She was gathering all her psychic resources into a pinpoint—as focused a measure as calling up her knife.

Her reservoir of power opened, supplying her with only a fraction of her usual allotment. She gritted her teeth. *What you have, you use. No sense worrying about what isn't available.*

Suddenly Ka-Zar groaned. Betsy hissed in pain. A strident hypnotic command pierced them from one side of their brains to the other: *Stay there. Don't move.*

For the span of two heartbeats, Ka-Zar's hands were immobile on the reins. Their mount soared on in a straight line. Sauron bore down. The villain may have been too rattled back in the cavern to cope with Cannonball's fusillade, but he was in the clear now, able to concentrate.

But Sauron, for all his psychic talent, was not a full telepath. She was. She quashed the mesmerizing voice, first in her mind, then in Ka-Zar's.

"Duck!" she blurted.

Ka-Zar jabbed his knees into the pteranodon's sides. The creature tucked its wings. They slid under Sauron's outstretched talons so narrowly Betsy lost several strands of hair.

Sauron screeched and circled back toward them. "So precipitously you pursue me! I am not spent yet! And you are oh, so sluggish aboard that poor, overburdened beast!''

Psylocke put more juice into the mental force field she had erected around herself and Ka-Zar. Sauron had found a way to accentuate his attack—by using spoken words rather than silently projecting his wishes.

"He's trying to intimidate us into giving up," she told Ka-Zar.

"I know. I can feel it. Here's what I say to that!'' As Sauron streaked in, the jungle man hefted the weighted net that had been attached to the saddle and flung it.

The net struck Sauron on the upper beak, forcing him to shut his eyes. Ka-Zar banked the pteranodon and Betsy used a martial arts block to deflect one of Sauron's sharp rear feet. The other foot and its talons gashed the pteranodon's neck.

Their mount screamed. As it rebounded clear of Sauron it began flapping wildly and bucking. Ka-Zar clung tightly to its neck. Betsy clung tightly to Ka-Zar. The landscape wobbled crazily below them.

They were easy targets now. Betsy tried to locate Sauron, but amid the flapping wings and lurching changes of direction, she saw only clouds, horizon, and a great big fall if she lost her grip.

"Veer left!'' called a familiar voice.

Ka-Zar yanked fiercely on the reins. The pteranodon veered left. A shadow passed over them.

Finally, their poor, wounded carrier responded to Ka-Zar's soothing murmurs and his firm hold. As they soared more steadily, Betsy glanced back and saw Shanna spiraling in toward Sauron. The villain had turned and was responding to her attack, momentarily ignoring the initial dogfight.

"My psychic shields can't reach her!'' Psylocke said urgently. "She's vulnerable to his hypnotism!''

LAW OF THE JUNGLE

Even as she spoke, Shanna ceased spurring her flyer. The pteranodon began to coast. The She-Devil came to her senses immediately, but Sauron was closing fast. She ducked, avoiding his talons. Her mount was not so lucky. The monster's claws tore great slices in its leathery wings. It screamed and slid into a nose dive.

"Shanna!" Ka-Zar shouted.

Psylocke swallowed hard. Shanna was unhurt, but she faced a lethal impact on the water below. But the pterosaur feebly extended its tattered wings, gliding/plunging toward the shore. It would make it, if Sauron didn't follow through.

They would just have to make sure of that. "Get me close to him," she told Ka-Zar.

Her ally was already doing so, pulling their flyer into a tight circle with the villain, preventing him from streaking directly at them. To close the gap and slash at them again would require Sauron to stay near for several seconds in a row.

That was the opportunity Betsy had been waiting for.

"No!" Sauron rasped, and squeezed his eyes shut.

Psylocke poured everything she had into the probe. Avoiding the deeply rooted defenses of his natural psyche, she seized the construct Brainchild had crafted and yanked on the places already weakened earlier in the cavern.

Suddenly she recoiled. One of Sauron's organic personalities leapt into coherency. She recognized it just as she was pushed from his mind.

"Lykos!" she screamed. "Karl Lykos! Help us!"

Sauron fluttered, losing altitude rapidly, jibbering and spasming. "I . . . I . . . where . . . ?"

"You are in the Savage Land, Karl!" Ka-Zar yelled. "Tanya is dead by the hand of your alter-ego! Do what you have to do!"

Sauron's eyes bulged. He coughed as if his heart were trying to crawl up his gullet. Abruptly he steadied, hanging in the air.

"I will," he said clearly. His voice was raspy, tortured . . . and human.

He kept the pteranodon shape, but he was no longer Sauron. Moving only to fold up his wings, he plummeted down like a meteorite. The impact of his body on the lake's surface sounded like a thunderclap.

Ka-Zar and Betsy stared silently below. Adrenaline still rushed through their blood vessels, but with no more need for action, their limbs merely shuddered and their mouths quivered, trying to form words.

Below, the splash subsided. A moment later the waters began to churn. Fins, tails, and long, toothed mouths broke the surface. A tremendous host of the lake's predatory fish and prehistoric marine reptiles were gathering. By the time they were done, they would probably have forgotten what prey they had come for, and many of them would be torn to pieces, claimed by a killing frenzy.

Blood welled up, turning the foam from white to pink. Sauron did not surface.

"Rest in peace, Karl," Ka-Zar said.

Betsy sighed. All at once, she realized a new winged shape had appeared, flying low over the water above the carnage. It was Warren. He circled three times, then climbed to join them.

"It seems to be over," he called solemnly. "I saw the bit at the end. Sorry I couldn't make it in time to help." He sounded incredibly weary. It was amazing he was still able to fly, and possibly a blessing that he had not had to fight.

He wasn't the only one weary, thought Psylocke, finally able to acknowledge the dead, wooden stiffness in her bones.

LAW OF THE JUNGLE

She knew without scanning that Ka-Zar was only slightly better off, and only that much because he hadn't had to expend himself using mutant talents.

"Not quite over," Ka-Zar called back. "I need to alert the villagers. We'll want them up at that cavern as soon as possible to deal with our captives and help out in case the mutates have any reinforcements to call upon."

"I can do that," Warren offered.

"I was hoping you could look after Shanna and Ororo."

Glancing back, Betsy saw Storm fluttering down to a shaky landing on the shore beside Shanna and her crippled pteranodon.

Ka-Zar patted his mount's neck, avoiding the gashes. "This animal needs its wounds closed up before it loses too much blood. We'll do that in the village, too. We'll see you when you bring the women in."

"Okay," Archangel said. "We'll be there as soon as we catch our breaths." The X-Man veered off, beginning a long, easy glide toward the shore near the swamp, where Shanna and Ororo were waving.

Betsy called upon the meager remnants of her psychic reserve to telepathically inform her friends of the plan, and then she slumped against Ka-Zar, grateful to have him to lean on as they coasted across the lake toward the territory of the Fall People.

They cruised over the stockade walls amid shouts of excitement from the youths manning the watchtower. The pteranodon flopped to a perch on one of the log benches of the storytelling circle and hung its head, heedless of the antic humans around it. Red rivulets trickled down from its neck. Not, Betsy was gratified to see, as profusely as the leakage had flowed during the battle.

Ka-Zar jumped out of the saddle and helped Betsy down.

Letting go of her, he turned and hailed the approaching warriors. "Victory!" he cried.

Betsy smiled.

The jungle lord explained the situation at the cavern, its location, and details of the battle. Betsy only half-listened, because she needed telepathy to translate the native language and that required too much effort just yet. Soon Tongah and a large knot of strong adult men and women jogged to the gates, leaving other tribespeople to gather needed material and spread the word.

Betsy saw the grim frowns and glinting stares of the warriors and knew that when they reached the enemy stronghold, they would be swift to begin the process of justice. Any raider lucky enough to escape execution would no doubt regret that he had been spared.

A healer began covering the pteranodon's wound with salve and poultices, while his assistants kept the beast calm. Betsy slipped off to the shade of the lodge. Ka-Zar soon joined her there.

"That was a fine coup de grâce you delivered," he said.

She shook her head. "My part was trivial. Sauron and his various alter egos did the real sabotage."

"No. Let's take credit for this one," her companion said. "We deserve it."

She chuckled. "Very well, sir. I thank you for the compliment, and hasten to add that I couldn't have done it without you. If you hadn't realized where to find that pterosaur aerie, the fiend would have gotten away."

She leaned forward, kissed him, then settled back on her heels, smiling.

Betsy noticed for the first time that Zira was standing a mere fifteen feet away, with little Matthew in her arms.

LAW OF THE JUNGLE

Betsy's cheeks grew so hot she could toast marshmallows. Ka-Zar glanced at the swept mud beyond the lodge poles. But Zira merely shrugged and winked.

"Doan whurry," she said, tousling Matthew's hair. "The little whun is too yhung to . . ."—she struggled hard to recall the English phrase, brightening as she did so—"tattle tale."

"Thank God," Ka-Zar muttered softly. "Otherwise we'd all see exactly why my wife is called the She-Devil."

CHAPTER 15

The feast began well before dark and continued into the night. A bonfire crackled in the center of the village of the Fall People. Children and young men and women pranced around the flames, seemingly immune to the jungle heat, laughing and chanting and exuding the aromas of incense and healthy sweat.

A day and a half after the fight, Cannonball was ready to believe they had won. No sign of Sauron had turned up in the lake. The mutates were imprisoned. The cavern had been explored and secured. The raiders, save for a few who had escaped early, were dead or confined to a peripheral grotto for imminent serving of justice.

The village had worked all day to prepare the celebration. Roasted pigs emerged from luau-type trenches. Blankets lay piled high with fruit. Tubs sloshed with beverages, many of them casting off wonderful, yeasty fumes of fermentation. Dancers exhibited the designs they had painted on their bodies. Singers and musicians, especially drummers, provided an exuberant background rhythm.

The X-Men added their touches. At dusk, Cannonball had raced in circles over the huts, glowing like a Fourth-of-July rocket. Not quite the display Jubilee could have put on, but he was proud of it. Now Ororo was air-conditioning the audience with zephyrs of autumnal wind and with spritzes of cool drizzle. Over between the huts, Iceman was renewing a three-foot layer of snow, and laughing as the village children showed their instant expertise at the previously unknown art of snowball fighting.

Allies from neighboring tribes shared in the festivities, but the stockade was only slightly more crowded than normal. Many of the resident warriors were still guarding the cavern, and others were en route to or from. Sam could cover the distance in a fraction of an hour at full-speed blasting, but on foot the journey took a full day even at the marathon pace some of these magnificent athletes could achieve. The Savage Land was vast. Sam, Warren, and Ororo had transported some by air, but couldn't do that for everyone, especially while trying to overcome the deleterious effects of the battle. Sam thought it was too bad the tribes didn't have pterosaurs to use as taxis. The people seemed reluctant to be near the reptiles, even though the mount who had served Ka-Zar and Psylocke so well was treated with respect and indulgence. Sam suspected the raiders had violated some sort of intertribal policy by making use of the creatures in their schemes.

The taste of roast pork and sweet potato clung to Sam's mouth, encouraging him to run his tongue over his lips. Good food, good scene. What more could a Cumberland boy want? Maybe two lovely native damsels, clad in not-much, to rub his bare feet? That was exactly what he had. And a fine job they were doing, too, dabbing his soles with coconut oil and working out kinks he hadn't been aware he had had. Must have come from all that walking in the foothills. With all the flying around he usually did, that ground search had taxed his lower extremities. He leaned back in his half-hammock and let his eyes fall partially closed, listening to the young ladies serenade him with their giggling conversation, all of it unintelligible to him, but intriguingly exuberant.

LAW OF THE JUNGLE

Iceman finished winterizing the playground and strolled back toward his buddy. He plopped down in the neighboring half-hammock.

"How's the headache?" Bobby asked.

Sam lifted the poultice off the bruise on his scalp. "Between the healer's herbs and all those ice packs you helped put t'gether, the swelling's pretty near gone. Considerin' the way I came out of m'last tussle with Sauron, I'm feelin' like a linebacker that's just won the Super Bowl. End of a hard season, but I survived and got m'winner's ring."

"Well, you sure don't look like you're suffering." Bobby grinned, dismissed his ice form, and clasped his hands behind his head. One of the lovely masseuses accommodatingly shifted over to him. He moaned delightedly as she kneaded the callouses on his heel.

"Now I know why you old guys kept the New Mutants under curfew so much," Sam said. "You didn't want us to know what a mint-julep kind o' life you led when we weren't lookin'."

Bobby stared up at the halo of fireflies dancing above the grass roofs of the huts, kept at bay by the smoke of the bonfire. They looked like agitated stars in the oh-so-dark overcast sky.

"The Savage Land has its moments," Bobby declared. "Maybe we should stick around a few more days."

Now that Iceman was in human form, Sam couldn't help but notice all the black-and-blue marks dotting his companion's body, temporary legacies of the pounding he had taken in the swamp. They didn't seem to be annoying Bobby any more than Sam's head and neck insults were distracting him. Not that either of them liked the damage, but right now those aches and pains, in their strange, profound way, made the pleasure and sense of accomplishment that much sweeter.

For the youngest recruit of the team, he had done okay. All the frustration of the first part of the mission, when he never seemed to be in a useful place at the right time, had evaporated. He had made the show after all, keeping the team's hope alive. Sacked the enemy quarterback.

One of these days, he was going to quit worrying about measuring up. A night like this put him most of the way there. He knew he belonged.

He gazed contentedly at his peers—yes, his peers, not his ''seniors''—arrayed throughout the village. Psylocke and Archangel were leaning against the shaman's hut, so lost in rapt conversation that they weren't even watching the Swamp People's fire-eater demonstrating his art a few steps away.

Ka-Zar and Shanna sat cross-legged among the crowd encircling the dancers, elbows intertwined, frequently leaning sideways to nuzzle each other. Little Matthew scrambled from lap to lap.

Sam's eyes widened as he observed a long gaze exchanged between Betsy and Shanna. They smiled like his sisters did when they bonded after a particularly heated argument. Not that Sam's sisters ever bonded very often where witnesses could see.

When they did, it usually meant trouble for everyone else in the family.

But not here. Not now. Tonight was magic.

Ororo was engaged in elegant, subtle weatherworking, the sort of indulgence she could never partake of during the heat of battle, and which had been utterly impossible while she repaired the damage to the Savage Land climate. From her chair inside the village grounds, she gently beckoned stray air currents from the lake, enriched them with moisture, and funneled them miles upriver to the celebration. With a casual gesture, she eased the heat on the brows of the infants in their mother's arms. She misted the hair of the dancers until they flung droplets with each shake of their heads. She banished any pockets of dead air that tried to collect between the huts.

It was so very good to be able to use her power again without feeling as though she were going to faint from the effort.

Hank McCoy emerged from a guest hut, his fur freshly groomed, his eyes far brighter and more alert than when Archangel had ferried him back to base after a long day spent tinkering with Brainchild's devices in the cavern.

"Your work went well today?" she asked.

"The inhibitor equipment seems to be functioning to specifications," he reported. "That Brainchild came up with some remarkable innovations for someone determined to create items of no honorable worth to society. Rather delicious to turn such mechanisms on their designer. I think we can leave the Savage Land confident that the X-Men's presence won't be required to keep him and his fellow mutates under wraps. They won't be bothering anyone while they remain down there, unless it's to annoy the resident bats with their whining."

And how long would that circumstance last? pondered Ororo. The tribal victims of the raiders had agreed that the best punishment, in the near term, would be to force Brainchild, Lupo, Gaza, and the others to endure a stout dose of the suffering and humiliation they had so readily given to others. Yet would the patience of the jailers last more than a day or two? The locals were not the "savages" the outside world assumed, but they lived by a code that did not become entangled in appeal processes, highly paid defense attorneys, and bureaucratic red tape.

"It's good that you could join us," Ororo said. "I was hoping I wouldn't have to order you to come out and have fun."

Hank raised a bushy blue eyebrow. "Speaking of which, shouldn't you put down your magic weather wand and partake of your own council, O goddess of the rain?"

She laughed. "Oh, Henry, I *am* having fun. I'm not exactly deskbound at a police station, filling out arrest reports, now am I?"

"True. And I might add that if you reported to work at a police station dressed like that, your boss might well arrest you." He turned and waved to Bobby and Sam. "We all refresh ourselves in our own way. I suppose to a deity and a leader of the team, what you're doing constitutes surcease from your labors, but to me you still appear preoccupied with the general population's comfort and welfare."

She blinked. Come to think of it, she had been tending to responsibilities a great deal that day, making sure matters were properly dealt with. It was her way of balancing the frustration of the weather disruption and her own capture.

"You did well," the Beast said. "Given the challenges Sauron and his brood had thrust in your way, only a perfectionist would quibble with any part of your performance these past few days. And you know of whom I speak. As Rogue would say, 'Lighten up, sugar. All's well that ends well.' "

A perfectionist? Ororo preferred the term "responsible" or "dedicated." But Hank had a point. This was a proper juncture to stop worrying about leadership or justice or consequences, and give herself a moment to just "be."

"Well, my friend," she said to Hank, tucking her arm in his elbow and strolling toward the heaped food for a second helping. "What would you recommend a lady such as I do to relax?"

"Why, when I am in need of serious recuperation, a rousing game of chess is just the thing. Ka-Zar has a very fine set of pieces, did you know? Had them made in England from some mastodon ivory that he donated."

Ororo chuckled. "Ka-Zar has a surprising number of modern-world possessions, tucked here and there. Shanna had some testy words to say about it at lunch."

"Oh, yes. The ladies' gab session down by the hot springs. How did that go?"

"I can't tell you. You're one of the boys." Ororo waved her hand above her head, gave the cooling breezes a burst that would keep them going a while without further attention, and pulled the Beast toward the lodge. "All right. A game of chess. But you know you'll win."

"That, my dear," said Hank, "is what is so relaxing about it."

Wolverine finished his third circuit outside the stockade walls. No suspicious noises intruded from the darkness, just jungle chatter or the buzz of nocturnal insects pollinating the garden. No drunk and disorderly tribesmen lurked in the shadows of the walls, needing a reminder to be cool. Most of all, Sauron did not come stumbling up to the gate, wings in tatters, soaking wet, and really mad at what he had been put through by the attendant squad of X-Men.

Logan extended a claw and scratched one of his long sideburns. The wolf-bite mark there still itched, though the wound itself, like those everywhere else on his body, had closed and knit back together, courtesy of his healing factor.

Sometimes sensations lingered—itches, tingles, heat—as scar tissue was absorbed and turned back into standard, good-as-new flesh.

He had to watch himself whenever he started to feel good. It made him want to scrap and tussle all over again. Wasn't that what all that vitality was for? That's what he would say, if asked.

But no one was asking. He didn't have to play the tough guy with himself. That would be too much like having a conversation inside his head, and he had already gone through enough phases like that.

Face it, bub, he thought, *you might have to take a break and enjoy yourself.*

He reached a corner of the cultivated rows near the main entrance, and recognized the plants as tobacco. He was admiring their lushness when a village woman walked up. She seemed to take his interest in the leaf personally.

"You grow this?" he asked.

She nodded proudly. She held up her hand. In it was a cigar.

"Bless you, darlin'," Logan said, and received the gift with reverence. The woman giggled and vanished back inside the stockade.

He examined his prize lovingly before pulling a match from his belt and lighting up. The natives of the Savage Land didn't put their cigars in plastic wrappers and tuck them into boxes with brand names. They grew their tobacco on tiny, individually-tended plots of land like the one next to him. They carefully nurtured the plants, dried the leaves in the open air, and rolled the final product by hand. No chemical fertilizers. No pesticides. Logan's healing factor barely needed to kick in as he drew in a soft, warm cloud and exhaled in a sinuous plume.

LAW OF THE JUNGLE

He hadn't smoked for a month before coming on the mission. Probably he would give it up again when he returned to the mansion—or at least, make a token attempt at it. But that was then and this was now. He filled his lungs again, closed his eyes, and smiled.

When he opened them, a pair of well-built warriors emerged from the forest, following the torch-lit path to the stockade. Logan recognized them less by their silhouettes than by their supple strides and no-nonsense pace. And, of course, by their scent. Smoking a cigar didn't deaden his mutant senses.

"Gelm. Aben." He spread his arms to greet the two Lake People warriors. How they must have run to have finished the journey from their territory in time for the feast.

The pair whooped and rubbed wrists with the X-Man, looking as pleased to put in their appearance as when they had helped him snare Lupo. Gelm met his glance, took off his velociraptor necklace, and held it out.

"Moshru," he said.

Logan raised an eyebrow. "So. You heard about me, eh? Sure. Be glad to." He took the necklace and placed it around his neck.

He figured an hour would be about right, then he could give it back. By then, Gelm's prized possession would be imbued with *moshru*, the essence of the god who had touched it. Logan found it somewhat embarrassing that the local people still thought enough of his previous visits to the Savage Land to regard him with such awe, but what the heck, anything for a friend. Besides, a bit of worship now and then sure beat the kind of treatment mutants received from the average citizen of the so-called civilized world.

The arrivals lifted their noses, inhaled, and smiled at the delicious aromas coming from the heart of the village.

"Whatcha waitin' for?" Logan waved them in. "There's plenty of grub and brew left."

The trio were drawn to the light of the bonfire and the cacophony of happy, singing voices. As they gravitated toward the banquet, they paused to admire the dancers, particularly the women, their hair twirling, their bodies glistening with perspiration and fragrant oils, their teeth blazing white inside smiles.

"Now *this* is my idea of a party," Logan declared, slapping his pals on the back.

Psylocke noticed Logan hanging with his native friends. She turned and saw that Sam and Bobby were still happily allowing their feet to be turned to putty. She telepathically sensed Hank and Ororo in the lodge deeply immersed in chess strategy. Their contentment overflowed into her. The Xavier Institute and the team's day-to-day responsibilities hovered in some distant corner, like a neglected cobweb on the verge of turning to dust. Leaving the Savage Land would not be easy for any of them.

Across the feasting grounds, Ka-Zar gazed at her, and she gazed back. She could have probed to see what he was thinking, but she already knew. It was the same thing she was thinking. They had gone from the intrigue of what-might-be to the wistfulness of what-might-have-been.

This was one of those times she knew she loved Warren all the more, because she stayed with him knowing she could, if she wanted, find herself in the arms of men as attractive as Lord Kevin Plunder. Choice made bonds strong. Ka-Zar knew that, too. The fact that he had chosen to be so firmly devoted to Shanna was, ironically, one of the traits that made him so desirable.

She leaned back into Warren, pressing him more firmly

against the shaman's hut, letting her feel as though she were melting into him. She tilted her head. Their glances met. No wistful might-have-beens here. Just love, fulfilled.

"You look like you slept well," she said, stroking his cheek. "No more nightmares?"

A vestigial dose of tension fled his shoulders. "No. No more nightmares."

"Sauron did you a favor, in the end," she said. "Had you not faced him, you might have always wondered if you had what it took to shut him out."

He nodded. "I would rather have found out in a less dramatic way."

"True. But we're X-Men. We don't do anything like others do. Regular people pay analysts two hundred fifty an hour to sit on leather couches in offices. We journey to exotic locales and beat up on super-powered villains for catharsis."

He chuckled. Suddenly he squeezed her, his hug so fervent that she almost wished she hadn't eaten so much of the feast. "Thank you for being here."

"And where *else* would I be, sir?"

"I wasn't very attentive to you this week. I wouldn't have been surprised if you'd felt a little abandoned."

"You think I stay with you just for the *companionship*?" She laughed. "That you're just a figurehead to keep me from being lonely?"

"Of course not," he said quickly. "Sometimes I feel too lucky to deserve you, is all. It seems a miracle to find you beside me, time after time."

"Have I ever given you cause to doubt me?" she asked.

His face rose into a smile. The expression looked so good on his blue-skinned, golden-maned features, she thought. She began plotting to find ways to keep him that way as often as possible.

"No," he said. "Not in any of the ways that matter."

She caressed his long, supple forearm. "What you said about not deserving me? Was that why you seemed so willing to sacrifice yourself back in the cavern? Were you so eager to die and leave me all alone?"

"No," he said. "Rather the opposite. I realized that thanks to you, I'd had enough beauty and grace in my life to die content, if that's what was needed." He placed his hand atop hers and held it gently. "I have to admit, I'm delighted it didn't come to that."

"As am I, love."

"It was more than coming to closure regarding Sauron," he said. "I was willing to face the unknown because I had already done it with you, when we forged the psionic link. Tell me, what do you think of the idea of building a new one?"

She shivered, unsure whether the reaction was fear or delight. Probably both. "There's no technical difficulty. With Professor X's help we could even make it permanent, like what Jean and Scott have. I've been considering it for quite some time now."

"But?" His voice grew tight with worry.

"I remember that moment in the cavern when I was sure you would be killed. The link was still active at that point. I knew if you died, I would feel it down to the core. Bad as it would be to have lost you at any other time, to lose you while we share the rapport would be the sort of anguish I wouldn't wish on my worst enemy."

"Then," he whispered, "you don't want the rapport?"

"Yes. I *do*," she said. She kissed him. "I have no question about that. But I'm scared, Warren. Tell me, can you be sure you want to take that step? To be able to feel me die from a world away, if I should be the one to go first?"

LAW OF THE JUNGLE

He glanced at the dancers. "I . . ." He sighed. "I'm not sure."

"Nor am I. Yet." She smiled gently. "We have time. If we feel it's right, we can always do it later. We could even craft temporary links in the meantime, like the one we used here, before Sauron ripped it away."

"In that case, we'll be talking about it again." He stood. "Elisabeth Braddock, will you fly with me tonight?" He held out his hand.

"Warren Worthington III," she replied, wiping a tear of joy from her cheek, "I thought you would never ask."

He lifted her in his arms, spread his wings, and they rose into the air, united. The village receded beneath them, the glow of the bonfire waiting for them like a candle in a window, lighting the way home. The Savage Land spread out in every direction, a haven of limitless potential. A symbol of the vast reaches, the dreams, contained within their hearts.

Dave Smeds, a Nebula Award finalist, is the author of the fantasy novel *The Sorcery Within* and its sequel, *The Schemes of Dragons*. He has sold short fiction to anthologies such as *In the Field of Fire, Full Spectrum 4, Peter S. Beagle's Immortal Unicorn, Return to Avalon, David Copperfield's Tales of the Impossible, The Best New Horror 7, Sirens and Other Daemon Lovers, Warriors of Blood and Dream,* and many others, including other Marvel Comics–related fiction in *The Ultimate X-Men* and *The Ultimate Silver Surfer*. He has also contributed to such magazines as *Asimov's Science Fiction, The Magazine of Fantasy & Science Fiction, Realms of Fantasy, Pulphouse,* and *Inside Karate*. He was the English-language scripter of *Justy*, a Japanese *manga* science fiction miniseries released in the U.S. by VIZ Comics. His work, called "stylistically innovative, symbolically daring examples of craftsmanship at the highest level" by the *New York Times Book Review*, has seen print in Great Britain, Germany, France, the Netherlands, Italy, Finland, Poland, the Czech Republic, Slovakia, Croatia, Greece, Russia, and Indonesia. With wife Connie and children Lerina and Elliott, Dave lives in Santa Rosa, California. Before turning to writing, he made his living as a commercial artist and typesetter. He also holds a third degree black belt in Goju-ryu karate, and teaches classes in that art.

Max Douglas did some art for Marvel in the 1980s and early 1990s, but he's feeling much better now, thanks. He's lately been focusing on book illustrations, with his black-and-white work showing up in *The Essential Phantom of the Opera* (a new, annotated translation of Gaston Leroux's novel), *The Ultimate Super-Villains* (an anthology of stories starring Marvel's bad guys), and *Blood Thirst: 100 Years of Vampire Fiction* (a collection of vampire fiction since the publication of Dracula). Max often lives in Canada.

CHRONOLOGY TO
THE MARVEL NOVELS AND
ANTHOLOGIES

What follows is a guide to the order in which the Marvel novels and short stories published by Byron Preiss Multimedia Company and Boulevard Books take place in relation to each other. Please note that this is not a hard and fast chronology, but a guideline that is subject to change at authorial or editorial whim. This list covers all the novels and anthologies published from October 1994–September 1998.

The short stories are each given an abbreviation to indicate which anthology the story appeared in. USM=*The Ultimate Spider-Man*, USS=*The Ultimate Silver Surfer*, USV=*The Ultimate Super-Villains*, UXM=*The Ultimate X-Men*, and UTS=*Untold Tales of Spider-Man*.

If you have any questions or comments regarding this chronology, please write us. Snail mail: Keith R. A. DeCandido, Marvel Novels Editor, Byron Preiss Multimedia Company, Inc., 24 West 25th Street, New York, New York, 10010–2710. E-mail: KRAD@IX.NETCOM.COM.

—Keith R. A. DeCandido, Editor

"The Silver Surfer" [flashback]
by Tom DeFalco & Stan Lee [USS]
    The Silver Surfer's origin. The early parts of this flashback start several decades, possibly several centuries, ago, and continue to a point just prior to "To See Heaven in a Wild Flower."

"Spider-Man"
by Stan Lee & Peter David [USM]
    A retelling of Spider-Man's origin.

X-MEN

"Side by Side with the Astonishing Ant-Man!"
by Will Murray [UTS]
"Suits"
by Tom De Haven & Dean Wesley Smith [USM]
"After the First Death . . ."
by Tom DeFalco [UTS]
"Celebrity"
by Christopher Golden & José R. Nieto [UTS]
"Better Looting Through Modern Chemistry"
by John Garcia & Pierce Askegren [UTS]
   These stories take place very early in Spider-Man's career.

"To the Victor"
by Richard Lee Byers [USV]
   Most of this story takes place in an alternate timeline, but the jumping-off point is here.

"To See Heaven in a Wild Flower"
by Ann Tonsor Zeddies [USS]
"Point of View"
by Len Wein [USS]
   These stories take place shortly after the end of the flashback portion of "The Silver Surfer."

"Identity Crisis"
by Michael Jan Friedman [UTS]
"The Liar"
by Ann Nocenti [UTS]
"The Doctor's Dilemma"
by Danny Fingeroth [UTS]
"Moving Day"
by John S. Drew [UTS]
"Deadly Force"
by Richard Lee Byers [UTS]
"Improper Procedure"
by Keith R. A. DeCandido [USS]
"Poison in the Soul"
by Glenn Greenberg [UTS]

LAW OF THE JUNGLE

"The Ballad of Fancy Dan"
by Ken Grobe & Steven A. Roman [UTS]
"Do You Dream in Silver?"
by James Dawson [USS]
"Livewires"
by Steve Lyons [UTS]
"Arms and the Man"
by Keith R. A. DeCandido [UTS]
"Incident on a Skyscraper"
by Dave Smeds [USS]
   These all take place at various and sundry points in the careers of Spider-Man and the Silver Surfer, after their origins, but before Spider-Man married and the Silver Surfer ended his exile on Earth.

"Cool"
by Lawrence Watt-Evans [USM]
"Blindspot"
by Ann Nocenti [USM]
"Tinker, Tailor, Soldier, Courier"
by Robert L. Washington III [USM]
"Thunder on the Mountain"
by Richard Lee Byers [USM]
"The Stalking of John Doe"
by Adam-Troy Castro [UTS]
   These all take place just prior to Peter Parker's marriage to Mary Jane Watson.

"On the Beach"
by John J. Ordover [USS]
   This story takes place just prior to the Silver Surfer's release from imprisonment on Earth.

Daredevil: Predator's Smile
by Christopher Golden
"Disturb Not Her Dream"
by Steve Rasnic Tem [USS]

X-MEN

These all take place shortly after Peter Parker's marriage to Mary Jane Watson and shortly after the Silver Surfer attained his freedom from imprisonment on Earth.

These two stories take place one after the other, and a few months prior to The Venom Factor.

LAW OF THE JUNGLE

This novel takes place over a one-year period, starting here and ending just prior to Rampage.

"On the Air"
by Glenn Hauman [UXM]
"Connect the Dots"
by Adam-Troy Castro [USV]
"Summer Breeze"
by Jenn Saint-John & Tammy Lynne Dunn [UXM]
"Out of Place"
by Dave Smeds [UXM]
   These stories all take place prior to the Mutant Empire *trilogy.*

X-Men: Mutant Empire Book 1: Siege
by Christopher Golden
X-Men: Mutant Empire Book 2: Sanctuary
by Christopher Golden
X-Men: Mutant Empire Book 3: Salvation
by Christopher Golden
   These three novels take place within a three-day period.

"The Love of Death or the Death of Love"
by Craig Shaw Gardner [USS]
"Firetrap"
by Michael Jan Friedman [USV]
"What's Yer Poison?"
by Christopher Golden & José R. Nieto [USS]
"Sins of the Flesh"
by Steve Lyons [USV]
"Doom²"
by Joey Cavalieri [USV]
"Child's Play"
by Robert L. Washington III [USV]
"A Game of the Apocalypse"
by Dan Persons [USS]
"All Creatures Great and Skrull"
by Greg Cox [USV]
"Ripples"
by José R. Nieto [USV]

X-MEN

"Who Do You Want Me to Be?"
by Ann Nocenti [USV]
"One for the Road"
by James Dawson [USV]
  These stories are more or less simultaneous, with "Child's Play" taking place shortly after "What's Yer Poison?" and "A Game of the Apocalypse" taking place shortly after "The Love of Death or the Death of Love."

"Five Minutes"
by Peter David [USM]
  This takes place on Peter Parker and Mary Jane Watson-Parker's first anniversary.

Spider-Man: The Venom Factor
by Diane Duane
Spider-Man: The Lizard Sanction
by Diane Duane
Spider-Man: The Octopus Agenda
by Diane Duane
  These three novels take place within a six-week period.

"The Night I Almost Saved Silver Sable"
by Tom DeFalco [USV]
"Traps"
by Ken Grobe [USV]
  These stories take place one right after the other.

Iron Man: The Armor Trap
by Greg Cox
Iron Man: Operation A.I.M.
by Greg Cox
"Private Exhibition"
by Pierce Askegren [USV]
Fantastic Four: Redemption of the Silver Surfer
by Michael Jan Friedman
Spider-Man & The Incredible Hulk: Rampage (Doom's Day

LAW OF THE JUNGLE

Book 1)
by Danny Fingeroth & Eric Fein
Spider-Man & Iron Man: Sabotage (Doom's Day Book 2)
by Pierce Askegren & Danny Fingeroth
Spider-Man & Fantastic Four: Wreckage (Doom's Day Book 3)
by Eric Fein & Pierce Askegren
The Incredible Hulk: Abominations
by Jason Henderson
    Operation A.I.M. *takes place about two weeks after* The Armor Trap. *The "Doom's Day" trilogy takes place within a three-month period. The events of* Operation A.I.M., *"Private Exhibition," Re-demption of the Silver Surfer, and* Rampage *happen more or less simultaneously.* Wreckage *is only a few months after* The Octopus Agenda. Abominations *takes place shortly after the end of* Wreckage.

"It's a Wonderful Life"
by eluki bes shahar [UXM]
"Gift of the Silver Fox"
by Ashley McConnell [UXM]
"Stillborn in the Mist"
by Dean Wesley Smith [UXM]
"Order from Chaos"
by Evan Skolnick [UXM]
    These stories take place simultaneously.

"X-Presso"
by Ken Grobe [UXM]
"Life is But a Dream"
by Stan Timmons [UXM]
"Four Angry Mutants"
by Andy Lane & Rebecca Levene [UXM]
"Hostages"
by J. Steven York [UXM]
    These stories take place one right after the other.

Spider-Man: Carnage in New York
by David Michelinie & Dean Wesley Smith

X-MEN

Spider-Man: Goblin's Revenge
by Dean Wesley Smith
These novels take place one right after the other.

X-Men: Smoke and Mirrors
by eluki bes shahar
This novel takes place three-and-a-half months after "It's a Wonderful Life."

Generation X
by Scott Lobdell & Elliot S! Maggin
X-Men: The Jewels of Cyttorak
by Dean Wesley Smith
X-Men: Empire's End
by Diane Duane
X-Men: Law of the Jungle
by Dave Smeds
X-Men: Prisoner X
by Ann Nocenti
These novels take place one right after the other.

Spider-Man: Valley of the Lizard
by John Vornholt
Fantastic Four: Countdown to Chaos
by Pierce Askegren
These novels are more or less simultaneous.

"Mayhem Party"
by Robert Sheckley [USV]
This story takes place after Goblin's Revenge.

Spider-Man: Wanted Dead or Alive
by Craig Shaw Gardner
X-Men & Spider-Man: Time's Arrow Book 1: The Past
by Tom DeFalco & Jason Henderson
X-Men & Spider-Man: Time's Arrow Book 2: The Present
by Tom DeFalco & Adam-Troy Castro

LAW OF THE JUNGLE

X-Men & Spider-Man: Time's Arrow Book 3: The Future
by Tom DeFalco & eluki bes shahar
   These novels take place within a twenty-four-hour period in the present, though it also involves travelling to various points in the past, to an alternate present, and to five different alternate futures.

PUTNAM *b* BERKLEY
online

Your Internet gateway to a virtual environment
with hundreds of entertaining and enlightening
books from The Putnam Berkley Group.

While you're there visit the PB Café and
order up the latest buzz on the best authors and
books around—Tom Clancy, Patricia Cornwell,
W.E.B. Griffin, Nora Roberts, William Gibson,
Robin Cook, Brian Jacques, Jan Brett,
Catherine Coulter, and many more!

Putnam Berkley Online is located at
http://www.putnam.com

●●●●●●●●●●●●●●●●●●●●●●●●●●●●●●●●●

PUTNAM BERKLEY NEWS

Every month you'll get an inside look at our
upcoming books, and new features on our site.
This is an ongoing effort on our part to
provide you with the most interesting and
up-to-date information about
our books and authors.

Subscribe to Putnam Berkley News at
http://www.putnam.com/subscribe